STEE

FLIGHT OF THE STARSHIP CONCORD

BRAXTON A. COSBY

STEEL REIGN

FLIGHT OF THE STARSHIP CONCORD

BRAXTON A. COSBY

Cosby Media Productions

Entertaining the Mind, and Inspiring the Soul

Cosby Media Productions ™

Entertaining the Mind, and Inspiring the Soul

TABLE OF CONTENTS

DEDICATION

To those who feel and appreciate the power of the winds of change and run fiercely toward it without fear or hesitation, convinced in their heart that destiny is defined by the purpose embedded within them… and that it bleeds from the soul.

ACKNOWLEDGMENTS

I must first give thanks and glory to God and His son Jesus Christ who has already given all of those who believe the victory over everything contrary to faith.

To my loving wife, best friend, and soul mate Shontel Cosby, who continues to be the very embodiment of a blessing in both the literal and physical form. My Father has delighted my soul with the presence of you. You give me the freedom to believe, live, laugh, and love.

To my amazing children, Selene, Avian, Sienna, and Sophia: your continual growth and development fill me with the joy I need to survive.

To Ma – You Are Loved!

And to the fans of The Star-Crossed Saga, of whom without there would be no more world-building, space battling, character loving, rain kissing, or hot-hydrogen spewing—my deepest and most sincerely a heartwarming Thank You is more than overdue. Thank you for enjoying my works and joining me on this journey of discovery and hope.

To everyone else, let's get reading!

A WORD TO THE READER

Thank you for purchasing this novel and welcome to the world of The Red Gemini Chronicles. This novel represents book 5 of the series, comprising *The Star-Crossed Saga Saga* and novella. The character Steel Reign was introduced in *The Star-Crossed Saga*, so you may want to pick up those novels as well.

Here is a link to the Series:

ALSO...

You don't know it as of yet, but you are about to be the willing participant in a social experiment. Well, not really, but something akin to one. Throughout the text, I have intentionally opted to exchange some words for numbers. For example, one may be the numeral 1 and two for 2, and so forth. This is my 16th novel, and as such, I decided to have a little fun with it. The purpose of such a trial is to keep your mind alert throughout the entire story so I do not lose you. I did this because, well, I REALLY like this 1 and I want you to remain as focused as possible. Trust me: I'm not illiterate; I earned and possess 3 degrees and multiple certifications. I just selfishly want you to LOVE this book because it is a fulcrum to connect the tale of William and Sydney in The Star-Crossed Saga to the upcoming larger project that I am currently weaving together in my Proxima Centauri Universe. And so, without any more delay, please enjoy,

STEEL REIGN'S story.

PROLOGUE

Somewhere in Deep Space

I did it.

I made a mistake.

I allowed them in.

Too many, too close.

Let my guard down, breaking all the rules of a good spy.

Against my own instincts, I trusted them. Now, I'll lose everything.

My sister Olia.

My lover Serias.

And anything I *thought* was family.

Don't worry Mother…and Father. I won't go out with a whimper. I'll do as you taught me and give 'em hells with every ounce of my last breath.

They'll feel me. I'll make them pay.

ONE

2036

Sirus Delta, Space Station Trading Colony

4 Days Earlier

"Good for nothing, Raider," **I yell, pointing at the huge hairy** beast sitting across the table from me. I watch as his eyes burn a dark crimson color and his fists tighten on the tabletop.

He leans in close as he yells back at me. "Who you calling good for nothing?"

A poignant, but stupid question, as we're the only two seated in my dump of a rental office space. It's larger than most, complete with a living room, kitchen, and bedroom that's big enough to be an office, but not large enough to house a bed, so I mainly bunk it on the couch right behind me. The smell of piss stains my nose, and I lean back to steal a bit of fresh air. Donthras are never known for having good hygiene, so his pungent aroma comes as no surprise. But, admittedly, I expected more from an Elite.

You see, there's a hierarchy to Donthra Military Clans. In general, basic military rank is based on experience. You can earn a few wings from time in the battlefield or solar cycles served. But not with Donthras. They base rank on two things: size and family, with each one carrying a certain measure of weight to it. The bigger you are, the more important you are, and the greater your value as a soldier. And although no self-respecting Donthra would ever freely admit it, familial genealogy carries a slight edge. Among the Donthras, it's the unequivocal age-old story of the "have and have nots" that genetically unites them to the rest of us devolved species. Either way you slice it, you're screwed by who your father screwed.

"You!" I bark back finally, the taste of the Cardack flesh still warm in my mouth. The Donthra stands and drags his knuckles along the table, intentionally knocking over my fresh plate of stewed Cardack and lime rice. It flings off the table and hits the opposite wall with a loud clang. This sears my brain to no end as it was most likely my last meal for the next two days, as preparation for my mission requires a 48-hour fast to pass Alliance inspection. "I can't stand your kind. There's a reason you all almost got wiped out during the Great War," I add.

The beast yells his name, incessantly, "Zayer, Zayer, Zayer!" and points at me. "You disrespect Zayer and his people. You owe Zayer a full apology." He stares at my left eye. "Or I'll pull that Optic Aug right outta your skull."

Sheat just got personal. No one comments on my eye unless I ask them to and a discussion like that is reserved for my doctor or a certified biotics technician. Neither of which this sack of sheat qualifies to be. My hand slips to my right thigh, where Martha is resting, strapped tightly to my leg, but not too much that I couldn't whip it out of the holster and fill this goon with enough hot hydro blasts to rip him in two. My fingers hover lightly over the strap, nestling Martha in her place. It'd be messy for sure, as Donthras spill blood like the warm streams of the Fabrician moon of Darbish. Their metabolism is 3 times that of my Torrian's, forcing stores of adrenaline to pulse into their 3-chamber hearts while actively coursing liters of blood through their veins per second.

And I hate making a mess. My hand relaxes at the thought of it and quickly begins to wither into a fist. Besides, it'd most likely be a waste of ammo as my last salvage gig only paid half of what I needed to re-supply my weapons cache. So instead of wasting either ammo or time, I choose the other best option and make my best attempt to calm him. "Easy, big guy. I didn't mean to disrespect you and your people. I'm just a little upset that you expect me to pay for an artifact that I haven't even laid eyes on."

"No, you choose to disrespect me because you consider Zayer less than you."

"No, no, no," I say, softening my tone. "I consider Donthras highly intelligent creatures that are equal to every other being in the galaxy. I just don't want to get swindled on another deal. Times are hard out here—for everyone—and I just need to guarantee that you can deliver on the goods, that's all."

Zayer beats his chest. "I always deliver."

"I know. That's why they call you the mailman."

"That's right. That's why you hire Zayer."

I slide my hand from my holster. "That's why I hire you, right." I sit forward and swallow the residual remnants of my meal, still lingering in the back of my throat and clear it. "So then tell me how we can come to a resolution. I want the artifact, and you need your money. But if you don't have it, then we both have a bigger problem on our hands."

Zayer looks down at his left wrist and fingers away at the screen of his Holo-band. "It's done. The artifact is on its way and will be here shortly."

I peer over at the clock across the room. It's a few minutes shy of 1300 hours, and my concern starts to rise. "How short?"

"They're close," Zayer says rather confidently. "Relax, Torrian. This deal will run smoothly."

"Smoothly, huh? Then what's the reason for the games?"

"I had to see how desperate you were to obtain the prize before I gave it up."

"Oh, you're one of those kinds of dates, huh? The make-me-beg type."

Zayer winks as his hand slides across the table and softly touches mine. "Only after we conduct business."

I pull my hand back. My mind quickly whips me back to the stark reality of the situation. Donthras are multi-sexual and are open to trying anyone and anything. "Sorry. I was only speaking metaphorically."

"What, Bounty Hunter? Not your type?"

"I don't have one," I say as I stand. "But, if I did, you wouldn't be it."

Zayer straightens and narrows an eye at me. "Too strong?"

I shake my head. "No, too hairy." Zayer cracks a respectful smile just as our exchange is interrupted by 3 hard knocks at the door.

"Ahh, my people," Zayer says as he makes his way to the door.

"Your folks make it a custom of hammering on people's doors?"

"They're not the polite type," Zayer says over his shoulder.

My eyes dart to the clock again, and I note the time. 1301. *We're late*, I think. My intuition ignites and reflexively my right-hand hovers over my thigh as my fingers tickle Martha's leather strap. Zayer finally makes it to the door, and just as he is about to open it, I scream out, "No!"

Too late again.

A wave of hydrogen blasts riddle Zayer's body, and I kick up the table on its side before taking cover behind it. I hear the sound of Zayer exploding as the smell of burning flesh coats the air. The mess I desired to avoid happened anyway, and I'm both down a meal and a meal ticket. This pisses me off royally. I close my eyes and listen for the sound of footfalls entering the door.

1, 2, 3 sets pass through the threshold. These goons are as good as dead. I whip out Martha and quietly turn the shot selector to 3 before standing to a half-kneel, just enough to peer over the edge of the table and aim Martha at all 3 assailants. My Optic Aug locks on to their heat signatures instantly, and I quickly unload one round of a triple spread shot that flattens them. Nice! The sound of the hydrogen rounds penetrating their chests is satisfying, but I can't relish in the victory yet as the rumbling of more feet grows louder down the hallway.

Before they can enter, I thrust the table with my foot at the half-opened door and pin it shut. Then jet over to it and lock the keypad before securing it with a long bolt across the top of the frame. "That'll hold," I whisper as banging commences.

"Open up," I hear a voice project above the knocking. This plants an untimely grin across my face. These guys really expect me to do that. I snicker at the thought of granting their request. Maybe we'll all go out to the bar afterward and down a couple of shots of Crilean Ale while we're at it.

My mind whirls to ascertain what just occurred. A deal for an artifact was on the table—a very expensive one mind you—that would've easily paid for the next 3 month's rent for my office along with fuel for the next few months. A dimwitted Donthra stalled for time and now lies prostrate on my floor, swimming in a pool of black blood along with 3 presumably Dagmas Clan holdovers looking to do what exactly: get in on the extravagant gig or collect that nice hefty bounty on mine.

You see, ever since the Torrian Alliance took back control of Fabricius a little over a solar cycle ago, Dagmas Clan stragglers have been starving for income. Alliance allies have made it their duty to wipe out the few remaining sects of Dagmas loyalists as to not allow for another uprising. And, well, that put a big target on me and anyone else suspected of playing a part in saving the Torrian Kingdom from ultimate destruction. Our solar system is Proxima Centauri, home of the now solitary Super-giant star Sarah—composed of 2 combined stars Mira A and B—and over 10 planets housing over 3 billion humanoid beings. The planets are separated by a large, dense cluster of asteroids known as the Belt of Aster. The 5 Inner Colony Planets come under the authority of the Torrian Alliance, while the 5 outer ones are divided amongst 5 Great Houses: Elixir, Primus, Cephallus, Kinu, and Alero. Initially, everyone joked that House Alero pulled the short straw owning the outermost desolate frozen planet of Ravinia. That is, until it became the single source of a rare mineral known as Oramite, the strongest metal in the known universe.

Fabricius—the homeworld of The Torrian Alliance—is nestled safely, smack dab in the middle of the Inner Colonies and is heralded as the most viable of all 10 worlds, making it the most sought-after. After the war for Fabricius, the 4 inner planets merged with the Torrian Alliance pledging their loyalty. The merger signified the official declaration of supremacy in favor of the Torrian Alliance and brought with it the alienation of the other 5 houses, leaving only resentment and hate from the outer planets.

For the most part, the last solar cycle has represented a time in which peace exists, with everyone cohabitating in harmony. That is, except for The Unit or The Third Faction, the mercenary conglomerate that makes it their duty to wage insider wars among the Houses and The Alliance to secure their own interests with the spoils going to the highest bidder of credits.

I was never considered a scholar, but history says I'm too young to recall the good old days of our system before war decimated almost everything, a time when things seemed a lot simpler. Eleven planets, three factions—The Torrian Alliance, the Dagmas Clan, and The Unit—two dying stars and one goal; system domination. But now, murmurs continue to swirl concerning more civil unrest across the planetary colonies as resources become more and more strained the farther you travel from the Star Sarah.

My eyes fall upon my clock again as I ponder my next move. 1305. Ten minutes before the last space transit disembarks from Sirius Delta and the ticket in my pocket is getting heavier by the second. But I can't leave yet, knowing full well that I desperately need that artifact.

The sound of knocking ceases momentarily as an argument erupts just outside my door. It's possible but not certain that the Dagmas boys have been informally introduced to Zayer's friends, and the artifact could potentially be within reach. Still, I'm down to 3 rounds left in Martha's belly and I know that I'll need more to keep from bleeding out if I get caught up in a slugfest. So, it's either roll the dice and duke it out, or abandon the artifact altogether, keep what little credits I had to purchase it with, and hope that a viable Plan B materializes in time to satisfy my end game.

As the sound of hydrogen blasts fills the air, I choose the latter and head for the back room where my backpack is located. I toss it over my shoulder and head for the hidden escape passage just behind my bookshelf. Yeah, it's predictable as hells, and anyone who *knows* me knows that I haven't read a book in ages. But with space at a premium, it's the only area of this dig where I could build the said escape passage. I flip open a small compartment along the wall and enter a 4-digit code. The bookcase slides sideways, revealing a darkened set of stairs and I input the second set of codes that initiates a self destruct sequence, just as the sound of shearing guns pierces my ears.

It'll take them about 30 seconds to cut through the door and another 20 for me to clear the area safely before the blast goes off, so I split the difference and set the timer for 25 before slipping down the stairs.

As I clear the flight of stairs and enter the alleyway, I look back one last time at my temporary home and shake my head. I'll miss the place, but it's better to have a head to lie down and lose the place to lay it than to have a place and lose your head. These words comfort me as I race down the alleyway and the sound of the explosion from my office rattles the still of the night. I guess I won't be cleaning up after all.

People scurry about to find the source of the explosion, and the sound of sirens immediately follows. I look down at my Holo-band

and note that I have exactly 5 minutes to catch my ride, but, fortunately, I'm only seconds away from the port. Sirus Delta isn't one of the prettiest of spaceports in the galaxy, but it's apparently one of the most durable. The thing can take a licking. I lost count of the many bar brawls, gunfights, and street revolts it's endured since it was opened several solar cycles ago. Heck, even witnessed a couple of dog fights that damn near slammed into the outer hull. When one ship finally bit it, the explosion was so close that it warped the exterior, pushing debris into the heavy metal framing. Every time I return, I'm tempted to place bets to see if anyone cared enough to make repairs and clean it up. But seeing as though I'm the kind of betting man that saves his change for things he can control, I never bring the subject up.

Space stations don't carry the reputation of being the nicest digs in the system. Still, they serve their purpose as a place for travelers to dock, restock supplies and weapons, find crew, try their hand at the mission boards, and lay their heads down for a bit before facing the darkness once more. Sirus represented the first of 7 stations that litter the system now: four in Proxima Centauri and three in two other nearby galaxies, next to large stars allowing for long-distance space folds for safe travel. It was an initiative spearheaded back in the day by the Torrian Alliance in hopes of uniting the planets of Proxima Centauri with these oversized pit stops. And even though people failed to rally behind the cause, you can't blame King Derry for trying.

As I close in on my destination, I step over a passed out drunkard lying along the sidewalk just outside the port and stop to download the latest solar news report to my Holo-tablet. The regular merchants greet me as I get closer to the entrance. "Register now to receive free information on the latest hydrogen repeater pistols," a tall man screams over the Techtronic music blaring in the background. He eyes me from afar and waves to garner my attention, but I ignore him and breeze past as quickly as I can.

Then I'm met by another merchant selling armor upgrade augmentations. "Hey, handsome, you look like the strong, adventurous type. Care to take a look at my wares?" a dark, frail-looking woman asks before quickly gesturing toward her small stand, just inside the entrance opening leading to the spaceport.

"No, thanks," I reply before brushing past her and ushering in line to enter the spaceport. Thankfully, the line is short since most travelers choose to fly by day instead of the dead of night like me. It's not until a few more seconds pass that a small child creeps into my periphery and catches my attention.

He hands me a new flyer and holds out an open hand. "One credit, sir," he says, beating me with wide glossy eyes. Although I just downloaded the same exact thing only moments before to my Holo-tablet, I dare not refuse and reward him for his diligence, seeing as though I always respect a good hustle. He smiles and scoots off before I can thank him. As the line sloughs forward, I glance down at the first page of the report. The title steals my breath away.

CIVIL UNREST LINGERS ON FABRICIUS AS KING DERRY VOWS TO UNITE THE COLONIES.

I shake my head. "William, give it up, kid," I whisper. A beautiful woman with long red hair, green skin, and purple lips greets me as I approach the desk and offer my ID and credit-jump drive. She flashes me a smile after she looks them over and hands them back to me.

"Welcome aboard, Mr. Reign. Will you need any other accommodations?"

I pass on stating the obvious seeing that I'm already pushing the time window for boarding my flight. But if there was ever a good reason to waste credits and take the next flight, she was it. "No, thank you, that'll be all…for now," I say with a wink.

I round a couple of long pristine white hallways and finally make the long trek down the cylindrical catwalk to the shuttle. It's all glass and oval top that ends at the bottom where the metal grating is covered with thin dark-blue carpet. From here, I can see every ship trickling from the darkness, docking on numerous landing pads extending from the central body of the space station—similar to that of a Gotesh sea creature on Rizen. Just before boarding, I look back once more to catch the Sun break over the horizon of the space station and set the entire skyline of Sirus on fire in a blaze of orange, red, and amber blooms. I hold a second just as the Sun dives out of sight behind the space station. The last fleeting bit of light disappears, and I take a deep breath and bask in the grace of the gods that I'm still alive to fight another day. The next stop: Neyas Jezpa.

TWO

The Gloria – Space Transit Ship

I hastily plop down into the first empty stall I can find and slide my bag over in the seat next to me. Although my office space is totally wasted and I lost my one shot at obtaining the artifact, things are looking up. I was probably one of the last people to board the shuttle, so I'm amazed to find a place to sit, much less rest my bag without anyone pushing up against me. The thing I despise most about public transports is overcrowding. They always overbook these flights, so I count my blessings that I can tow this stall alone.

"Welcome to *The Gloria*," a pleasant female voice announces over the intercom. "We hope you enjoy your trip to Neyaz Jezpa. Everyone is officially on board. The shuttle is about to depart. Please secure all belongings."

I check the safety on Martha and peruse my bag for the rest of its contents. Ammunitions: check. ID: check. Personal GPS: check. Datalogue: check. Encrypted Underground decipherer: double-check. The Underground is a digital bargain-basement of sorts, giving you enough options for Intel, weapons, information, and tech at a discounted rate that you'd be hard-pressed to find by any legitimate means. Sometimes, the items I trickle across give me goose bumps as one can imagine the lives lost or the risks taken to secure such assets. Beyond credits, information is the hottest commodity in the 'verse, and you can only find it on the Underground.

I'll need that more than ever if I'm to find a suitable item for trade now that I've lost the artifact. Stupid Donthra. Or should I be placing the blame on that gang of Bounty Killers? Ever since I helped the Torrian Alliance take back their planet from Dominic's reign of terror last solar cycle, I've paraded through space with a virtual bull's eye on my back. Any Dagmas Clan holdovers and insurgents are desperate for a chance to take me out and claim the bounty on my head. You see, once the Torrian Alliance took back Fabricius, Prince William Derry reclaimed the throne of his deceased father King Gregorio. A kingdom left behind after his assassination and one of the first duties William performed as King was to officially declare the disbanding of the Dagmas Clan, along with their allies, the Third Faction—the biggest group of mercenaries in the galaxy. That was a big problem for nomads like me, who prefer to roam the galaxy free rather than remain in the safety of the Alliance.

William even offered a place among his Royals as his first-tier security officer, but I passed. That type of position carries far too much responsibility and accountability, and I've never been the role-model type. Having kids look up to me makes my skin crawl. Queen Sydney attempted to coax me into taking another position in the royal guard, but seeing as though Jacques Oscillot procured the Captain slot of the Royal Armed Forces—the only position I'd find even remotely attractive—I chose to hit the open road instead. Besides, I have bigger fish to fry.

Admittedly, I do miss it all sometimes. And I can't lie; it's nice to have servants wait on you hand and foot. And there's nothing like a hot shower every now and then along with an equally warm meal. I even welcome the occasional adrenaline surge I get in my gut when I think back to that last battle. But it's quickly drowned out by the image of King Gregorio's wilted body after Dominic assassinated him right before my eyes.

I pause from my reminiscing as I pick up the last of the contents in my bag. Golden Holo-locket: check. I click the button along the top of it, and it quietly opens. A picture of my half-sister, Olia, fills the frame. Her radiant purple skin blazes before me. Although the original picture was taken when we were both in our childhood many solar cycles ago, Holo-locket technology has default settings to project an image of what the person would look like in the present. I crack a smile and slide my finger over the button along the side. The picture fades and then restores Olia to her original age— somewhere between 8 and 10 solar cycles. My smile widens as my eyes dance across her two side ponytails. She always did love that style.

My moment is broken by the presence of someone over my shoulder. I close the Holo-locket and straighten up without looking back. "I hate when people enter my personal space, unannounced," I grumble.

"Oh sorry, man, I was just—"

"Not minding your own business," I say as I turn to find a chubby human staring back at me, sporting a leather cap. A lock of blazing red hair drapes just above his nose. I slip the Holo-locket in my bag and zip it closed.

"Naw, see, I actually—"

"Need to leave, right?"

"Well, I wasn't going to say that—"

"Well, you should."

"If you'd let me talk, I'd actually tell you what I was going to do—"

"And that nothing, you hear. Do me a favor and find a seat somewhere else."

"Well, actually, that seat right there is the last one on this shuttle," he says, pointing at my bag.

Anger races through me. "Well, I paid double for extra storage for my bag, so you're sheat outta luck," I lie.

"Well, see…that's not entirely true."

"You calling me a liar?" I ask, standing now. My chin hits the annoying male just above his forehead, and I'm certain it's enough to drain at least a few drops of pee from him. By the fearful look on his face, I'm somewhat encouraged that he'd leave me alone now. But to my dismay, he babbles on.

"I've got this little gadget here, and it says that you didn't pay for jack," he replies, pecking away at a small black box in his hand.

I snatch it from his hand, turn away, and gaze at the words on the screen. Upon closer inspection, the box is more cube-shaped and the screen on one side is more oval. I gaze at the image before me. The ship's manifest stares back at me containing my stall number along with my name in bold and my purchase order. "What the hells is this?"

He taps me on the shoulder and calls my name. "Mr. Reign, can you please give that back to me? It's my mother's."

"Bullsheat," I reply. "Your mother a hack too?"

"Taught me everything I know." He taps me on the shoulder again. "Gifford's the name, by the way."

"Great, but I didn't ask." I turn around and hand his gadget back to him. "Nice one kid. I'll give you an A for effort. Now do me a favor and get the foo—"

"Not so fast, big guy. There are kids in this cabin." His eyes fan about the cabin and I notice that everyone is staring at me, taking in our conversation. He's right. Among the crowd of 20, at least 6 or so youngsters hang on my every word. I crack a light smile and then take my seat. After a few seconds, I notice that Gifford is still hovering. If I didn't have an audience, I swear I'd lose a few more rounds from Martha into him just to keep her nozzle warm. Instead, I kindly look up at him and ask, "Can I help you?"

"The bag, Mr. Reign. Can you move it, please?"

I narrow my eyes and notice that Gifford doesn't flinch one bit. He's got balls of steel, and I'd be impressed had I not been so annoyed. I sigh heavily and pick up my bag before sliding over into the seat closest to the window. Gifford slumps down next to me. "Thank you, Mr. Reign."

"Whatever," I grunt.

Gifford peels off his backpack and pins it in his lap before opening a pocket and placing the black gadget inside. He looks over at me. "Fancy device, right? It's called a Daedallus Cube. I can get you one if you need it. I know a guy…or 2…or 3."

"Daedallus Cube?"

"Yeah, it's named after the ship that Prince, well, King William now, flew in the last war against those pesky Dagmas clowns."

"Why is it named after the ship?"

Gifford wears a proud smile. "Because its data encryption is so fast that it can fly under the radar and steal secured files so classified that you'd swear you were getting burned by a star."

"But the name Daedallus refers to flying close to a star, feeling the heat and not getting burned."

"You see, that's just it. When I hack, I get all hot and bothered," Gifford whispers as he leans in.

"Save it," I say, throwing a hand in his face.

Gifford snickers. "If you want one, I got you."

I nudge him back with my elbow to free up some space. "I'm good. Back up."

"I'm just saying—"

"Way too much."

"Is it your way to always cut people off when they're trying to help you out?"

"No! But you're not helping anything. And, besides, I'm sure you couldn't give me a damn thing that I need."

"Shoot your shot, playboy. Try me. You'll never get those codes without the right currency."

The room falls silent. I stare at Gifford so hard that I swear I burn a hole into his skull. "What did you just say?"

"I said, you need codes, right?"

"What codes? Did you hack me?"

"I did."

Before I can control myself, my hands are wrapped around Gifford's neck, and I stand, pulling him along with me. Gifford screeches in an attempt to scream, I think, but my hands tighten around his windpipe to quell any chance of him uttering a single word. Gifford grabs my wrist with one hand and his backpack with the other. "In case you hadn't noticed, punk, I'm tired of playing games," I mutter as I free up one hand to secure my bag as well. I know I'm on limited time now as Gifford's face is beginning to turn blue beneath his pale skin, so I half-walk, half-shimmy us out of our stall and into the aisle of the cabin. Eyes fall upon us, and I quickly make light of the situation. "My friend has had a little too much to drink and is feeling a little ill. No cause for alarm, everyone. I'm going to take him out for a little fresh air. We'll be right back."

We exit the cabin and spill into one of the larger common areas of *The Gloria,* where concessions, ticket booths, and souvenir stores occupy the majority of the space. A sea of strangers lies before us, but I do my best to navigate through them and into the nearest bathroom. "Scram!" I yell as I'm met by a couple of old men inside. They run out, and I release my grip on Gifford's neck and toss him against a wall opposite from the entrance. I turn and lock the door behind us. As Gifford crouches over and struggles to catch his breath, I draw Martha from the holster and line the sights squarely at his head. "Talk or bleed."

Gifford chokes on fresh air a few more times before finally straightening. He lifts a pair of goggles from around his neck and places them over his eyes. "Let me explain, Mr. Reign."

"Stop calling me that!" I yell.

"What do you prefer I call you?" Gifford asks, holding his hands apologetically at shoulder height.

"Daddy!"

"Daddy? You into some ole kinda freaky sheat?"

"No, it's Daddy because I may not have brought you in this world, but I sure as hells have the authority to take you out of it."

"By whose authority?"

"The Torrian Alliance," I reply with a smile.

Gifford bursts into laughter. He pauses momentarily, only to speak. "For real? Is that what you think? And for a spy, you suck at lying."

I slowly cock Martha's hammer and set the dial to two. The rapid-fire setting, double kill. "Who the hells are you? Talk now, and I mean it."

Gifford stops laughing and raises his hands once more, this time, high above his head. "Okay, okay. I'll talk. Just give me a moment to hit the John."

"What?"

"Yeah, man. All this rough sheat got me needing to pee."

Now he needs to pee. Is this clown serious? I sigh as I replay the words of my defunct father. *Untimely success is only as good as a failure.*

THREE

My grip tightens on Martha as I patiently wait for Gifford to finish pissing. The toilet flushes, and on cue, Gifford pops out. He offers me a hand, asking for his black gadget cube.

"You kidding me? Wash your damn hands, bozo," I hiss.

Gifford makes his way to the sink and wears a look on his face as if he has the right to be offended. "Okay, okay." He proceeds to wash as he talks over his shoulder. "You know, I could be a big help to you if you let me in."

"Shut it! And keep cleaning."

Gifford cranes his neck in my direction. "Wait. Now you're judging my hygiene habits?"

"You're the one who tried to walk out without washing your hands," I reply in disgust.

He turns halfway to make eye contact. "I was merely going to take my cube. If I soiled it, it's my right to do so." He shoots me a half-grin. "Not like I washed my hands any other time before handling it."

I toss him the cube as quickly as I can. "Nasty ass."

Gifford catches it, places it down, and begins to dry his hands one by one on his pants legs. "You Alliance guys are all the same."

"What do you mean, and speak quickly?" I grunt.

"You're not the first project I've taken on." Gifford pauses and brings the cube closer to his face. After examining it for a few seconds, he pecks at the screen and then turns it to face me. "See that right there?" An image of 3 faces fills the screen. A woman and two males, neither of whom I recognize.

"Am I supposed to know who they are?" I ask.

"You might. But I'm not surprised that you don't. They're ex-military. Served before you came back to help out in the Battle Solstice."

"That what they're calling it now?"

"Yes. The day Fabricius destroyed the Dagmas Clan…for good." He pauses and shoots me a raised brow. "But not really, right?" he asks jokingly. I hold my tongue, chomping at the bit to know what he's driving at. "Evil always has its rightful place," he continues.

"As long as that place is far away from me, I really don't care. You mentioned something earlier about codes. What's the deal?" I pause and aim Martha at his head. His narrow eyes converge on the sight as my finger starts to squeeze on the trigger. "Start talking, and don't skimp on the details."

Gifford slowly raises his hands at his sides. "These 3 soldiers are now dead. Apparently, they were stealing classified files from the Torrian Alliance and giving them to the Dagmas Clan just before

Dominic's coup. They served under Jacques. Coincidentally, there was a leak of some kind as Dagmas seemed to know every move the Alliance made before they did, allowing easy infiltration of highly-classified security documents." He takes a deep breath and continues. "Codes and such. Many people suspected that he was the lead."

"Who?"

"Jacques."

I chuckle. "That's crazy. He's as solid as they come."

"Even the solid ones falter from time to time." I knew what Gifford was getting at. A memory rustles up in my mind from a time when I carried similar doubts. Being a spy is never easy. You choose sides only on the surface and remain loyal to your creed. And along the way, you learn to live with terrible outcomes of horrible decisions, even if the people closest to you get hurt. "For a while," Gifford starts again, this time slowly dropping his hands back to his side. Either he's mistaken me for a man with a conscience who cares about killing random techies, or he's accepted the fact that surrendering stops speeding hot hydrogen blasts no more than wet tissue paper. "Many people thought that Jacques was behind it, but after all hells broke loose and he proved himself during the war, everything settled down and the leaks were isolated. And that's where I came in," Gifford finishes. He stops and slides his jacket sleeve back from his right wrist and up to his elbow. A symbol of a black hawk with a bionic eye greets me.

"Cute," I muse. "You're a spy too."

26

"Outer Rim affiliation," Gifford says smugly as he rolls his sleeve back down. "Just beyond the Belt of Aster," he continues. "You know, the line of demarcation between the rich and poor colonies. I helped them hunt down the traitors and it led them to an even bigger counteroffensive that was being conspired." Gifford shrugs a little. "I'm kind of a hero."

I narrow my eyes, curious now to know more. "Call-sign?"

Gifford pokes his chest out a bit. "The Sons of Sarah," he chimes in a stern voice.

"No offense, but I've never heard of them or you," I snarl, trying my best to sound unimpressed.

"I wouldn't expect you to. Most haven't. We like to do things quietly. In and out—"

"Hit, don't miss," I say, cutting him off. It's basic Spy Creed gibberish for sure, and although any space hacking nerd could unearth it, it's not something that's heavily publicized—mere whispers across the Wave. But if Gifford was trying to convince me of his alliances, that was enough to do the job.

Gifford nods respectfully. "And you know more than most that the only way to be a true spy is to hide in plain sight."

He stares at me with a pause as if awaiting a positive response that would somehow unlock the invisible door of tension between us. So I toss him a bone. "So you're on the Alliance's dime?"

"Not full-time. They contract me when things really hit the fan. When they can't afford to waste credits on people who make promises they can't keep."

"And who's flipping the bill for you to follow me?'

Gifford chuckles. "Actually, no one. Let's just say I took a special interest in you."

"Of me? For what?"

"Well, Alliance gave me access to their most secretive files and dossiers after Solstice. So I started poking my way around."

I wave a weary finger at him. "Snooping, where you shouldn't have."

Gifford cocks his head. "You can say that. That's when I came across your file. Steel Reign, the ex-spy turned rogue, then hero, back to rogue again, and finally nomad. Your story piqued my interest. I thought to myself: why would a hero leave the sanctuary of such plush accommodations? Was he running from some-*one* or looking for some-*thing*?"

"Easy, genius," I warn.

"Over the next year, I followed closely behind your tracks, hacking into what trail you left behind. And it wasn't an easy feat, mind you. You tend to leave a lot of sheat in your wake, studly. Odd jobs here and there, off the record interrogations," Gifford says with a smirk, making air quotes when he says the words "off the records."

"I was confused as all hells until finally, you left one clue that pointed to the place of your desire. Your heart."

I swallow silently. This guy is good. Irritating…but good. Maybe too good, though. That worn tattoo on his wrist was a bit outdated, from a time when I rolled through the system taking out prized targets. I earned a couple of credits on their dime from time to time, made a few friends too. But I never slept for long enough in the bed to be too smitten where I'd sacrifice my skin for a linking relationship. And I was wise enough to know that partaking in such an act would have been spy suicide. I take a deep breath and slide my finger off the trigger, loosen my grip on Martha and slowly begin to lower her to my side. "And."

"And, well, I realized you were looking for someone of the utmost importance. But not just anyone. Family."

My eyes narrow at him dangerously as I fight off the thought of pointing Martha again. "And what key clue did you stumble upon?"

"That hit job on Boshin Rowe. You slaughtered 30 men but left that one behind. A child. Female. Pelorian. Groomed to be a fine Sintock warrior." With each word, images of a beautiful purple-skinned girl paint my thoughts. "I enacted a Phishing Protocol with your personal data and, before long, information on your half-sister materialized."

I holster Martha and begin to clap sarcastically. "Great. Fantastic job. Now I'll be leaving. You've seen my resume, kid. Consider yourself lucky I didn't kill you." I turn to exit the bathroom and hear a set of heavy feet scurrying after me.

"Wait, Mr. Reign," Gifford says. He beats me to the door and bars it with his body, arms splayed at his sides. "I can…I mean, I want to help."

"Don't need it."

"That's naïve of you."

I flash teeth at that and growl for effect. Gifford cowers a little and closes his eyes as he continues to talk. "The mere fact that you say that proves you have no clue what you're getting into," he says quickly in a high-pitched tone. "Forge and the *Eclipse* is a death sentence if you lack the proper technological assistance."

I turn away and look for some other means of escaping the impending uncomfortable conversation. "I fly alone, buddy," I grunt.

"But you don't have to," Gifford says faintly. I can tell from the direction of his voice that he had moved from the door and was solely diverting his attention to me. "And, well, to be honest, you're hitching a ride, not flying at this point."

The anvil weight of the truth crashes down on my head, and within the murky details of my present situation, clarity begins to settle in. Quite possibly, the kid's help could give me the nudge I need in the right direction. If not to lend a *technological* hand as he insists, at least to be a decoy to mask my true intentions along the way if anyone came snooping. "Okay, you're resourceful, I give you that. But I know for a fact that you no longer have Alliance clearance or they would've come for me the second you pulled my dossier. They've been begging for me to return, which is why I have both good and bad guys on my ass. I can always get tech anywhere. The Underground is wide open.

"And as you can see, I'm very talented at getting what I want." I begin to walk toward Gifford. "So, tell me." I close the distance between us, meeting him nose to nose. "What could you seriously have that I need?"

"Credits."

"I've got that too."

"Not enough," he says.

"Not enough?"

"Not if you're trying to get aboard the *Eclipse*. They changed their entry fees after last year and ramped up their security. Something about a precocious Prince breaking out."

My eyes widen at that. "How do you know how much I have, anyway?"

Gifford wears a look of a proud child, who had against his father's wishes, somehow broke into his storage closet and fixed his broken pulse rifle. "I checked your account."

My blood boils at that, and I shake my head vehemently. "I'm done," I grunt. "This conversation's over. I think I'll manage on my own from now on. Thanks." I press for the door. "Step aside." I try to pry Gifford from the door, but he tightens his grip on the frame and pulls back.

"Please, Mr. Reign, I really want to help, and I have more than enough credits to get us what we need."

This makes me pause. Deep down inside, and I mean deep, I know I need the help. That artifact was the monetary Hail Mary I needed to get me back in the black. And with that option all but zeroed out, I was running on fumes for cash now. It would only be a matter of time before I'd be dragging back to the bounty boards to collect monetary rewards in exchange for heads. And that would run me a half-solar cycle off my timeline at best.

For the most part, Gifford is right. I need to get on the *Eclipse* to save Olia, and without sufficient credits, I'm merely swimming in a pool of dreams. But to carry him with me is a huge risk because I always roll solo. With both Alliance, Dagmas goons and who knows what else on my ass—if Gifford got this close, it makes me ponder whose next—things will continue to get tight; wallet included. "Okay," I say finally.

Gifford's face relaxes, and a wide smile blooms across his jaw that I'd swear would outshine Star Sarah. "Really?"

"Yes, really. You can tag along, but first, I need a moment to stop off at my old dig on Neyaz Jezpa."

"Of course, you do. How else will you refresh your ammunitions?"

My eyes narrow dangerously at Gifford. "You know the last time I took a crap too?" I ask.

"Ugh, you really want the answer to that?"

I shake my head and lift a hand. "Spare me. I was there."

"Mr. Reign—"

"Stop calling me that!" I yell.

"Aww, you're back to cutting me off. I like that. It reminds me of the first time we met."

"It was only moments earlier. There's nothing nostalgic about that."

"I know, but call me sentimental."

"Mental, for sure. Don't know about the *senti* part."

"All right, Reign then. How's it sound?"

"Just like every fooking other person does when they say it."

"Delightful, I'll take it. I'll keep practicing until it sounds just right. Maybe there's a cool accent or emphasis I can place on parts of the name."

"Don't strain too hard. It's one syllable. I think you'd just be wasting your time."

Gifford wags a finger at me. "Don't go doubting me, Reign. You'll find that I can be very surprising when given a chance."

"I'm drowning in anticipation."

"I knew you were."

"So just how many of these *enough* credits does it take to get onboard the *Eclipse* anyway?" I ask.

"Oh, I don't have enough credits to get us on the *Eclipse*. They don't accept credits for entries anymore. Forge is a Space Pirate of exquisite taste, and now he only accepts items of great value for trade. My credits will get us where we need to go to obtain one of these items."

"Let me guess. One of these items serves as a payment for you helping me, right?"

"Everyone has a price, Reign."

"Aww. And here I was thinking you just wanted to help me because of my celebrity status," I say in a whiny voice.

Gifford looks down at his black square tinker box and pecks at it. "That's a 2-for-1 deal. The item we need to obtain will be traded, so we will lose it once the deal is settled. What I need is, well, a little different." Gifford finishes pecking just as he stops talking.

He offers me the cube once more. When I take it, the image on the screen makes me cringe. "Why do I have a sinking feeling I'm about to lose big." I shake my head. "You want the *Eclipse*?"

"No. Just the Dark Matter engine protocols."

"What are you going to do with it, disintegrate?"

"The first thing you need to know about a hacker is that any respectable one hacks just for the joy of winning, not *obtaining*."

"You say *obtaining*, and I translate that into stealing. But I'm sure a hacker of your caliber would balk at such a term. Am I right?"

Gifford points at me. "Bingo."

"And the second thing I need to know?"

"What?"

"About hackers?"

Gifford raises an eyebrow. "We always win."

FOUR

Neyaz Jezpa

After a few hours of travel, *The Gloria* finally slows to make the final approach to our destination. Gifford was kind enough to occupy his thoughts by exploring the rest of the massive shuttle, frolicking about, and making small talk with the other passengers. I, on the other hand, took the opportunity as a fantastic time to add some much-needed sleep to my tiring mind.

As sharp as Gifford is, he's way too trustworthy as he left all of his belongings—backpack and gadget cube—in our stall. I don't bother it, though, as I'd expect mutual respect if I left my things with him. Still, it says a lot about Gifford's character. Either he's bullsheating me to death and setting me up for a double-cross somewhere down the line, or he's offering me a trust olive branch— something most spies never do.

I know a little something about his Spy Guild. They pride themselves on honor and trust among fellow spies—even if they're from another sect. It's been both their strength and Achilles' heel as they've lost thousands of great members to slippery characters like myself. But I'll never tell him something like that unless he asks.

36

I'm awake, but just as I contemplate trying to grab a few more minutes of sleep, a female voice breaks across the intercom. "Ladies, gentlemen, and everything else in between, *The Gloria* is making its final approach for the planet Neyaz Jezpa. Please make final preparations to retrieve your things and prepare to disembark. We hope you enjoyed your voyage today, and please consider flying with us again."

Her melodic voice is soothing and warm. It reminds me of someone. Olia's. In fact, for the last year, ever since William told me of her whereabouts, everything does. From the hue of purple on the ceiling of our stall that matches that of Olia's immaculate skin tone to the petite but muscular frames of the many females I've slept with in the past. And then there are those big, strong hands of hers. Massive like mine, large like our father's. Could easily grab hold of a man's neck and strangle him to death in seconds or simply snap it for good measure.

They all remind me of her. But her memory doesn't make me sad, it keeps me strong. I've never shed a single tear ever since Olia went missing many moons ago. Only because she left on her own terms. She dictated her future and her own destiny, so I was cool with it. Even a bit envious. But now, fighting as a prisoner on the *Eclipse*, serving as one of Forge's dogs, I know the option of freedom is a mere flicker.

Olia's a creature of moods. Hot like a star one minute and sweet as Lexus pudding the next. Like her mother. I didn't know her that well, but our father always referenced her similarities when Olia misbehaved. He'd jokingly poke fun at her, but behind those angry eyes, I saw a deep admiration for her spunk and tenacity. Something he couldn't tame, nor could he train.

Gifford rounds the corner, and reflexively I reach down and grab his bag. I hand it over to him and he takes it with a smile. "Thanks, Reign."

"Don't mention it," I mutter. Gifford remains standing, and I instinctively slide over to the window, giving him a chance to sit.

The view from here is pretty amazing. Our window opens out to the common area of *The Gloria*, but technology being what it is, I'm able to tap on the glass and scroll through various images from the external cameras. I filter through a few until choosing the front one. The image of the half planet of Neyaz Jezpa looms into view. Its shape resembles that of a crescent moon with the majority of the inhabitants living on the light side along the convex end. The main city nestles in the center, with tall towers that kiss the sky, spewing billowing clouds of black smoke skyward, mixing with a sea of gray ash, flowing from the opposite concave side.

"I'm always impressed by the sight of this one. It never grows old," Gifford says from behind.

"You make a living off of gazing over folk's shoulders?"

"Now, you know I don't want to answer that." I can feel Gifford's breath on my neck as he speaks, and the image of lips taints my brain. "Don't act like you're not impressed too, Reign."

When I can't ignore his proximity encroaching on my personal space any longer, I shrug and give him an elbow to shore up some room between us. "Whatever. Seen one junk planet, you've seen 'em all. And trust me...I've seen 'em all."

"Like this one?"

"*Just* like this one." I relent on upholding the lie. "Well, maybe not exactly."

"Chunks of planet adrift in space, trapped in a makeshift orbit around the remaining half." As Gifford speaks, my gaze wanders across the outlining forest, crowding the city, drowned in dark ash. From here, I swear I could hear the trees screaming out for clean air. "Sorry, Mr. Reign. There's only one Neyaz Jezpa. It's documented in the archives how that meteor split it in two. And a nearby star's gravitational pull slowly wrenched it away."

"What are you now, some tour guide?" I ask in disgust.

"No. I took you for a man that likes to be enlightened."

"Well, you read that one wrong. Know it alls drive me crazy and make me feel uncomfortable." I look over at him, and my eyes fall on his bag. "Didn't your all-knowing cube tell you that?"

"No. Just my...never mind."

Gifford quiets, and his head drops as if for the first time since meeting him, he's actually ashamed of his babbling brook disease. "This is the home of some of the most dangerous traders, scavengers, bounty hunters, and mercenaries looking for side jobs that pay in pounds. No easy money here, kid. Every cent must be earned. So stay on your toes," I say to lighten the mood.

Gifford looks back up at me. His eyes are bright again. "See, I knew you were a connoisseur of information."

"Yeah, whatever."

I feel the rumbling of landing gear lower as *The Gloria* begins her descent, and the image of Neyaz Jezpa fades, replaced by the external docking harbor. Multiple ships drop and rise, crisscross one another in a beautifully choreographed dance without a single one even skimming their external Parry Shields.

Moments later, we're down, landing safely at our port. I grab Gifford by the arm just as he tries to stand. "What gives?" he asks. "I don't want to get caught in the bottleneck trying to get off the ship."

I caution him. "There may be others shadowing us. Give everyone a chance to exit so we can take in all the passengers and free up our backsides. I want to see them coming—*if* they're coming."

Gifford seems to get the gist of what I'm saying with little fanfare, tossing me a silent nod. Our cabin empties, and I look out the window to watch the rest of the passengers spill out into the common area. As the crowd disperses, I'm satisfied that we've made it safely. "Let's roll," I say in haste.

Gifford and I grab our things and make our way to the line for the Admissions Counter in the main docking bay. People buzz around us in a low hum of idle conversation that doesn't do the job of drowning out Gifford's continual mumbling on tech stuff that fails to stick even the slightest to my uninterested mind. We fall in behind a massive crowd that forms multiple single-file lines, which converge into numerous desk counters with security workers.

Despite the large crowd, we make good time on closing the gap between us and the admission desks and, before long, we're mere whispers away from the front. I've never been pegged as a patient man, but the wait is more than worth it. Getting back to my pad and shoring up some fresh ammo and munitions is both comforting and satisfying. I'd rather have sore feet from standing than a hydrogen-riddled back from Dagmas grunts.

I take a slow, heavy drag of filtered air into my lungs. "You smell that, Gif?"

"Smell what?" he asks.

"The heavy scent of death. It's ripe in the air. Stay close and enjoy the clean air while you can. Once we step outside, your lungs will be feasting on contaminants."

"Can't say this nose is as good as yours, but my ears worked like clockwork. Don't think I didn't notice you award me with a nickname." He smiles wide. "Giff…I like it."

"Consider it a slip of the ton—"

"Not buying it," Gifford says, his eyes settling on mine. "See, I've even earned the right to cut you off too now."

"No!" I reply harshly. "You really haven't."

We step forward as the woman behind the counter waves us forward, a Pelorian with long dark hair. Memories of Olia pierce my mind again. But at least this one sports a light blue skin tone, so the resemblance is not as stark. We hand over our IDs. "What business will you have here on Neyaz?"

"Nothing in particular," I answer.

"Well, is there anything I can do to make your stay more…enjoyable?" she asks me, her eyes batting wildly. The idea of being with a Pelorian—especially one who reminds me of my sister—makes me gag. I slew a few before but only those of red and gold tones. But never anything in the blue or violet visible spectrum.

I feel Gifford lean in. "Well, since you're offering—"

I elbow him sharply. "That'll be all for now. Thank you."

Gifford reaches for his ribs, and I hand him his ID pad before leaving the counter. He lags behind a bit and finally catches up when we exit the safety of the spaceport and enter the outer bands of the woods. We're met by a faint shower of gray ash that lightly falls from the sky. It's a holdover from the destroyed half of the planet that was slammed into by the runaway meteorite. Gifford dons his goggles and comes alongside me. "We grabbing a ride or do you have one?" Gifford asks.

I shade my eyes with one hand and crack a faint smile as I nod him over to a cropping of dark green and brown bushes in the shadows, just a hundred or so yards from the main road. I reach forward, and my hands break the image, causing ripples and waves to disperse in all directions. I whistle a specific tune with separate cords and, instantly, the image dissolves, revealing a single-seater motor-pad, complete with a side compartment for another passenger. I step inside, open the middle console and pull out a pair of goggles of my own.

"Fancy, schmancy," Gifford says. "Full of surprises…spy."

"Clam up and hop in. We should have just enough juice to get us home," I say.

***

We arrive at my home. It's a small pad just beyond the main road, up in the hills with two entrances—one in the front and the other in the back. The outside is dirty like my past, covered in inches of ash from Neyaz Jezpa's atmosphere. When asked in the past if I ever thought of scrapping it away, I quickly tell others no, touting that it gives the house character. But I know the real reason. I prefer the obscurity it gives off as it drives away would-be thieves and deters bounty hunters.

I approach the front door and open a side compartment to reveal the retinal scanner. It's old tech, but it still works like new. After a few waves of green light across my good right eye, the door slides open, and the lights immediately turn on overhead. I make my way to the kitchen, pull open the fridge, and snatch a bottle of water. As I start to chug it down, I notice Gifford taking in the space. It's a one-bedroom dig, complete with a den and kitchen. "Toward the back is my work station," I say, breaking his gaze.

"How'd you know what I was looking for?"

"A geek like you. Heck, what else could I offer to feed that busy mind of yours."

His eyes pass over me as he continues to peruse the surroundings. "Does it happen to have a 4-D printer?"

"Top of the line Alpha-Quatro build," I say proudly.

Gifford's eyes bulge from his skull. "No way," he says.

I move from the kitchen and open the adjacent door that leads to the back shed. I wave a hand. "See for yourself. You're welcome to take a look."

Gifford briskly rubs his hands together and follows the broken trail to the shed. This gives me a moment to break away to my bedroom to secure more ammunition and, for the first time in a while, some privacy. I crash on my bed for a few seconds and take in the smell of my freshly-scented linens. Liane, my automated cleaning robot, breezed through on my last visit just a few months ago and sanitized the place from head to toe. I can still smell the evidence of her hard work, and it warms my soul.

Cognizant that I'm not alone, I pry myself from the bed, move over to my storage closet, and quickly make haste to reconcile my weapons cache. As I enter the closet, the lights turn on and a large metal box ascends from the floor. It rises to knee-level and opens another tier as the entire container stops just short of my waist. I place my hand over the fingerprint scanner and it opens with a hiss.

Inside are all the fixings you'd expect to find from a ragged, aged, veteran spy. Guns, you name it. Single-handed pistols, assault repeaters, and shoulder cannons all await wary and hungry eyes. Grenades—frag, stun, and smoke—by the barrel hug the right corner, haphazardly stacked on one another.

I pass up the explosive eye candy and secure what I really came for: ammo for Martha. I grab 3 or 4 clips and stash them in my backpack. Each one carries enough liquid hydrogen to gun down an entire battalion, which would be the equivalent of two to three-hundred rounds. I consider grabbing a few grenades or even a hand cannon but remember that I'm no longer going it alone, and it'd be just my luck that Gifford mistakenly sets off an explosive and creams the both of us. So, instead, I take a semi-automatic repeater to satisfy my craving to let off a few rounds if we get into a skirmish.

The sound of the door sliding open cues me that Gifford is back inside, so I close up shop and return to the kitchen area. He greets me with a bright row of teeth along with a glowing orb in his left hand. "You like?" he asks.

"I don't know what the hells it is to know if I like it or not," I reply.

"I made it with your 4-D printer using a program called Illuminate. It's a Light Disc. Catch."

Gifford tosses it to me, and I snatch it out the sky with one hand. I peer at it closely. "Did it just dim on its own?"

"Yep. Very observant of you," he says with a boyish charm that's halfway cute.

"Can't take all the credit. My Optic Aug's pretty nice," I say braggingly.

"Well, that baby is going to pay for itself," Gifford says, wagging a finger at it with a heavy sense of pride. "It brightens and dims automatically, scaling appropriately to the darkness of its surroundings. In the light of day, it will completely shut down."

I toss it back to him. "Fancy. Speaking of shutting down, take a moment to make yourself at home and grab something to eat from the fridge. We don't move out again until the morning. I'll take some sheets and rummage up a pillow for you so you can get ready to make your accommodations here on the couch."

"Couch?"

"Yeah. You got a problem with roughing it, spy-boy?"

"Not at all. But I don't wanna take a nap, Daddy," Gifford jokes. "We still have daylight, and I kinda want to explore the planet more."

"You step outside that door, and you may find more than you're looking for, kid," I growl. "Trust me, this place isn't worth the effort. Scan the Wave on your Holo-tablet to learn more about it if you really need to feed your curiosity. It'll be much more rewarding and safer to boot."

Gifford takes his backpack and stows his disc inside. "All right, you've convinced me. So what do the plans for tonight entail?"

My eyes narrow as my heart rivets in my chest. The thought of seeing Olia again gives me life. "Tonight, my friend, we start to map out all the pieces we'll need to get on to the *Eclipse*."

FIVE

Neyaz Jezpa – Reign's Home

After chatting a few minutes more with Gifford I feel the sudden urge to catch another couple hours of sleep and excuse myself from Gifford's company after preparing his couch for bed. I get a sense that Gifford isn't crazy about me leaving him to his own devices as he continually comes back and forth to my bedroom door to ask questions that I'm certain that mind of his fully knows the answers to, but that doesn't stop him from asking. Where's *this* or *that* fill his barrage of attempts of conversation, and after I wear him out with a few well-timed grunts and barks, he finally gets the picture and settles down, leaving me alone.

I drift off into a deep slumber soon after, and before long, my Optic Augmentation powers down and transitions into sleep mode. And that's where things get very strange. Augmentations are rare in Proxima Centauri, reserved only for those with high credits and status. Up until lending a hand in freeing Fabricius from Dagmas Rule, I had neither. But the Torrian Alliance is very generous to those who show fidelity. So after I contracted a near-fatal infection from scouring the bowels of the planet while infiltrating the

Palace—allowing William to kick the evil dictator Dominic to the curb—I received my reward for well-doing in the form of a hefty credit cache and a replacement for my infected Optic nerve.

But it turns out that my fading vision wasn't age or wear-and-tear related. Deliterious X or DX for short was the culprit.

That's the name of the virus that vied for my life. A nasty little booger indeed, DX guns for the host's nervous system first in an attempt to shut down all volitional control. Normally, it's a silent killer, but once the dust settled after the war, everyone was issued a complimentary medical examination from head to toe with each crack and crevasse excavated and analyzed. It didn't take the fine doctors of Ontarius long to pick up on the subtle symptoms of my failing Optic nerve to know I had contracted it. But exactly how or when, they had no spacely idea. They said that the treatment will force the virus to go into a dormant mode, and it should never awaken as long as I don't become immune-compromised. They injected me with a cocktail regimen through IV over a few days and then let me go, giving me a half-solid clean bill of health.

Although they caught it before it could spread, it was too late for my right eye. The myelin sheath had already disintegrated completely, all the way from the shaft to the insertion on the back of my eyeball, but just 2 millimeters shy of my occipital lobe. The doctors told me that I was a couple of hours shy being slapped with a death sentence, so I considered myself fortunate. And while science can never 100 percent replicate the original manufacturer's birth parts, it damn sure does come close. I can see at least 100 times more clearly than normal during the day and at least 50 percent at night. And it's littered with various upgrades from night to thermal and even amphibious vision, allowing for superior clarity during the most demanding environments.

But during sleep mode, my mind downloads every image my Aug recorded, even those things that my conscious mind ignored. Consider it a sort of backing up of information onto the server of my mind that's only accessible in my dreams or by a skilled neuro-scientist at a brain matter center. That is, unless I'm fortunate enough to recall any of it on my own and store it in my long or short-term memory.

Inside the darkness of my mind, random images flash by at light speed. Faces and still images I hardly recall ever seeing bloom before me, fighting for pole position with my normal dreams. I'm not sure how much of the dreams are mine or the augmentation's but in the past, when I try to make sense of it, I develop a splitting headache. So I've relented to just allowing my brain to sort it all out until I determine it absolutely necessary to explicate.

After tossing about for an hour or so, I finally wake to a bed of sweaty sheets and the familiar sensation of cool metal in my right hand. Martha. She's strapped to my palm with an automatic safety gauge activated by my fingerprints that only adheres to my mental impulses. In other words, it preserves my life while allowing me to take another's at a twitch of a finger.

I crawl from my bed and saunter into the kitchen to see Gifford squatting at the table, munching down on a bowl of fruit. "Where the hells did you get that from?" I ask as I scratch the top of my head.

He's finally lost the leather cap he's been sporting since meeting him on *The Gloria*. His skin is peach, and his hair is dark red, playing off the light blue of his eyes making him come off as the cross-breed of a humanoid prism. He's all curls and dimples as he slides his Holo-tablet across the table in my direction. "I made it."

"Let me guess. My 4-D printer?"

Gifford points at me with his free hand as if aiming a gun. "Bingo." He puts his hands behind his head shortly after as I pull up a seat and stick my hand in the bowl. "You can thank me later," he says.

"I'll do it later," I say, tearing a few grapes from their stems.

"There are roughly 3 ways to get onto the *Eclipse*," Gifford says with a sense of finality in his voice.

"Hold the hells up. I don't recall asking anything about Forge or his ship. I just want to eat right now."

Gifford leans forward. "I know. Just thought I'd beat you to it. I had to find something to occupy my time while you slept the day away."

"So spit it out then," I say.

"One, we already know about. Credits. Gotta have 'em. Lots of 'em at that."

"And you got 'em, right? Don't renege on me now."

"Of course, I do, but we need to have back-up plans for our back-up plans if we're going to make good on this deal. Agreed?"

I lean back and swallow. "Agreed."

"Agreed. The second way is by sneaking on. I was able to hack some old schematics of the *Eclipse,* which shows a weakness in the ventilation system that is propagated by the Dark Matter engines. The ship has to release gas every 24 hours to depressurize the internal systems and allow the ship to maintain life support at optimal levels. Consider it a sort of 'spaceship fart' if you will."

"Spaceship fart, great. Thanks. Just when I was starting to take my life too seriously, you offer up a dose of ludicrousness that immediately breaks the tension."

"I told you, thank me later, Mr. Reign. I mean, Reign." He pauses with a smirk. "Anyway, when that happens, I can lock on to the highest source of natural gas released from the vents and if we could get in close enough, we can make our way inside."

I shake my head. "Won't work. The rotating struts that encircle the *Eclipse* and create the Dark Matter shielding rotate at ridiculous speeds. Anything that comes within a hair's breadth of those things is instantly obliterated."

"Don't go breaking my resolve, Reign, I've got a plan for that too. But I'd rather exact it for our escape, not our entrance. Fighting your way inside is a lot more difficult. And, besides, half as fun of the third option."

"So what'll be then? Something fancy, like crashing a spaceship into it, or teleportation?" I ask with a snicker.

Gifford leans in closer, his elbows resting on the table. His eyes are bright, and his smile is wide as the day, although it doesn't touch his ears. "No. They invite us on board."

"Invite, ha!"

"That's right, red carpet and all."

"I take back what I said before about you. You are suicidal."

"When did you say that?"

"Doesn't matter, we're going with the first option. Which reminds me, when are you going to show me these...credits?"

Gifford shakes his head as if he's disgusted by my doubt and retrieves his Holo-tablet. He pecks away at the screen for a moment, and when he is done, he slides it back over to me and cocks his head. The number of zeroes on the screen makes me lightheaded. "Well, damn."

"Well, damn is right. Believe me now?"

"I do. But with this amount of credits, why the need for a back-up plan?" I slide the tablet back over to him.

"The credits only give us collateral and credibility. But we need a lot more to get on. You see, two solar days from now is the Day of the Solstice. A day everyone pays homage to the Battle Solstice on Fabricius. And...it's also the greatest gambling day in the galaxy. A day that Forge makes his largest credit haul of the year by placing bets in the Arena of Sport, otherwise known as The Gauntlet. Only the highest of high rollers are allowed on board."

The words "Arena of Sport" send a wave of prickles down my spine. Thoughts of Olia ring in my headspace. She's there, competing in it, or has been competing for a while now if she's even still alive. "So what do we have to worry about? By the looks of that Holo-tablet, you'll be one of the high rollers anyway."

Gifford waves a dismissive finger. "Ah, ah, ah. They only accept rare items for a wager." He picks up the Holo-tablet again, and his fingers begin to play.

"Let me guess, that's where the third option comes back in at, eh?"

"We're going...to use...this." When Gifford finishes playing this time, he flips the Holo-tablet around and holds it with two hands to flash the screen at me. "Behold, the *Concord*."

I'm instantly in love. The image of the beautiful ship spins slowly on the screen, demanding my attention. It's sleek, shiny, and hella sexy, sporting a two-man cockpit, half-pike wing deflector shields, and twin cannons mounted underneath each lateral wing. I swallow hard to curb the saliva filling in the back of my throat. All gray, no wait, more like silver that shimmers like waves of diamonds as the image of the ship pulses in artificial light of the Holo-tablet. With orange highlights evenly scattered along various sections of the fuselage, I come to the stunning revelation that I've never been more enamored by a ship in my life. "The *Concord*," I repeat in a whisper.

"Yes, the *Concord*," Gifford adds. "And it's yours."

"You own it?"

"No."

"You're giving it to me?'

"No."

"Okay, so how do we get it, or where do we get it from? You got another 4-D printer somewhere that can fabricate a ship of that size?"

"Not exactly," Gifford says with a slight shrug. "It's a little more complicated than all of that."

"How much more complicated?"

I feel of pang of regret swell in my chest for even chasing Gifford down this rabbit hole of conversation, but my curiosity quickly outweighs any neon flashing caution signs. "Slightly."

"Okay, then. How do we get it? Spit it out already, will ya?"

"It's owned by Princess Varia of the Toshin."

"So, do you know her?"

"Not at all."

A heavy sensation of dread returns and weighs in on my stomach. "So, how are we going to get it?"

Gifford's eyes lower, and a smile breaks the right side of his face. His grin shakes me to the bone. I know the news is not good. "We're going to get onto her ship and take it for ourselves."

SIX

"Ha! I knew it, you are bat-sheat crazy," I say, with a fair dose of satisfaction in my tone.

"What do you mean?" Gifford asks.

"Let me get this straight. You want me to steal a ship from a Princess in a gambling freighter and somehow escape without being detected?"

"I never said we wouldn't be detected. And who said anything about stealing?"

"I could've sworn you did."

"I said, take it. With a strong possibility of returning it once we are done," Gifford says with a shrug.

I lean back in my chair and gaze at him. "You got balls, kid, that I can't deny. Either that or you're smoking the strongest grade of Gochie powder ever made."

Gifford shakes his head. "You know what your problem is, Reign?"

I stand in frustration. "No, tell me, Doc. Matter of fact, let me park over on the couch over there while you break down my fractured psyche and dissect how growing up in a broken household led me down a path of reckless abandon."

"I don't think I possess that kind of skill set, nor do we have time for that sort of thing."

"And neither do I, *Doc*," I reply, my voice rising. "Please try not to take me seriously when speaking about family and mental instability."

This strikes a chord with Gifford. Up to this point, he was all smiles and candor. But something in my words stymies his laughter for a moment. Does he have familial issues as well? "Family? I thought that's what this was all about. You doin' this all for your family?" he says in a low tone.

"I…" I pause and sit back down. "I am. But this plan is beginning to unravel. You may not see it now, but, trust me, son, I've been involved with a lot of these sorts of missions. And this one stinks more than anything I've ever been a part of in my entire life."

"How do you know? You've barely let me explain how it could work."

He's right. I did cut him off. I've always been a run and gun personality. It's just my style. There's safety there. Hiding behind the walls of doubt and never allowing optimism to dominate my thoughts. It's preserved me. But why? Why do I think that way? Maybe it is about my father. He always scolded me for my impulsivity and compared me to my Uncle Darwin. He got locked up at an early age, and my father held that over my head for the extent of my entire teenage rearing. If I strayed outside the lines, even a little, he'd chastise me saying, 'There's a warm bed with your name on it, boy, right next to your uncle. Keep up this behavior and you'll be there soon enough.' So, quite naturally, anyone trying to call the shots of my life easily earns a bulls-eye for my resistance ammunition. And I've got an endless supply of that.

Gifford shifts in his seat and folds his arms across his chest in frustration. The tension between us rises, and I realize that I'm the source of the contention. He's only trying to help, and I've all but pissed away any chance of getting Olia back without that artifact, so it's not like I have a ton of options available. I sigh and lean forward, elbows on the table. "You're right, kid. Go ahead. I'll hear you out."

Gifford's eyes light up. "Fantastic," he says, rubbing his hands together. "While you were sleeping, I pondered a most excellent plan that I'm sure you'll..." Gifford stops talking as he stares back at me. He must notice the lack of enthusiasm written across my face and decides to cut to the chase. "Right, you're not interested in that part." I nod, and he continues. "Well, I've been doing some research about Princess Varia's ship, *The Sunset*. It's a space yacht...and a nice one at that. Rather large, with a full complement of up to 10 or so marines on board at all times. 4 levels with 3 docking bays: 1 interior for smaller ships and 2 external ports that extend from long tubular catwalks. They maintain an airtight seal to accommodate larger vessels. The *Concord* is a gift to the Princess, but she never flies it. No one does. Word has it that only a few pilots possess the skill to manage the controls. They require a neuro-interface that does a number on the brain."

"Who the hells made something like that?"

"The Scrappers of Volgin Prime, in the outer planets. They gave it to the Princess as a gift when her father, King Savin, died. Her mother, Queen Alarquin, took over and now allows her daughter to travel about the galaxy forging her own path."

"Some gift. If someone gave me something I couldn't use, I'd kill 'em." I ask the next obvious question. "Why the hells does she have it then?"

Gifford's head quivers as he muffles a laugh behind his grin. "That's because you lack the pedigree of the Royals and their geocentricism."

I raise an eyebrow. "Geo-what?"

"It's the belief that the universe revolves around one plane. And, come on, man, you've been around much too long to be naive. I know that you know how the minds of the rich work when it comes to the 'verse. In a Royal's mind, the universe revolves around them."

"Not all Royals share this sentiment."

"True, but the vast majority does. They're trained to do so. It's the only way they can survive. Hierarchism and such," Gifford says, flailing his hands in the air. "They want things that no one else does just because they can have it."

"Oh, I see," I say with a hint of sarcasm, trying my best to be somewhat interested. "Well, you were getting back to this fabulous plan of yours."

"So, the Princess is still searching for a suitable pilot. She's having an open house for interviews. She decided to host the event on her ship tomorrow, and we are invited."

"I know about the spy gig, but you didn't tell me you were a pilot too."

"That's 'cuz I'm not."

"And so how did we...wait, let me guess. You hacked us in." Gifford nods in a half bow. When his head lifts, his eyes meet mine, searching for some degree approval in my face. I take the bait and offer him something more than that. Praise. "Okay, I'm impressed thus far. What's next?"

"So this neuro-link is quite sophisticated. Artificial intelligence onboard was crafted to be self-modulating, always looking for a mind that can challenge its sense of plasticity." My eyes widen and then narrow. Gifford knows I'm lost. He sighs. "The A.I. can adapt to various challenging changes in its environments so that it is always in a position to generate a superior, desired outcome."

"Quite the egotistical booger, isn't he?"

"It's a female, notably fashioned after the personality of the Princess. That's why she loves the ship so. The pilot must sync with the A.I. from the start for the link to work."

"What qualifies a pilot to sync in this fashion?"

"You mean, what separates the Elect from the Aces? That's easy. Only Pelorians possess the mental fortitude to handle it. Something about a gift called—"

"Teleonotioning," I say, cutting him off.

Gifford seems surprised at my sudden interjection. A sense of pride washes over me. "You know of it?"

"I should. My sister Olia has the same gift. Sensing and seeing things ahead of time." I can feel my head quivering as I speak, similar to the way Gifford was doing when he was speaking earlier. "How do you think she's lasted this long on the *Eclipse* competing in that Arena of Sport?"

"Your sister's some intellectual stud." His eyes trace my body one time and then fall to the table. I know what he wants to say before he says it, and so I beat him to the chase.

"I know, I know. She inherited the brains, and I got the brawn."

"I wasn't going to say it."

"But you thought it. Please, proceed," I say, waving him along with my hand.

"I've accessed the dossier of pilot applicants, and only one is of Pelorian heritage."

"So the rest of the applicants are wasting their time then."

"Not really. If nothing else, they'll all get an opportunity to rub elbows with Royals for one night. And who doesn't want to do that?" Gifford asks with excitement in his voice.

"Me," I say.

"Well, don't rain on our parade. The last time I was around Royals was when..." Gifford pauses for a moment, and it's hard to tell in the dimness of the room, but I swear that his face pales a little. What is he hiding? "Well, when I hacked a few for odd jobs," he continues with a snicker.

"Who's the pilot?"

Gifford grabs his Holo-tablet and taps the screen, then hands it over. "His name is Jeffrey Mire, aka Stink."

"Stink?" I lay down the tablet. "Wonderful. Just like this plan of yours. How fitting."

"Ha, ha, ha! Very funny." Gifford wags his finger dismissively. "No, you haven't gotten to my plan yet. You only have a concept of it."

"And you are going to get to it at some point, right?"

Gifford sighs. "Right you are. The *Concord* is usually kept inside the inner docking bay, but on this night, it will occupy one of the external docks so that the pilots can take turns interfacing with it. That's phase 2 of their interview. The first phase involves a barrage of questions and tests by the Princess's Royal Nobles. She won't abase herself by participating in such a frivolous task. During the time between phase 1 and phase 2, we will *recruit* the Pelorian."

"And how do we recruit him?" I ask, making air quotes when I say the word recruit.

"Credits Reign, lots of credits. I scanned his bank accounts and found out that he needs credits. A sheatload of them to be exact. A couple of reports across The Wave indicate that he also owes quite a bit of pocket change to some rather nefarious characters. He'll come on board, trust."

My jaw tightens. The number of variables working against this plan is mounting. I want to leave now and do things my way instead, which normally involves blowing everything up and carrying away anything of value that remains. And, although I'll never openly admit it, Gifford's confidence is infectious. "Trust, huh?"

"Yes, trust, Reign. Try it on for once. It may fit you a lot better than you think." I don't respond, holding my peace and refusing to offer even the slightest twitch of a single facial muscle. "Anyway, when the Pelorian partakes in the interfacing portion of phase 2, we'll zip away."

I chuckle. "This is where the plan falls apart. Won't they have some sort of tracking mechanism onboard?"

"Not if I disable it first. While you're participating in phase 1 of the interviews, I'll slip away and deactivate it."

"When who does what?"

Gifford smiles; he's all teeth and tongue at this point. "Our relationship isn't much different than that of you and your sister, Reign. You're the brawn, and I'm the brains. Unless you have some hidden degree in mechanical engineering that I don't know about?" he asks casually.

"No," I mumble.

"You're going to have to start carrying your weight around here on these missions if we're going to be successful," he jokes. "Remember, this is only the first leg of this journey. The real fun starts on the *Eclipse*."

I don't share his witticism, but I am one who respects the level of care it takes to forge such a plan. Could it work? Possibly. I nod and begin to clap my hands. "I can't offer any objections at this point."

"Great! So tomorrow, we need to go into town and grab some suitable attire for the occasion. You and I need to look our best, you know?"

"No need. I'm sure I have something suitable in my closet. Recall that I rubbed elbows with the Royals in my past life. I chose to walk away."

"And that's why you have a slew of Dagmas rejects hunting you down. Why'd you do it?"

"For one, I needed to find my sister. And two…two…it. It's just not my style," I lie. After Battle Solstice and the death of King Gregorio, I couldn't stand to live in the Palace anymore. Everything reminded me of him. The burden of guilt was suffocating. And even though there was nothing I could've done to stop Dominic from killing him, Gregorio still died on my watch. No real spy could ever live with that.

"Don't talk to me about style. Style, it seems, isn't your strong point. I already looked in your closet, and, well, let's just say that you need a real overhaul. But that's for another time. For now, I've got the credits and eye. So we'll get you looking the part in no time. By the way, our shuttle leaves around noon. It's a half-day's trip, so we'll arrive at *The Sunset* just as things pop off."

"Shuttle, huh? Didn't you think of everything?"

Gifford points at his temple. "Wouldn't be the brains of this outfit if I didn't. I assume you approve of my plan?"

"I…do."

"Fabulous!" Gifford stands and extends his arms wide as he stretches. "Time to get some sleep now. My *couch* is waiting. Oh, and you can thank me later."

I roll my eyes. "Noted."

SEVEN

Space Freighter – Opus

3 Days Earlier

We wake the next morning and make haste into town to pick out a few items before embarking on the route to the *Opus*. This shuttle was a little classier than *The Gloria* and faster too. Lavish cushioned seating rounds out the individual cabin, complete with a bathroom that offered a shower if need be. It's complimented with gold-trimmed faucets that spew warm vapors that can cut away and remove even the peskiest dirt and grime in minutes.

They remind me of the ones back on Fabricius, in the Palace. I recall the first time I used one to blast my back with pulsing waves of water, as multiple shower heads placed just above eye-level, projected from the wall before me. I lathered the rest of my body with a charcoal soap and allowed the jets to remove each solitary sud from every inch of my skin. Smooth as the day I came from my mother's womb. I could've sworn it removed a few layers of skin in the process. And maybe even stripped away a few solar cycles as well.

There's an overhead storage area to accommodate our personal belongings, although we don't really need them since we checked in the two large luggage pieces in the belly of the ship. You'd be surprised what they'll let you check-in for the right amount of credits. As long as your artillery is strapped down, it's yours to manage.

Both my grenades and Martha should be safe, especially since I locked them in steel cases that only my retinal scanner can open. Gifford pecked away on his Holo-tablet as normal for the majority of the ride, zeroed in on any last-minute details that we may have overlooked in our conversation last night. To our surprise, our scheduled half-day trip turned out to be a few hours shy of the originally planned trek to the *Opus*.

"Honored travelers, thank you for choosing Safe Net Travels as your means of transport today," a young man's voice rings out from the overhead intercom. "We will be arriving at the *Opus* within a few moments and docking shortly. Please have all your belongings, as well as one form of identification available before disembarking. We hope you enjoyed your trip and please choose us to be your number one choice for travel in the future."

I walk over to the bathroom and take one last look in the mirror. Admittedly, I clean up well, and truthfully, I have Gifford partly to blame for that. Long black lapels run the length of my body elongating my torso as the tailored suit hugs my frame. I'm crisp to the eye, donned in all black, from the neck down to my pants, which meet perfectly at the top of my shoes. Gifford handed me a pair of diamonite cufflinks before we left Jezpa and begged that I wear them. Initially, I refused to pour on the sophistication too thick, but he wasn't having any of it, emphasizing that everyone would be clean to the gills and I had to do my part to fit in or the mission could be ruined.

Thoughts of Olia were the only thing that convinced me to follow his advice. I snatched them from his hands and pinned them at my wrists. The glare from the stones is damn near blinding as it reflects the light. This sort of gaudy thing is nothing like me. Nothing like the place I'm from.

I'm a creature of the night. A child of the cold, dark ghettoes of Overlight—the birthplace of everything cruel and evil—a moon of the outer planets so war-torn and savage that it beckons civil unrest like men desire power and greed. I lived there until the age of 14. That's when my father shipped both Olia and me off to stay with our cousin, Bosko, who lived in the Inner Colonies on the moon Teir, just shy of Fabricius. That was the last time I ever saw him. The monumental time of my life that forged me into the beast of a man I am today. Fate, it seems, is not without a healthy degree of karma as Overlight soon after was decimated by Civil War. A series of nuclear bombs ravaged the moon and destroyed nearly half the population.

Most believe it was the brainchild of a government so corrupt and debauched that they were determined to purge the planet and start over. So decades later, after the fallout dissipated, the planet recovered. Somewhat, allowing the new government of Magistrates and Governors to reign in a more democratic society where popular, majority votes dictate decisions.

In another world, I may have turned out to be someone else. I often think long about it, especially after living in such close proximity to the Torrian society while doing covert missions for the King. Everything was under the radar. I served as a spy back then with no one, and I mean no one knowing my true identity—not even King Gregorio.

Talk about prime living arrangements. Plush amenities with large, healthy horses that run along the multi-acre grounds with ponds and lakes filled with all kinds of beautiful fishes. The water is clear enough that you can stand on the surface of the center of any lake and see straight to the bottom. And don't even talk about the flowers and lush vegetation that populate the many gardens and fields of the property.

It was how I could have been, would've been had I not been kicked out of school. My cousin Bosko had an in with the principal of the school and had me placed on the Elitist Tract. I was to receive an education in Sophisticated Robotics and further learn everything it took to blend in with other like-minded students. That was until I punched Delvin Cook for touching Olia inappropriately. Split his bottom lip in two. There was no coming back from that. You see, his father was the head Dean of Second School, and no one was going to tolerate such behavior, especially from a dreg like me from Overlight.

So my love for Olia got me cast out, and I was forced to take on odd jobs here and there to help pay bills. "Everyone has to pull their own weight," I recall my cousin saying back then. He had deep sagging bags underneath his eyes and the skin on his hands was coarse like sandpaper from numerous late nights of working at the factory. He took me with him one day to see where he worked and offered me a few credits to lend him a hand. I dove right in and pulled my weight for a bit, helping him hoist metal rudders from crates—used to guide hover ships for tourists on the Ring Planets— and placing them in large boxes to be shipped off-world. I hauled as many as my narrow legs could bear until finally giving out and sending me barreling to the floor, with one of the beams pinning my finger beneath it. I screamed but held back an ocean of tears as I wiggled my hand free and ran off to the bathroom to rinse off the grime and run it under the cool water to ease the pain. Uncle Bosko, as he made us call him later, finally caught up with me and after he checked me out to make sure all the digits could still move, he put me on light duty in the office stacking papers and helping out the administrative assistants. I felt like I punked out, but at least I still had my fingers.

Weeks slipped by as my resentment for my father abandoning us grew, etching small scales around my heart. I hated it at the time, but looking back, I realized it was the best decision for both me and Olia. Living without love gave me tough skin, and either good or bad, it forged me into the man I am today. A survivor.

As for Olia, she shined like a star, graduating in the top 10 percent of her class before shipping off for Secondary School. Seeing my sister flourish in the brokenness of our circumstances pinned a permanent smile on my face, always. But it was equal parts bitter and sweet because it marked the time of our separation. And seeing as though Olia was headed down a positive road, I took to finding my own path. And that's when I was recruited for my first infiltration job by the Thieves Guild.

Credits by the bushels. That's what they promised me. And for the most part, they delivered. But one thing you learn about running with thieves is that there's no honor among them. After a few solar cycles of earning enough bucks to carry me for a couple more, they turned on me and leaked my identity to multiple other competing guilds in the galaxy. It wasn't long before I fell on the radar of Bounty Hunters, so I had to think fast if I was to live another day. A good buddy of mine suggested I contact the Spy Guild for work and sanctuary. Ironically, they bore the name Thieves of Light, so I considered it to be a sign, either of my impending death or my resurrection. But without any other options, I followed his lead and linked up with their leader, a man named Tannan. On the day of our meeting inside an old bar of an abandoned platform space station, he grilled me on my past experiences as a thief. My resume was long and impressive, but it didn't move him one bit. I remember staring at Tannan as he sat across the table from me. His skin was dark like honey, with a set of high cheekbones and deep-set eyes that gave him a look of permanent derision. As words spilled from his mouth,

I could barely make out movement from his lips, which were completely shrouded by a thick red beard.

By the time the interview was over, I was flanked by 4 more visitors, armed guards of Tannan. But I didn't panic because our hour-long conversation had gone better than expected. I credit my checkered past more than my bountiful resume. Tannan and I, it seemed, were kindred spirits after all, both growing up on Overlight, with the exception that he lived through the Civil War losing his mother and being the only survivor of 4 boys. He escaped with his father in his late teens and landed on a mining planet in the outer planets. There, he eventually buried his ailing father who was suffering from dementia due to being exposed to an excessive amount of radiation from the nuclear fallout. He completed the remainder of his days there before shuttling off to start the Eastern District of the Spy Guild. We shared a few laughs and even tears over our circumstances before he welcomed me with open arms as a brother.

No one fooked with me after that. He completely erased my identity and deleted any file across the Wave that carried my likeness or history. I became only a figment of the imagination.

"Ready?" I hear Gifford's voice ring from behind as I glare at the unrecognizable image of my own reflection.

"Always," I reply as I turn to look at him. Gifford is nothing like me, he's young, full of excitement and energy. His eyes take in everything in his surroundings, but he's as naive as a Cardack infant. In the few days of being around him, he's grown on me like a fresh handful of moss. I've never had a little brother before, and except for Prince William, I've never been a surrogate older sibling to anyone at that. But as it stands, for now, I'll serve as Gifford's, at least until this little alliance is over.

"I'm really excited about this event," he says, straightening his bow tie around his neck. Even in the muted light of our cabin, his purple suit blinds me, only buttoned at the bottom as to reveal the red-line colored shirt underneath, with matching socks and black shoes.

"You should be. This is your idea. Stay close and try not to talk too much."

"As if you have to warn me."

"I do," I grumble.

Our shuttle comes to an abrupt halt as the sound of the external airlocks magnetizes to the outer hull. It's not long before we're all shuffling into the disembarkment pier at the front of the shuttle, in a single file line that runs the length of the ship. Gifford and I are first to exit as he paid extra for priority deboarding. We make our way to the baggage area and quickly grab our things, which consist of only one backpack apiece.

As we begin to enter the *Opus*, we're met by a tall, beautiful female Furling with shaggy orange hair that runs along her bare shoulders and arms. She's wearing only a loose-fitting, elegant white gown that straps around her neck and falls to the floor, covering her feet. I wonder how she'd run in that garb if this ship was to go belly up from a Space Pirate attack and picture her falling flat on her face, long canine teeth impaling the floor. The image in my head forces a smile across my face. But I quickly shed the thought as she addresses Gifford. "Welcome aboard, gentlemen." She holds out her hand, revealing carefully filed nails to make her appear less intimidating. Furlings are close cousins to Fanglings, minus the ability to grow five times their size in a fight like Prince William's comrade StarKozy. It was that primal ability that saved him runs through the Arena of Sport and helped William eventually escape the *Eclipse*. "Boarding passes and invitations please," she says with a lisp.

"Of course," Gifford says, pulling the documentation from his bag. He hands it to her, and she quickly scans it with a metal device the size of a toilet paper roll.

When she's done, she hands it back. "Thank you for this." She gives a slight bow. "Please enjoy your stay, pilot," she says slowly as her eyes pass over me.

I almost miss my cue to respond, forgetting for the moment that I'm supposed to be a pilot and Gifford a handler, but Gifford shoots me a look that beckons me to jump into character. "I'm sure I will," I reply in a flirtatious tone.

Large, expensive vessels such as these have alias call-signs to hide their whereabouts from the unindoctrinated, Gifford explained earlier when I questioned if we were headed to the correct ship or not. For the regular folk, it's called *The Sunset*, but to people like us, it's the *Opus*, at least for one day. We enter the large oval galley of the *Opus* and everything is as advertised. From the inside, you'd have a difficult time believing you're in space. Tall columns dwarf both of us, reaching the 30-foot ceilings, which sport countless dangling chandeliers, each one adorned with hundreds of precious amethyst and opal crystals. Gold walls surround us, and red curtains border the edge of the fake Holo-graphic windows, that flash scenery of tranquil forests, countrysides and even deep space itself. My eyes sweep across huge, cream-colored marble tiles as they sprawl before us and run the span of the floor, where not 1, but 2 pianists play music from the twin baby Grande pianos. A pair of harpists sandwich them in as they tickled the strings of the platinum instruments.

The sound of the music is breathtaking. Whether intentional or not, the music is relaxing, and I take a moment to enjoy the soft tones. If there's any truth to the saying that *music soothes the savage beast*, I will wager to believe it at this point. As beautiful as everything is, nothing is distracting enough to pique my interest and break my focus. That is until a female voice cries out my name from behind. Not Steel, but Cassius. I turn.

A stunning woman with dark hair pinned in a knot on the crown of her head and wearing a long red dress approaches. I stop breathing as she pulls up short a foot away from me, clutching a small gold bag with both hands. As she bats her eyes, her sultry voice speaks. "Mr. Reign, it's been a long, long time. We have much to talk about, I'm sure."

EIGHT

"You're as pale as a ghost," Gifford mumbles next to me."

I elbow him away and finally speak. "Serias Canus. Fancy meeting you here," I say.

Serias walks closer to me and offers her right hand. "Cas—"

"Shhh," I whisper, pressing my index finger over my lips. "That is a name long left for dead." I place a soft kiss on the back of her hand.

"Ahh, yes, I remember now. A time before you joined the Thieves of Light." She smiles and slowly pulls her hand away. I stand, and our eyes finally meet. "How long has it been since we last...spoke." Her eyes narrow, and I pray that Gifford doesn't notice her flirtatious act.

I swallow and slightly turn to see if he's paying attention. When I do, he quickly looks away and whistles to himself. I'll have some explaining to do later. "8, maybe 10, solar cycles ago," I murmur as I turn back to face her. My eyes narrow a bit. "But I still remember the time as if it was yesterday," I whisper. "Tell me. How were you able to track me down after all this time?"

The corner of her mouth rises wickedly, and her nostrils flare. I know that look all too well. She's pissed. "Don't flatter yourself, Cassius."

"I was never one for flattery," I say. "I was merely asking a question. That's all. Feel free to hold your tongue."

Serias crosses her arms and speaks. "Oh, the gods…Yes, you were never one for flattery nor for manners, Cassius, so I'll take the onus of the responsibility upon myself to school you in the latter." Serias begins to slowly pace sideways as she speaks like an alpha Cardack does his prey. "In the outer planets, it's common courtesy to speak when spoken to and to never, and I mean never, answer a question with another question. So I'll offer you an answer to yours." She comes to a stop and tilts her head as she glares at me through narrow slits. "And since you're asking a question, then it'd be rude of me to simply ignore you. So I won't. I hunted you down, *Master Spy*."

Her last two words send a chill across my body that brings with it the unexpected result of giving me a slight boner. "Hunted me down? All you had to do was call. My number never changed," I say. The energy between us is palpable. As it was long ago when we were an item. Serias, named after the brightest star in the sky Sirius, from constellation Canis Major, was just as the name implied. A beautiful, shimmering, and radiant beauty. When we met, I was already a member of the Thieves of Light, and she was a newly dubbed recruit. They assigned her to my sect, and I taught her everything she knew. Well, almost everything. Anything dealing with seduction and pleasure came to her naturally, and she never disappointed.

While she demonstrated perfection in the sack, I excelled in the field. Guns were my specialty, and she was an adept pupil. A quick learner. That's what attracted me to her, minus her stunning looks. Before long, she was shooting stink flies off the backs of Cardack with repeater pistols without even singeing a single follicle of fur. We even ran a few missions together for the Guild. Infiltration and dissemination were our favorite assignments. I brought the power and she brought the skill. Our names became famous among the whispers of Guild elders and it wasn't long before murmurs of us inheriting the reins left behind if Tannan were to be reassigned. But that was just a dream.

"No, I think it was more like 7. But who's counting," Serias says dismissively. She remains still, holding both hands at her waist, still clutching her gold bag and only offering a slight nod in Gifford's direction. "Hello."

"The pleasure's all mine," Gifford says with a childish smile.

"What?" she asks.

Gifford's face turns red. "I said," he starts with a chuckle, realizing no doubt that she never offered any words in his direction that would necessitate his untimely response, before abruptly finishing with, "the pleasure is all—"

"Don't hurt yourself, son," I say with a laugh as I barge in. "So, again, I say Serias, fancy meeting you here."

"Not really. You know full well the circles I run in Cass—I mean, Steel," she says, correcting herself this time.

I quickly look around before dropping my gaze back on Serias. "Actually, the circles you run in never approve of Holo-graphic windows and harpist. At least, last, I remember. But what do I know…that *was* 7 solar cycles ago. Right?" I ask with a wink.

"Right," she says without returning a wink. Serias' eyes momentarily bounce around the room too, and when they land back on me, she finally speaks. "What is it that you want with the Princess, anyway?"

"You know me. What else do I long for?" I ask.

"Winning," Serias answers.

"Precisely right," I say.

Her eyes run the length of my black suit. "And what, you a pilot now?"

"Maybe," I say.

"And what would you be winning?" she asks.

"Everything, of course," I reply confidently.

"Not *everything*," she says, tilting her head. Her words are laced in a bitter tone, and they strike at my soul. She knows what I felt for her. What we felt for each other. What they took from us, I could never get back again. My hands fist at my sides as I squeeze until the pain in my chest resonates into my fingers. The Guild shuns relationships among members and although we kept our relationship as low-key as we could, eventually, they found out and separated us as only the Spy Guild could. In death.

At least that's what they thought.

The funny thing about trying to kill a person who's waiting for death to appear at their doorstep every waking moment of their life is that you'll never do it unexpectedly. And on the fateful day when I saw Death's face surrounding my ship, I pulled the eject cyclic, catapulting myself some 300 feet in the sky while simultaneously initiating the self-destruct button. Lit the entire hangar bay of Delvis Chong ablaze.

But I was safe, cleared of the blast and descending slowly in a parachute—caught in a down-draft from the snowstorm that day—which landed me some 1000 yards outside of town. Everyone counted me as dead since the blast left no survivors. So I did what any good spy does...I went ghost. I wasn't sure if she got out alive, and it was our code to vacate and survive—a term affectionately coined as *Kill Streaking*. From that day on, I never saw Serias again.

"You're correct. Winning everything isn't always possible. You have to compromise some things and take what Lady Fate gives you," I finally reply.

"Funny, I never thought Lady Fate could keep you warm at night," Serias says.

There's a sudden silence between us that seems to even drown out the background music of the musicians. "Speaking of warm," Gifford says, piercing the quiet, "we need to be getting in line for the interviews, Mr. Reign."

"How is that speaking of warm?" I ask absently.

"Because you're already on fire with the preliminary questionnaire, and I'm quite sure you don't want to lose the momentum and sit around waiting while your neurons get cold." Gifford takes me by the arm, laughing as he tightens his grip. I look down at his hand as his grip loosens and as my eyes dart over to him, he speaks again. "Right, Captain?"

Suddenly, it comes to me. Gifford can see it as plain as the nose on my face. Serias is doing it to me again, intoxicating me with her beauty and her seductive ways. "Yes," I say in agreement. I look over to Serias and grant her an agreeing nod. "We must be going. It's time to win." I crack a smile. "Good day."

Before Serias can answer, Gifford whisks me off to a side hallway heading to God knows where. "Focus, Reign," he stammers.

"I am focused!"

"Yeah, on winning pussy, not on winning the *Concord*," Gifford says. He must notice the glazed over look on my face and speaks again, attempting to shake me from my stupor. "Remember Olia. She's on the *Eclipse*."

Gifford's words shake me free from Serias' grip. "Fine, dammit. You're right," I say harshly. "You're right," I repeat, my voice lowering.

"Yes."

"What is she doing here?" I murmur.

"What?"

"Is the Spy Guild working this case too?"

"Who cares! We've got our own mission to tend to, Reign, and don't have time to get caught in the crossfire. In and out, remember? Whatever her play is, let it be. Let her have at it. She's got her thing—"

"And we've got work to do. I know."

"Exactly! So act like it." Gifford looks back down the hallway. "She is fine, though," Gifford says, nodding, his smile breaking to both of his eye sockets.

"Silence."

"Right."

"So how do I pass these interviews?" I ask.

Gifford chuckles. "Did you not hear a word I said earlier on the shuttle over here?"

"Not really. Well, I heard you, but I really wasn't listening."

"You're only supposed to stall during the interviews. Answer the questions as best you can and then when they ask you about something you have the slightest idea about, you talk about sheat that has nothing, and I mean nothing to do about flying. I need you to buy me some time to hack past the security hall that leads to the external docking clamps for the *Concord*."

"Right, right," I say with a nod. "Point me in the right direction. The sooner I get the fook outta her, the better."

"Outta *here,* boss," Gifford repeats glaring at me with a heavy sense of concern washed across his face.

"That's what I said, outta here," I reply, annoyed.

"No, boss, you said, outta *her.*" His eyes expand. "That has a totally…totally different meaning."

"I didn't say that…and even if I did, whatever. You know what I meant."

Gifford takes me by both shoulders. His grip is firm. "Snap out of it, big guy. I need you here. 100 percent. You can't have an ex-girlfriend on the brain if this is going to work. There can't be any distractions."

"We play this by the numbers. I'll do my part. You do yours. Give me time frames. I'll be *where* you want *when* you want. Not a second off."

Gifford lets me go as his hand strokes his chin. "Fine."

***

We spend the next couple of hours enjoying our time aboard the *Opus.* The entire ship is buzzing by this time, with scores of people bustling about, with standing room only. Gifford, enjoying a drink or two of his own and even trying his hand at Veniserian Toss, a game in which the contestant tries to ring the freshly shaven horn of a baby Cardack from some 100 yards away, managed to win a few credits for his efforts. Pocket change for an affluent lad like him.

He mingles with the crowd a lot more than I'm willing to do, unable to shed my disdain for these high rolling fools, drunk on their obsessions of both being seen and talked about. Their lack of self-control and frivolous spending make my stomach turn. With some luck, I'm able to avoid Serias as much as possible, hopeful of shaking whatever remnant of feelings that swirl inside my belly and threaten to bubble out of my gut and make me do something stupid like telling her how much I've missed her.

I finish my 5th cup of purified Cantalean water and slam it on the bar as a robotic drone floats by and collects the empty glass before I can blink. Normally, I'm a regular hooch hound for Crilean or Kinuian Ale, but up to this point, I exercise restraint to keep my wits about me, unsure of when I might be *persuaded* to buss off a few shots from Martha's muzzle if things go south. Just then, a female waitress saunters by with a tray of the tasty-looking stuff and I swear the back of my throat grows desert dry. I could drink the entire bar full right now and still catch a boner the size of my leg. I chuckle to myself at the idea of this impossibility and just as I do, the Princess Varia sweeps by, quickly rushed along by an entourage of 10 or more underlings. The majority of which bark at the crowd to make room while two or three others carry the train of her gaudy gold and silver colored gown that hangs from her shoulders and droops low enough from behind to reveal the house sigil tatted on her mid-back.

They clear the crowd and make their way to the back of the ship atop a fleet of spiraling stairs for a makeshift interview with some galaxy reporter, no doubt detailing the purpose and expectation of the night's events. I gaze at the Princess' lips, revisiting my skills as an expert lip reader to pass the time. As she babbles on about rumors of war and her family's dedication to maintaining the peace of the outer planets, an odd thought flickers in my mind. It flashes back to the vision of the Kinuian Ale atop the tray of the waitress. Kinuian Ale fetches a pretty credit on the Inner Colonies, and here it is being served by the droves aboard the *Opus*; a Toshin vessel which is the property of House Alero? Every house in the outer planets persists in a perpetual contest to control any and every resource available— libations included. So why not here?

Just as my skepticism meter begins to climb, Gifford's voice chimes in from my right. "Hmm, do you have a timer on you?"

"No," I reply, my voice slightly savage. "I'm a spy, remember. I have an automatic timer in my head. When I focus, this entire place could be involved in an orgy and I can still count to 100 forward and backward with perfect timing."

"Okay, you made your point," Gifford says. He claps me on the shoulder. "Fabulous imagery there, by the way."

"What's the sudden obsession with time all about anyway?" I ask.

Just as Gifford is about to explain, my Optic Aug begins to ping as a flashing orange circle floats along the wall behind him. I focus, blocking out Gifford's words and zeroing in on the circle as it slows and begins to blink as if locking on to a target. I brush Gifford to the side and sharpen my gaze. Seconds later, the walls of the hallway become translucent, revealing a vessel off in the distance, several hundred yards away. It's sleek, laced in seamless, shimmering metal that's grayer than silver, with patches of orange and brown along the hull that run the length of the vessel and converge at the tail and wings. Twin canons hang from the tips of each wing, and the red heat shield of the cockpit is fully protracted, hiding the interior. It's the *Concord*.

"That's it," I say faintly.

Gifford stops talking, turns, and follows my line of sight. In a flash, he's standing beside me, gazing in the same direction. "Yes, that's it, Reign. Impressed?"

"Easily."

"Well, that's where I'll be going soon, while you'll be," he pauses and spins me in the opposite direction, "headed that way."

"Right," I say.

"What's the mission again?" he inquires.

"Distraction."

"Excellent."

I open my backpack and look inside, checking on Martha, nestled behind my Holo-tablet. "You sure you'll be able to disable the ship's locking mechanism on our weapons?"

"I will, in due time. Don't worry, Martha will be ready when it's time to take the prize," Gifford says confidently.

I close the bag and look at him. "And how much time you think you need to do all this?"

Gifford's eyes flutter as if some surge of electricity is flowing from his neck and up into his brain. After a few twitches, he answers, "55 minutes, give or take. Can you manage it?"

"Whatever you say. Consider it done."

"Perfect." Gifford reaches for my bag, and I protectively pull it away from him. His eyes widen. "Come on. You don't think you can go into the interview packing, do you?"

"What if I did?"

Gifford shakes his head in disgust. "Don't worry, Martha will be safe. Find me once you finish."

I begrudgingly hand him the backpack and nod. "What about the real pilot?" I ask, looking around the room.

Gifford looks down at his wrist, eying his Holo-band. "I've already got a lock on him. He just boarded."

"How do you know?"

Gifford reaches into his pocket and pulls out the Daedallus Cube. "This is linked to this," he says, alternating finger points between the cube and his watch. "The cube started vibrating the second he got off that second shuttle. I'll be *pimping* him soon."

"But you've only got 55 minutes."

"Right! 35 to pimp, 15 to grab a drink and mingle and 5 minutes to hack."

I raise an eyebrow at that. "5 minutes?"

"Who do you think I am Reign? Do I look silly enough to drag you along in this mission if I couldn't hack some basic Space Cruiser's security protocols?" Gifford cuts his eyes at me, filled with a flicker of pain in them. For a brief second, I feel guilty. It's not until he glares back at me again, and barks, "You can thank me later," that I'm overflowing with frustration with my present circumstances and determined to end this ordeal as swiftly as possible.

That's when my patience wanes, along with my confidence in things running smoothly. "Have those doors open when I'm finished. We're going to blow this joint."

NINE

I was 21 when I mistakenly sacrificed my first life for the Thieves' Guild. I say mistakenly because thief jobs are never supposed to end in death. Our talents lie in deception, trickery, and stealth, not killing. So when I say that the incident changed me forever, I don't mince these words lightly.

Lionessus Dioneecy. I remember his name as if it was yesterday. His memory painted against the back of my brain, unmovable, stark, and prevailing. It was my first taste of the royal life. My handler had successfully gotten me on board his luxurious space palace, affectionately known as *Twilight*, hanging in pristine orbit of the planet Adonis. A day pass as a tourist only lasts for 6 hours, so I had to act fast. The target: a Horintian Crystal necklace. A precious family heirloom. A 24 total carat weight gem of unfathomable value.

The plan was simple. Get in, make friends, lift a key card from some foolish lackey, penetrate the vault, bypass the security system and take the spoils—replacing it with an item of equal weight, a gold figurine replica of the Thieves' Guild shield.

I'd done it numerous times before that I swear I began to successfully pull off a similar mission with my eyes closed. That is when things were normal. And by that I mean, the kind of normal dealings that involve arrogant fools, drunken on the libations of greed and lasciviousness. It made it easy to steal from them. It made me hungry to do it again. But this time, things were nothing close to normal. Something lost in the details.

First of all, someone failed to tell me that Lionessus had a child. A little boy, 6 solar cycles of age, who took to me from the moment I set foot on board. He said I was the coolest thing he'd ever seen. Apparently, he's half Voshin and possessed the talent for detecting those with checkered pasts. Said he felt sorry for me. That somehow he could sense that I carried a lot of pain in my heart and that one day, I must find a way to heal.

Second, the foolish lackey person of interest this time was a female Pelorian, dressed in a long emerald gown with long sleeves that covered the entire length of her arms and draped down to the floor, hiding her feet. She was disfigured in the face by a birthing accident that left her with a scar that ran at a diagonal from the top of the right side of her face to the opposite side of her neck. She reminded me so much of Olia back then. Young, frail, and vulnerable.

Third, Lionessus wasn't supposed to be on board.

These 3 variables shocked me off course, fooking with my head, causing me to lose my mental focus.

I had only one hour left before visiting time was done, and I made my final attempt to close the deal. So I broke away from the child and started snooping around. My footsteps led me to the arboretum, a large space just outside the holding place for Lionessus' vault. The area was virtually empty, void of anyone other than the Pelorian and me. She was gracious enough to allow me to manipulate her into giving me a private tour of the vessel. I laid on my charm only half as strong as what was necessary to pull off the job, and she ate it up like a starving slave child from the bowels of planet Rizen. She wore a girlish grin the entire time, and I relished in the power of my candor.

Taking advantage of people like that used to bother me in the early part of my career as a thief. But over time, my remorse quickly faded, replaced by the desire to eat and live. But even more than that. Thrive.

Paydays were few and far between, and it was either swim or sink. What is she feeling right now? I thought back then, and she played to my advances and hung on my every word. That this is the moment when we partake in some magical, intimate moment? That possibly things would advance beyond just a simple meet and greet and that I'd whisk her away from this life of subjugation?

No. I recognized that smile and the naïve look on her face. She's thinking of something more. Something powerful. Something like…love. She pointed over to a large, gaudy, hand-painted picture of Lionessus on the far wall and leaned slightly into me as she shared details about the famed artist and the elegant strokes he used to create the vision before us. As her shoulder pressed into my chest, she turned away and snickered. When she turned back, our eyes locked. That's when I had her. If I wanted to. My eyes dropped to the key card dangling from the lanyard hanging around her neck. The object of my true desire. But when it came time to lift the key from her, I failed, finally succumbing to the pang of guilt seeping into my headspace as memories of Olia overwhelmed me.

I leaned away and asked if she could get us something to drink. She graciously abided and headed out, leaving me alone with my thoughts. That's when I found my resolve again and began to search for an alternate way to enter the vault. From the original dossier, the vault was hidden behind Lionessus' portrait. But how would I get in? I could attempt to utilize my lock picking skills and disengage the tumblers. But it's a slow process, and the Pelorian would no doubt be back before then. As I continued to ponder my options, the boy wandered in.

His eyes were bright as plasma cannons. And low and behold, he held a key card in his hand, extending it out to me. He told me that he knew of my intentions, but that my heart was true and that I was honorable and more deserving of the riches inside the vault than his very own father.

I considered it a trap until the moment the Pelorian returned. She held two glasses in her hand, filled to the brim with blue Joserian Liquor. But something was different. The key around her neck was missing. That's when I notice that it's the same one in the boy's hand. I cocked my head, but the Pelorian nodded me forward, beckoning me to take the key and finish the job. I pause and shake my head dismissively, but she explained that Lionessus was a mean-spirited man who undervalues everything he touched, including both her and his own son. She placed the glasses down on the marble floor and slowly pulled back one of her dress sleeves, revealing deep, purple and black bruises that cover her forearms and biceps. The boy lifted his shirt and turned his back to me, showing similar handwork of Lionessus.

My hands fisted at my sides. I fumed inside and wanted to burn the entire place down. And more than that, I wanted to kill Lionessus slowly and intimately as the people he hurt looked on. But, instead, I knew I had to control the rage burning within. I had to do things the smart way and finally chose to hurt him in the pocket instead. So I recommitted to the original plan of opening the vault while the Pelorian watched the entrance.

I made the swap and placed the Horintian Crystal necklace in my bag and sealed the vault door shut. As I handed the key card back to the Pelorian, she released a loud shriek, and her body went limp before me as black smoke wafted to the ceiling from behind her. I caught her just before she hit the ground and gently placed her head on the cold floor. When I looked up, Lionessus stood before me, clutching a repeater plasma pistol. With green and yellow markings along the shaft, the designation was unmistakable. A custom-modified version, no doubt, tricked out with a stabilizing upgrade. He couldn't miss me from this distance if he tried.

The boy ran to his father's side, gripping his leg as he shed tears and wailed aloud. Lionessus cocked the gun and kicked the boy to the ground, blaming him for the Pelorian's death. He promised to teach him a lesson later. Promised to make him pay. Promised that he'd never betray his father again.

He was right. The boy would never have to worry about doing anything to disappoint his father, ever.

Before Lionessus could aim in my direction, I activated my jet boots and flew directly at him. The blast rung out, sending a volley of plasma in the direction of nothingness. I reach out, grab hold of his arm, squeeze the wrist clutching the weapon, and drive my other elbow into his gut. We fell aggressively to the ground and began to tussle, me holding on as my life depended on it and Lionessus as if his legacy did.

As the boy cried out my name, Lionessus continued to scream, threatening words at him. Rage flooded me, and I fail to curtail it this time as my survival instincts took the driver's seat, with logic riding shotgun. I land a punch to Lionessus' jaw and quickly slip a hydrogen blade from my shoulder sheath with my free hand before ramming it in his stomach. As Lionessus squealed, I pull and drag the blade upward until it finds his jawline. Lionessus gurgled something unintelligible through a pool of blood and the plasma pistol fires one last time.

But it didn't hit me. The volley found its mark, emptying into the little boy. He dropped to one knee violently, holding his belly. I sprung to my feet and ran toward him. But before I could catch him, his limp body fell to the floor, dead on contact.

Escaping that day was the easiest part of the gig, as I accessed the ventilation shaft and weaved my way to the docking bay before anyone could lock down the vessel. I buried the memory deep within my psyche and promised to never unearth it again.

That is, until I met Serias. I don't remember how long it took for her to work it outta me, but, somehow, she did. It was the last time I can recall shedding tears for anyone, and Serias told me that I never would again. That she would carry the pain in her heart for me. She vowed that no soul would ever be able to hurt me like that, and if they did, she'd send them to the gods faster than light speed.

It's those memories that burn more now than ever. The betrayal she must feel for me when I left her all alone back on Delvis Chong, never to return. But I did it all for her...at least, that's what I told myself. What I convinced myself of. "The worst lie you could ever believe is the one you tell yourself," I recall Tannan telling me on the first day of Spy Guild training. And it rings true to this day.

Seeing Serias here, now, makes everything more complicated than ever before. I could give it all up, possibly tell her the truth and pray she'd take me back. But what would I ransom in return? Olia's life for my happiness? As I mull this decision while I stand in line for interview registration, I catch a glimpse of Serias strolling by in my periphery. She's still as stunning as the day I laid eyes on her. I watch and wait, hopeful that she'll turn and give me a look. Some flicker that I still haunt her memories as much as she does mine.

"You, step up," a voice grumbles before me. I shake from my daydream and approach the table, holding out my ID card. A man reaches forward and takes the card from me, scans it one time and hands it back. He points to a row of chairs to my right and flicks his wrist, ushering me over. Only one other person is seated. "Have a seat over there and wait quietly. You're next. The proctor will call you when ready."

I nod and take the ID card back. And as I step out of line, I look back, hopeful of finding Serias, but she is nowhere to be found.

TEN

"The next pilot is Cassius Reign," I hear an android announce as it steps out into the waiting area. I stand and approach the tanned synthetic, and it hastens to lead me down a long hallway with seamless, cream-colored walls that end at a solitary red door. A retinal scanner rests at waist-level along the right side of the door. "Please, look into the scanner. You'll see 3 flashes of green lights. Once it's over, the door will open. Good luck."

I follow the android's instructions and take a peek. And just as expected, my right eye is pummeled by 3 quick flashes of green light before a loud pinging noise erupts from the door just as it slides open. My mental clock starts the countdown. 35 minutes and counting.

When I enter the room, I'm met by a sprawling flow of alternating black and white marble square floor tiles that converge at a long table where four people are seated: one woman and three men. Two guards stand on either side; each one strapped with black and red assault rifles. Prime military-grade, no doubt. Why am I not surprised?

The whole thing reminds me of a primitive game I once played when I was a child, where you advance a piece across the board with the intent of removing your opponent's essential pieces first—the king and queen. The winner is only crowned as such when you successfully take the king of your adversary. Ironically enough, I'm overwhelmed by the sudden feeling of being played.

I look up, and the woman waves me forward. She's pretty, garbed in a white suit with long, flowing red hair that's pinned atop her head. She dons a pair of purple glasses that make her look twice as hot. While most guys don't find it attractive, I dig the nerdy-hot look on women, as it makes them come off as more intelligent. Some prefer a nice rack or a firm tail, but give me brains any day and I'm good. That's why Serias has her hooks in me so deep, lacking nothing in either department. Body like a goddess and brains like a professor.

The 3 men flanked alongside the redhead babe are thin and wiry-looking, like walking pipes. One sits to her right while the other two are on her left. They stare at me like a piece of prime meat, sporting the same color white on their uniforms as the woman, save for a few subtle differences. They wear vests, ties, and long-sleeved shirts versus her full suited attire.

At closer observation, I notice something odd. The 3 men are identical matches. Clones? Replicas? Or triplets? I'm not quite sure, but one thing I'm certain of, I'll find out soon enough. As I get closer, my eyes bounce between them, looking desperately for some sign, some minor differences in their facial features, like hair, nose, and eyes. But I come up empty. I cross the floor and come to a halt at the table. As the woman greets me with a smile, I'm confident that the 3 men are only here as a distraction. She alone is the main event.

"Octavious Champion, powerful name," the woman says. Our eyes meet, and I fight back a smile at the sound of the alias Gifford assigned me. The staging area for questioning is private. Here, they'll only know you as the person of your choosing. And, hopefully, my android escort won't tip them off to my true identity. Its hard-wired programming forbade it, but hells, it ain't like people are good at following the rules in Proxima Centauri, so why think otherwise of androids?

The one man on her right slides a Holo-tablet over to her, and she taps the screen. "In looking over your file, your resume is quite impressive." I have no idea what she's talking about. Gifford obviously fluffed up some sheat about me being a pilot, and I failed to prod him for the cliff-notes before boarding. So, I wait for her to speak again before answering, and when she does, I lay it on thick as molasses. "It says here that you flew for the Queen—"

"Yes, yes," I say, cutting her off. "I've logged over 50 cume space days of escort runs and cargo routes combined for royals during my career, but my biggest accomplishment lies in what I did between the sheets." I shoot her a wink to throw her off. "Know what I mean?"

The woman flinches a bit and rolls her eyes, but the 3 men seem unfazed by my arrogant approach, remaining silent and unmoved.

This intrigues me because if they remain noncommittal to this brand of dirty chivalry, I'll peg them as Replicas for sure. You see, Replicas differ from clones because in one conclusive trait—they lack a sense of humor. While clones utilize live brain tissue of the host, Replicas don't, relenting to utilizing focal memory implants that "mock" similar behaviors of the primary donor. Because of this, clones are reserved for only the special, only the filthy rich. They're possibly purchased by the Princess to be permanent friends, who never disagree but stroke her ego and build her confidence as supreme royalty, primed and groomed to take the crown. Or maybe they belong to someone else, this woman perhaps, and are here only to assist in the interviews, utilizing their natural intuition to separate the wheat from the chaff, the liars from the honest. Either way, they'll get neither from me. I don't deal in truths with people I don't trust, and I loath anyone trying to play me even more.

When the woman gathers herself, she cocks her head to the side and waves her hand in a direction behind me as a chair rises from beneath a sliding floor tile. "Please sit," she says.

I stroll over and oblige her request, but turn the chair around and straddle it, leaning forward on the backrest. This frustrates the woman to no end as her eyes widen at my defiance for the basic protocol. But, there's nothing *basic* about me, baby. If she thought the first interviewee was a challenge, she's in for a rude awakening with me. "So how long you guys been doing this?" I ask, my eyes darting across the 3 men's faces.

"We'll ask the questions," the woman says. Her lips form a tight line. "If you don't mind, would you please turn the chair around?"

"What, I thought this interview was supposed to be informal? But the way this set up is, it's like…nothing like that," I say.

"While this interview is somewhat informal," the man on the woman's right starts.

"The selection process is nothing of the sort," the man closest to the woman on the left finishes.

"And if you think that this is going to be some joyride gig from the outer planets, you're sadly mistaken," the last man adds.

As silence sweeps over the room, I begin to fume, insulted. But I keep my cool, determined to break them before they do the same to me. I give a nod and play as if I'm submitting to their requests for conformity. My mental clock kicks in—30 minutes left and counting. I've only been here for 5 minutes, and I'm already bored. "I get that," I say, "and I'm prepared to do what is necessary to land this job." I give a half bow. "Please forgive me. I was only trying to break the ice."

"Forgiven," the man on the right chimes.

The woman lifts the tablet and quickly slides her fingers across the screen as if she's looking for something. The pause between our conversations seems like forever, but in actuality, it's only 60 seconds. Finally, she stops her screen pecking and speaks. "Dear candidate, as you know, you've been cordially invited to participate in this interview process with a chance of successfully landing the most prestigious position of a pilot for Princess Varia," she reads. She babbles for another two minutes about how the procedure will run, asks if I accept the terms of the possible agreement, and if I give them permission to sign a non-disclosure about the events that will take place tonight. I agree with a nod, but she's not satisfied with that alone. "Mr. Champion, we are recording the interview, so you have to verbally agree aloud."

"I do," I belt.

The woman sighs and then proceeds. "Great. Let's proceed."

Red—as I refer now to her—pelts me with a barrage of questions about my past life as a pilot, which is a knee-high pile of sheat and I hold serve, slinging back an equal pile of manure that unexpectedly produces a smile across the woman's face. The triplets remain stoic, and I'm convinced even more that they're Replicas, which makes them somewhat dangerous in these types of situations. Their lack of facial expressions dampens my ability to provoke them, which makes my intention to bullsheat them less effective. That could force me to do the one thing in this interview that I don't want to—take them seriously.

8 minutes have passed, and the woman continues the interview, moving on to what she terms as Phase 2. "Let's move on to more personal questions. What about your upbringing?"

This strikes a chord. "What about it?" I mutter, my voice more raged now.

"Your records here are very scant. Says that you matriculated from the outer planets and finally spending the majority of your solar cycles on Fabricius, but we need to know more." She turns the Holo-tablet face down and leans forward. "So, please, chronicle the journey."

"Well, to be honest, I actually don't remember much of my youth. My father was a trader, and my mother died when I was very young," I lie.

"A trader," one of the men to her left chimes. "Not much of an affluent heritage there."

My blood begins to boil, but why? This entire story is fabricated, but if there's one thing I hate, it is when ritzy folks turn their noses up at me. And this guy is dangerously straddling that thin line. "Yes, I agree. I jumped that sinking ship as soon as I could," I reply with a chuckle. "Can't stand it."

"Who could? They give me hives," the man says, cutting an eye at his twins.

"They're so rough along the edges," the man next to him says. "Not like us, you know. Not like royalty." His eyes narrow at me. "They offer nothing of interest."

"Present company excluded," the first man rebuts.

"No offense," the other man says.

"None taken, of course," I say as my eyes lock back on to the woman. Her fingers nervously twitch as she tries to bring her hands together.

"Do you have any family, Mr. Champion?" she asks. "This job requires quite a bit of travel, as you might assume and, well, a family can be a…liability."

"If you're asking about a wife and kids, the answer is no. But, obviously, I have some family," I say. "It's not like I just materialized from dust and spit."

Oddly enough, this brings a roaring chorus of laughter from the triplets.

The woman waves a hand to silence them and smiles. "Good."

"But what about siblings? Sister? Brother?" the man to her right asks.

5 more minutes have passed. "No brothers…not like you," I bounce back.

"Like me?" he asks.

I nod in the direction of the other two men. "You know, like your halflings over there."

The man's face flushes red. The wheels in my head start turning. He's not a Replica. They never respond like that. Last I knew, they cannot react to emotional stimuli. But he can't be a clone either as none of them has intentionally laughed at a single word I've said except in a mocking tone after I referred to the old tale of the creation from dirt and spit. I've never been mistaken for the comedic type, but I gotta admit that most of this sheat-fest of an interview has gone so sideways that even the most stringent stick in the mud would have at least cracked a smile by now. Before they can answer,

I pose another question. "Tell me, what's the pay like for this sorta thing?" I ask, directing my attention solely to the man on the right.

"They're not halflings," he replies, ignoring my question.

"Okay, they're not. I apologize. Can you answer my question now?" I ask.

"We're not finished asking our questions yet," the man says, his voice rising. "Do you have siblings?" all 3 men ask in unison.

Ahh. And with that said, it all comes to me. They're not Replicas or clones. They're not reared from some test-tube or Petri dish experiment. No, they operate from a hive mind of one. An artificial intelligence strung along by some mainframe in this ship, probably somewhere in the command center or bridge. They're not human, either. They're Synthoids. Half man, half android. Fueled by zillions of advanced circuitry, bathed in ultrasonic fluid, transmitting endless pulses of information throughout their bodies, in a best effort to simulate the physiological composition of Terrans. The Inner Workings—the electronic guts—were manufactured to tolerate being saturated in the viscous fluid without rusting out. As the male Synth's mouth hangs agape as if waiting for me to respond further, I pound my hands on my thighs. "This interview is over," I say, standing.

The two guards step forward and train their rifles on me as the woman stands too, screaming, "Halt! Lower your weapons." The guards ignore her and continue to slowly press forward. "We need to complete the interview."

This was unexpected. "I don't answer to Synths, my dear," I say.

"They are not halflings," the man continues and joins us by standing. His brothers follow. Why does this guy have such a hard-on for halflings?

I swallow hard. My mental time ticks away—10 minutes left. I take the initiative to tank on the final Q & A of the interview and bow out, raising my hands above my head and slowly walking backward. "Easy guys, let's just call it quits for now. We've all got a little hot-headed, and it's obvious that I'm not your guy."

"They're not halflings," he repeats, his voice sounding more and more artificial. All 3 Synths move from behind the table and make a B-line straight for me.

"Do they even know what halflings are?" I bark in the woman's direction. She wears an inflammatory smirk.

"We are not halflings!" they scream in unison.

"Can you turn them off now?" I shout, again directing my focus to the woman.

Red picks up the Holo-tablet and starts to peck away. I pick up the pace, quickly backpedaling to the entrance but careful not to make any sudden moves as I'm certain that the trigger-happy twin guards to my right and left are itching for an excuse to release some hot hydrogen rounds. Suddenly, the 3 Synths stop dead in their tracks and collapse to the floor with a thump. The woman clears the table and runs over to the one that was sitting on her right. She kneels next to it and begins to peel away the skin on the back of its neck. "Crud. It was overheating."

One of the guards turns to speak with her while the other one remains locked on me. "What can I do to help?" he asks.

She looks up at him with desperate eyes. "Send for a maintenance droid while I contact the bridge to perform a reboot," she replies.

"And what of the pilot?" the other guard yells over his shoulder.

With fire in her eyes, she says, "He's no pilot. Get him outta here."

ELEVEN

My father was a burly man, with strong hands as big as landing gear and massive legs like those of Pittimore trees. Tall, dark and imposing, he towered in at around 6 feet and 7 inches and peaked at around 275 pounds. But he wasn't a tub of lard. He was solid, like the hull of a freighter and just as tough. When you spoke to him, he demanded respect and coached me to always make eye contact, whether in trouble or in celebration. And I did just that with no questions asked.

Olia always joked that I got my size from him, height-wise, that is, minus the weight. He was a man to be admonished, working hard to feed his children and care for those he loved. At least, that's what I saw. That's what I felt. He wasn't the mushy type and never expressed how he felt for you. He only showed it through hard labor on the trading routes that took a toll on his back, forcing him into early disability. Times were already hard on Overlight and when things got worse, I began to do what I could to help out by way of thievery. And I was damn good at it too. I could steal the crack off your behind if you weren't looking. And when my father finally found out about it, he threatened to ship me away.

Multiple times he made those threats, and when he failed to follow through on his promises, I realized his definition of whatever he deemed to be loved was the only thing keeping me home. But when the Civil War came knocking at the door, he played the only hand he could to keep both Olia and me alive.

I hated him for it. I was too young to understand, too immature to comprehend the sacrifice until much later. Until it was too late. Until after I developed a deep resentment for the man who gave me my name. The one who brought me into this pitiful world, with 2 dying stars, Mira A and B. But as I got older and worked in the Guilds, I realized how worse things were. After I stripped away the already filthy, dilapidated exterior, I saw the ugliness of its gooey, sickening center. I've seen governments overthrown, spouses conspired against and murders—all the while placating as accidental manslaughter—and houses pit against families. All in the name of…what, I'm not sure. Whoredom, lies, murder, rape, incest, and backstabbing; those were the jobs I took on early in my career, paying witness to not only the lowly in stature but the Royal as well. There's something to be said about being behind the scenes of such a fiendish enterprise. You learn something, out there in the black, watching the memories of stars' burning light as they pass by with each space-fold. You learn that heavenly bodies burn just as brightly in life as in death. And it's just the same as us.

As I stand here with Gifford, my only thoughts fall on Serias. Is there still hope for us? Can we too burn a brighter tomorrow if she could find it in her heart to forgive me?

"What the hells happened?" Gifford asks, grabbing my trigger arm.

I jerk it back as my hand fists at my side. "Easy?" I growl.

"Sorry, it's just...like, what the hells happened? You, I thought we had a plan?"

"We did," I reply through clenched teeth. "But, well, things kinda fell apart right about the time that the Synths went berserk."

"Synths? They have Synths on this ship?"

"Yeah. The inquisitive kind. Some redhead babe in charge of the interrogation, I mean, the interview, was sandwiched in between 3 of them, along with a pair of armed guards."

"Aww, sheat!" Gifford says.

"What does that mean?"

"It means that things are about to get a little more interesting now."

"Why?"

Gifford sighs and then motions me to a side corridor before speaking. When we're alone, he finally talks. "Synths were decommissioned a while back, maybe half a solar cycle due to multiple malfunctions. Mainly, the kill your family kind." Gifford rolls his eyes. "Yes, there are always mishaps when using any artificially operated machinery, but the standard deviation for accidental death is slightly more narrow than basic mistakes. And things escalated way high when it hit home, and high-ranking officials began to come up either missing or severely injured."

"Foul play?"

"Of course. Conspiracy sites on the Wave began to circulate stories that Synths and Replicas might have been hacked and used as pawns of espionage."

"Damn!" I stammer. "Makes sense," I say with a shrug. "Who's behind it, Giff, Third Faction?"

"Ding, ding, ding," Gifford replies. "But you know you can never pin anything on them as there is no true leader of the Third Faction. It's a following; a hive mind of people across the galaxy that follows the basic mantra of every self-serving enthusiast. Get mine and forget yours."

I fold my arms across my chest. "I've been out the loop for over a solar cycle, and things still haven't changed," I bark.

A set of footsteps creep up from behind us. "They sure haven't," a female says. I turn to see Serias standing there, arms crossed, shaking her head. "I see you're still causing a ruckus."

"Serias!" I feign ignorance. "Come on now, baby, I don't know what you're talking about."

As usual, she doesn't buy it. Serias closes the distance between us and speaks in a low tone. "I just got word that they threw you out of the interview."

"Really?" I say sarcastically and shoot Gifford a stupid grin. "That's weird, I thought I aced it."

"I bet," Serias says. "Security's looking for you now."

"For what? They asked me to leave, so I did. Better consider themselves lucky that I didn't get physical," I say.

"Cassius, what did you do?" Serias asks.

I look over at Gifford. "You two never formally met. Giff...I mean, Gifford, this is Serias, Serias, meet Gifford."

Gifford nods in her direction wearing a schoolboy smile. "Nice to meet you."

"Let me guess, the pleasure's all yours?" Serias answers, forcing a splash of burgundy across Gifford's cheeks.

"Gifford, but only Reign calls me Giff," he jokes to quell his embarrassment.

"I didn't ask," Serias says.

I shoot him a look. "A minute, please."

"Sure thing, boss," Gifford says as he steps away.

"You may want to find a new running buddy," Serias tells him.

I take Serias by the shoulders and lean in close. "Let me explain."

"Make it quick. You don't have a ton of time on your hands, Cassius."

"Can you stop calling me that?" I growl. "It's Reign. You know that."

"Cassius seems more appropriate, don't you think, seeing as though the Reign I once knew died off a long time ago. What 7 to 8 solar cycles ago?"

"Things aren't what they seem."

"They never are with you."

"I'm not a pilot, Gifford is not my handler, and we're not here to join the Princess' squadron."

"Duh! Didn't take a genius to figure that one out." I narrow my eyes at her. "Carry on," she says with a flicker of her wrist.

I sigh heavily. "I'm here on a mission to steal the *Concord*."

Serias' eyes bulge to the size of frag grenades. "Steal? Are you serious? You part of the Thieves' Guild again?"

"No. It's...it's about Olia. She's on a ship called the *Eclipse* fighting in some dangerous arena of sport for some Space Pirate named—"

"Forge!" Serias says, interrupting.

"You know him?"

"Know of him. A very dangerous fellow indeed from what I hear."

"Well, I'm dangerous too."

"Not like this guy. He's fiendish Cassius. Trust me; you don't want to tangle with him. He's got people in all the places: low, middle, and high. His gambling ring reaches across this and other galaxies. And he's not the bargaining kind."

"He's got my sister, Serias." My eyes fall to the floor. "I've got to try to save her."

"Not to come off negative but, do you even know if she's still alive?"

My eyes lock with hers. "Don't know for sure, but Gifford's Intel points to all signs of her still being on board, and even if she's dead, I need to take her body and give her an appropriate burial."

Serias' eyes soften. Behind that rigid exterior, I get the sense that something has broken free. "I'm so sorry to hear that, Cassius. But what do you need with the *Concord*? You can barter a ride from any spaceport."

"I need the ship to barter for access onboard the *Eclipse* so I can try to rescue her." Serias shakes her head in disgust. "Why don't you come with us? We could sure use another gun hand."

"What? Are you kidding me? Your sister hated my guts from what I last heard."

"Hate," I take a step back and chuckle, "hate is such a strong word."

"And Olia did it strongly."

"I'm sure that she's over that little *tiff* you guys had on Gamma Torres."

"If you call vowing to take my eyeballs out and feed them to a pack of Cardacks a *tiff*, well, yeah, okay. She blamed me for losing her scavenger droid on that Seek and Destroy gig. How was I supposed to know not to jettison the droid to give us more lift to break orbit?"

I nod. "She really did love Stella," I say jokingly. Serias glares at me dangerously. Against the artificial light of the inner corridor, her honey-colored skin looks as immaculate as ever.

"I'm not laughing."

"And neither am I. I need your help."

"I can't…even if I wanted to."

"You can't—" I say just as Gifford steps back into the conversation, holding his Holo-tablet.

"Boss, your lady friend is right. She can't help us," he says. His eyes are narrowed to slits, and he stares at her in a way that's foreign to me thus far. Up to this point, as little as I've known Gifford, the threatening scowl plastered on his face is a new one. It sends a light chill down my back.

My eyes dart back and forth between the two of them. "What do you mean?" I ask, finally settling on Gifford.

Gifford turns the face of the Holo-tablet toward me. "She's part of the personal security detail for the Princess."

"What! Is this true?" I ask Serias.

She nods weakly. "I took the job some half a solar cycle ago. I've been watching after her ever since they put this plan in motion to recruit pilots. I knew the second you came on board that there would be trouble Cassius." She looks away momentarily and points at her ear. "My IEPCS alerted me to the intrusive interview and I was called to check it out."

"Inner earpiece communication system, huh? Primitive by today's tech, but smart and sexy," Gifford says with a smile. "Kinda like you." Serias and I shoot Gifford a surprised look. "Oh, I'm sorry, did I say that aloud?" he asks, his face burning red.

"So you *can* help us then?" I insist.

Serias turns back to me. "Have you been listening to anything I just said?" she asks. I shrug. "They don't just want you out of the interview; they want you off this ship. There's a shuttle on the way to pick you up with about 20 battle troops to escort you out of here. I was ordered to follow you around and make sure you didn't *break* anything until they arrived." She makes air quotes with her fingers when she says the word break.

"How long do we have?" I ask.

"Twenty minutes tops," Serias says.

Gifford turns his Holo-tablet back around and begins to play. "Well, that gives us exactly 10 minutes to pimp and 10 to dive. That is, 5 to kill those soldiers guarding the *Concord* at the external docking bay and 5 for me to hack the controls for the door," he says mildly. He hands me my bag.

I reach inside and check on Martha, taking the gun out and holding it to the light. The weight of the weapon reassures me of her power, and I take a measured breath and sigh before staring down the sight one last time for good measure. She appears to be just as I left her—shiny and unused. "Weapon's free?"

"Yep. You can thank me later," Gifford says.

"Noted," I say. Gifford and I synchronize the time on our Holo-bands to 19 minutes. "You get the pilot, I'll map out a route."

"Got it! He's on the upper deck now." Gifford steps away.

When he's out of sight, Serias and I are finally alone; a place I'd been longing for since seeing her again. "Serias, I really need your help."

"Cassius, please," she says faintly.

"Can't you see? What are the odds of meeting here again, on this vessel, at this exact moment? After...after all these solar cycles."

Serias closes her eyes as she huffs. And after a few seconds, she opens them again. Just as she does, a fist connects with the left side of my chin. I see bright spots in the back of my skull as my vision dims and then returns. The blow drops me to one knee. I don't need to ask where it came from. I grab my jaw and smile. "Still got the meanest right hook in the system."

Serias kneels next to me and leans in. "In the galaxy," she whispers.

TWELVE

"I take it this means you forgive me?" I ask as I attempt to stand.

Serias wiggles her hands underneath my shoulder and assists me back to my feet. "What makes you say that?"

"It's how we always made up," I reply, massaging my jaw. "Well, not *always*."

Serias shakes her right hand and rubs her knuckles. "I'd say so. And you've still got the hardest head I know."

As the world stops spinning before me, I drift away from her and stand on my own. When I'm confident, my legs will support me, I speak. "You've been talking to my shrink?" I ask sheepishly.

She flashes me a smile that strokes my ego and then lays a compliment on me for finality. "Nice optics, by the way? Torrian? Latest-model?"

I can't help but smile back. "You know me."

"Well, it's probably got a couple of upgrades then."

"Some. But I'm not one to brag."

"Really?"

"So we good now?"

"Maybe. We'll talk later."

"Cool." I look around, surveying our surroundings. "How 'bout a kiss to seal the deal?"

Serias rolls her eyes. "As I said, nothing's changed."

"All right, you've got the layout of this place. So how should we play it?"

"You head down to the lower deck, aft of the ship. There you'll find several rows of crates stacked along the walls. I need you to climb up on top and search for a ventilation shaft. Duck inside and follow it toward the right. You'll wind around a bit and finally come to a split. Take that left. It will lead you up. You'll be directly under the catwalk leading to the *Concord*. Wait for my signal. I'll do the rest."

"And what about you? What are you going to do until then?"

"Check in on your nerdy friend. If he can't find a way to convince your pilot to jump on board," Serias pauses as her hands rise to meet her breasts. She gives them a slight squeeze. In that dress, they show off the perfect amount of volume and lift to make a man's mouth water. "I'm sure I can find a way to coax him to join."

I swallow hard, staring. "Hey, don't try too hard. I got first dibs."

She smiles. "And last." She hands me an IEPCS. "You'll need this. Now go."

I find my way down to the lower deck, just as Serias instructed and follow her directions to a Tee. Worming my way down the tortuous path of cool metal finally spits me out to my desired destination. Before long, I'm nestled directly underneath the catwalk leading to the *Concord*, eyeing the two soldiers guarding the entrance.

From here, my Optical Aug gives me a clear view of everything of interest in the catwalk. Up close, it's larger than I assumed, made up of 10-foot tall glass whose half-moon clear dome separates us from the emptiness of space. The distance from end to end is no longer than 100 yards and a long bench bookended by two artificial pots tall enough to make Gifford feel inept, split the distance between the openings. The pots house two taller plants that stretch the entire height of the catwalk. Hosferian Ferns if I'm not mistaken.

I lie on my back inside the shaft with Martha in my right hand, cocked and ready to burn. There's a vent door just a few feet ahead of me, but I hold my position, careful not to give away my location. I peer at my Holo-band one last time. "1-minute left," I mumble to myself.

My internal clock continues to run. 30, 29, 28…I'm not sure about Gifford, but Serias is never late, so it won't be long now. Just then, the sound of inertia rockets firing stab my ears as a ship roars in the distance. The aforementioned shuttle carrying my personal escort has arrived. Adrenaline surges through my veins. 5, 4, 3, 2, 1.

It's on.

I snake my way toward the vent door and prepare for gunplay but pause as the sound of high heel clatter trickles along the metallic floor, along with two other pairs of footsteps.

Bingo.

"Soldiers, I am Lady Serias of the Princess' personal security. I have strict orders to allow passage of these two men, handler Gifford and pilot J.C. Edwards," I hear Serias say.

"Many pardons, Lady Serias, but we've received no such clearance as of yet," one of the soldiers' replies. "If you will, allow me a moment to radio in and verify—"

"Maybe you didn't hear clearly what I just told you, soldier. I am head of Princess Varia's personal security, and I am the clearance you need. Now, please allow me to pass immediately or suffer the consequences of your defiance," Serias says in a commanding tone.

"Yes, ma'am, at once," the soldier says.

The soldiers step aside as the pressurized door leading to the *Concord* slides open with a hiss as fresh air from the corridor slips inside. The pair of soldiers ease away and head toward the *Opus*. Serias, Gifford, and who I assume to be the pilot all file inside as the door closes behind them. I hold my position.

"Reign, we're in," Gifford says over the IEPCS.

I tap my ear. "So I see. I think we've got company. Freighter pulled in seconds ago. How much time are we looking at?"

"Not sure. It's outta my hands. It's up to the pilot now," Gifford says. "We're jacking him into the system now. It will take a few to assimilate and test for compatibility."

"Cassius, the troops just debarked and are scurrying about the ship. It won't be long until they head this way," Serias says over the comm.

"Roger," I say. "I'll wait here until—"

"Too late, the soldiers have notified the troopers of our location. They're all headed this way!" Serias screams.

"Keep hacking," I say as I slide out of the vent shaft. "I'll handle this!"

The thunderous sound of heavy footfalls erupts along the catwalk as I throw a shoulder into each of the large planters to tip them over. They fall with a loud crash, and I make haste to slide them together, rolling them toward the center of the catwalk before the soldiers can file in. From the sound of it, they're equipped with basic hand pistols and SMG armament. No need to carry any hand cannons or rockets. And why would they? At this range, a stray shot of either could be catastrophic. Why risk destroying the *Concord* or even the docking port, for just some deranged thief or spy? I assumed they'd think.

The planters create a makeshift barrier between them and me and, hopefully, an impenetrable one at that. I peek out over the top of my cover and eye them from a distance. To my disappointment, Serias is right and I'm half wrong. They're all equipped with red rifles and handguns. And there's a sheat-load of them. Rows of 5 soldiers fill the corridor from right to left. This somewhat plays to my advantage as they'll have to shoot their way through the man in front of them if they are to have a tear at me. But, somehow, I don't think that is a smear of concern for any of them. Soldiers in this depth of space have a level of dedication and sacrifice that hints back to a time of military excellence the system hasn't seen in decades. Desperation will do that to you.

Before the fireworks begin, a lone female steps forward. It's Red from the interview. "Mr. Champion, or should I say Reign."

With the stress of the situation slowly beginning to rear its ugly head, I take a moment to dabble in a game of words to take the edge off. "All right, you got me. Only my favorite playthings call me Champion."

"Please step forward with your weapon deactivated," Red requests, sounding annoyed.

"Aww, sheat mama. You skipped right past the foreplay and went straight for penetration. I'm not even wet yet," I shout sarcastically over the planters.

"You're far away from Fabricius Reign, and I'm sure that King Derry would very much so like to have you returned in one piece. It'd be a pity to have to send you and your little friends home in duffel bags," Red replies.

"That would be bad, but I don't work for King Derry. In case you didn't get a chance to glimpse over the Cliff Notes, I'm a loner. Somewhat of a rebel," I say.

"That's not what the bounty on your head is saying. You make quite the headlines across The Wave nowadays. Many want a piece of you. I'm offering something else. Safe passage for you back home," Red says.

"And what of my friends?" I ask.

"They will be dealt with separately. Serias has much to answer for," Red says.

My blood boils as my thumb starts to slowly rotate the dial on Martha until it stops on the 3 setting. "That deal doesn't sound too appealing to me. I think I'd rather make a counteroffer. You ready?"

Even from this distance, I can hear Red sigh in frustration. "Let's hear it."

"How about you and your men back off the catwalk? If we start slinging hot hydrogen fodder around here, someone's likely to get hurt, or worse, sucked out into cold space once this glass goes bye-bye. And seeing as how I forgot to pack my heavy thermal underwear, I'd rather not freeze my package off."

From the sound of Red's sigh, I gamble that the frustration was slowly rising inside her—the thing I wanted the most at this point. I've dealt with people for a long time, especially women. For the most part, they're more dangerous than men—that is, when they operate with a sense of healthy reason. But more often than not, they live in the realm of make-believe and emotion. And if you prod them enough with pesky words and smack talk, you can get them teetering just enough to nudge them off their game. And that's when you win. Apparently, Red was starting to bite.

"Come off of it, will you, Reign? This is taking way too long and your stalling won't bring you any closer to getting outta here alive," she yells.

"I'm not sure too what you're barking about, but I'm doing my best to barter a deal that works for both sides. If you give me a moment, I can get on the comms and chat with my people. This will allow me to talk it out with my crew on the *Concord,* and once we come to an agreement, I'll get back to you," I say.

"As I said, you're stalling, Mr. Reign, and I don't have time for games," Red says. "Send them in!" she screams.

"Them?" I mutter.

Before I can ponder any further, the sound of 3 pounding footsteps rattles the metal flooring beneath me. The words, "Not halflings, not halflings," follows.

"Aww, sheat!" I scream, as the 3 Synths from earlier quickly rain down upon me. I let off a round of triple shots that miss hitting any of the Synths entirely. Luckily, my salvos manage to barrel down the extension corridor and connect with a pair of soldiers instead. And it's a good thing; I hate wasting ammunition. They drop like flies, and the splattering sight of human flesh unwaveringly slapping the metal surface is satisfying.

With a flip of the wrist, I reload Martha again and take a drop step backward to open some space between me and the triplets. They're quicker than before, performing flips and darting haphazardly from side to side to confuse my aim. Admittedly, anyone with only a pair of human eyes would have easily lost track. And that would've been a problem over a solar cycle ago.

But not now.

Luck and irony mix well together in this scenario, as my Optical Aug hones in on one of the Synths just as he lunges forward from the right. I paste him with a double shot, and he absorbs the entire clip, head first. What used to be it's face quickly melts away, revealing the metal exoskeleton shells that protect the delicate inner circuitry. The hot hydrogen rounds burn through that as well, exposing the gel metric brain that pops from overheating. The gelatinous goo showers around me as I raise my forearm across my face to protect my eyes.

Another flip of my wrist and Martha's ready to spray, just in time to pelt another Synth barreling upon me from the center. I squeeze the trigger, this time choosing the single-fire variant just so people won't say I wasn't playing fair. As if that mattered. But what's playing fair when dealing with artificial intelligence. They haven't earned the rights of humans, and I've never been the crusading type to help lost causes. So, I'm cooking these jerks tonight. *And besides, who's cheering for decommissioned walking tech anyway,* I think as the second Synth's head slides clean from its frame when the solo hydrogen shot pierces its neck. That's technically two headshots now, and I can't shake the silly idea that somehow I deserve some special achievement award, akin to one I might've earned from an adolescent video game.

One last flip to reload Martha, and I quickly scan the area for the last one but come up empty. My heart rivets in my chest as my head cranes toward the *Concord*. The door slides open and the Synth slips inside before I could let off another shot.

The door closes behind it. "Serias!" I scream over the comm.

No one responds. I've never been mistaken for a holy man, but I'm praying for a miracle right now as it may be the only thing that can actually save our skins right now. My head whips around again as a few bullets whiz by and pings against the corridor in a burst of electricity. They're using stun rounds. I allow myself a moment to chuckle at the thought. This is when it gets fun.

I roll my thumb once more and slide the dial to the two position. *Deuce Deuce.* After a few more combinations of weapon's fire and wrist flips, I down half the Princess' Troops with light speed. I'm in a dream state of euphoria, as I haven't had this much fun gun combat in over a year.

"Stop!" Red yells, and the rest of the troops mysteriously fall back down toward the *Opus* end of the catwalk. I duck behind cover once more and take a moment to catch my breath. I tap my ear and listen. Only static rings over the IEPCS and my optimism starts to wane at the thought that Serias or Gifford may have been killed, extinguishing any hope of saving Olia.

"Come on, guys, can you hear me?" I whisper once more. With my back to the remaining troops, I stare in awe at the pressurized doors leading to the *Concord.* To my dismay, they slowly slide open and Serias appears, but she's not alone. The lone Synth clings to her neck from behind with a blade pointed at her temple.

Sheat just got real.

THIRTEEN

"And so now, it looks like *this* halfling has the upper hand. How do you Terrans say it?" he pauses, and his eyes flutter at a blistering pace before he resumes, saying, "Yes, …it seems that I *hold all the cards*."

I half kneel, doing my best to not to let my wounded pride show while I slowly clocked the distance between us utilizing the Nav feature of my Optical Aug. 10 meters. "Touché. You made a wonderful joke. Want a cookie?"

"No, I want something else. Perhaps we make a trade. Your life for hers?"

"Not gonna happen. Not until I know the status of the other crew members inside the *Concord*."

The Synth cocks his head sideways. "Other crew members?"

Sheat! "I meant to say, if there are other crew members on board, I need to see them."

"Don't take me for a fool." The Synth tightens his grip on Serias' neck, and she squirms to pry her hands in between his forearm and give herself room to breathe. "If there are others on board, we will find them. They cannot hide, nor can they fly this ship either. It takes a skilled pilot. And no one on the list of applicants possesses the gene to perform such a feat."

My heart pounds. Is he for real? Before I can contemplate any longer, I follow Serias' eyes as they converge to a point just beyond my gaze. I crane my head and note that 3 more soldiers are slowly creeping into the vicinity. One load, and two trigger pulls are enough to send them retreating to their redhead momma. "So tell me…whatever your name is—"

"You can call me Alpha," he says.

"Okay, Alpha. If no one on the list of applicants had the gene, why go on with the interviews?" I ask.

"Because, silly, there are credits on the table, and no one in their right mind walks away from credits, even if it means to abandon your teammates." Alpha jerks Serias closer as if taunting me. "You know that, don't you…Spy?"

"I don't know what you're talking about," I reply.

"Are you sure? Your file says contrary." He cackles. "Need I remind you about…Delvis Chong?"

Serias wears a frown of sorrow that stings me to the core. It's as evident as the nose on my face. She still feels the pain of that day, just as much as I do. Maybe even more. Empty of the truth, it must weigh as heavily in her mind as it does in her heart. "Keep chattering, tin can, and I'll make quick work of you soon enough."

"Reign…keep stalling," I hear Gifford whisper across my IEPCS.

Instantly, I'm reenergized. Gifford and Mire are alive, somewhere hidden inside the *Concord*. I pray that Gifford can see me through the external cameras, so I don't speak, but only tilt my head slightly forward. "So make me another offer, Alpha," I say.

"Almost ready," Gifford says, his voice rising in excitement.

Alpha's eyes flutter once more. "No more offers. My superiors have lost their patience, and you have lost time. You have only one more option. I am going to count to 3 and if you have not dropped your weapon and surrendered, this female will feel my steel."

"You don't have to do—" I say.

"One!" Alpha yells, cutting me off.

I stand and slowly begin to lower Martha to the floor. "Give me a second, dammit."

"Two!" Alpha blares.

"No!" I say as I drop Martha to the floor and kick it over toward Alpha.

His head snaps toward the spinning pistol, and a wide smile splits his face. As the gun slows to a halt just outside his grasp, his eyes dart ahead. But not in my direction. "Did I do good, Mother?"

"Yes," Red's voice snaps across the catwalk. "Now, kill the woman, she won't be needed."

"What!" I bark.

Alpha reels back the knife hand and is about to strike just as the doors to the *Concord* open and out rolls the Light Disc. "Cover your eyes!" Gifford screams.

As the Disc stops, an explosion of light fills the catwalk, blinding everyone in sight, except for both me and Serias, who followed Gifford's instructions and shut our eyes just in time. I can only imagine the pain those who gazed at the blinding light of the device must be feeling as my eyelids flash red, and I reflectively squeeze harder to resist the pressure closing on my pupils.

The sounds of clanging metal fill the room as Red and her goons fall to their knees, writhing in pain, dropping their guns as well. I follow suit, holding a crouched position as I seek shelter from erratic gunfire. After a few rounds whip overhead—blasting the walls around us—the unsettling feeling of depressurization fills my gut, and I pause to blindly grab at the floor in hopes of slipping my fingers into slits metal gratings. But to my dismay, I come up empty as my digits tickle only cold, smooth steel.

I crawl on my hands and knees in Serias' direction. With my good eye shut, I rely only on my Optic Aug for sight, which has spontaneously activated the internal shaders to filter out the brightness and restore my vision. Alpha wails in pain as he claws at his eye sockets, stumbling about to secure good footing.

When I reach Serias, I take her arm with my left hand and swipe Martha from the ground with the right. I roll the dial on the side of Martha and set the trigger variant to *Triple Shot* for maximum impact as I point it square at Alpha's head. As if sensing its demise, the Synth stops wrestling with the light and stands completely still, gazing in my direction. I squeeze the trigger without another second's hesitation and explode its head against the glass of the catwalk. It splatters in a glorious discharge of purple ooze.

The Light Disc begins to dim as the doors of the *Concord* shut again. I tap my ear. "Giff, what gives? Get those fooking doors open!"

"I'm trying Reign, that ain't me. Someone's taking over the controls," he yells.

The soldiers begin to stir from their temporary haze and retrieve their weapons from the floor. The sound of ammo loading motivates me to find cover once again and momentarily ignore the sealed doors of the *Concord*.

I aim over the planters and pop off a few more rounds at the soldiers, who have now fallen back to the edge of the catwalk, returning fire from protective positions. I take a moment to glance over at Serias. She grabs the bottom of her dress and gives a strong tug, ripping a split in it the length of her entire thigh, all the way up to her hip, revealing her toned muscles.

"Shouldn't you have a pistol holstered there as all the sexy assassins do?" I ask.

"Sheat, I don't even have on any panties," she says as she holds a squatting position, her back against the planters as she pants for air.

I swallow at the idea of that and distract my primal thoughts by asking the most obvious question. "You good?" She nods and offers me a thumbs up. I reload Martha and gaze back at the soldiers, firing off countless rounds of hot liquid hydrogen, daring them to advance.

Finally, Serias speaks up again. "You won't hold them off for long."

"There you go once more, gushing with pessimism," I scream.

"They have marines on board with heavy shields and riot gear that can repel small cannon fire."

I swallow hard. "You mean like the big black ones with red trim along the edges?"

"Yeah, how'd you know?" Serias asks, gasping.

"Because they're barreling down the catwalk straight for us," I reply.

A small detachment of 8 to 10 marines hold an arrow formation and slowly advance our way. I duck and tap my ear again. "Giff, what you got?"

Static returns over the IEPCS just as the *Concord* detaches from the catwalk and peels away, full burn. "Some partner you got there, Cassius!" Serias says. "Funny, I never thought I'd have a chance to witness the look on your face when someone leaves you stranded for dead," she gloats.

I glare at her in silence and don't pass judgment. She operates from a place of ignorance, and I take the blame for it, 100 percent. With a team of marines closing in on us from one end and the void of space at the other, my mind whirls, desperate to conjure a plan of escape. But it comes up empty. I eye Martha. "If I set the trigger to maximum overload, I can use Martha as a frag grenade. It'll probably take out half the marines, but most likely open a hole inside the catwalk, sucking us both out. At a distance this far from the nearest star, we'll freeze instantly and die, suffering a painless death."

"That's the best plan you can come up with?" Serias stammers.

"Trust me, doll," I say weakly. "It's the better alternative to what you'll experience if the Toshin gets a hold of you. They don't take kindly to treason."

Serias flashes me a grin and shakes her head. "I never thought I'd go out like this." Tears form in her eyes.

"Like what?"

"Us...together, dying...side by side."

I kneel at her side. "If it means anything to you, I dreamed of a day like this."

"No, Reign, it doesn't mean sheat to me," she whispers behind a wicked smile. "Charge that damn gun and toss it true."

I look down at Martha, turn the dial, and press the button to initiate the sequence. Suddenly, Serias swats my hand away and points over my shoulder. I turn to find two fighter jets screaming in our direction. "Move out!" I scream, jumping to my feet and snatching Serias with me.

The marines drop their shields and race in the opposite direction as cannon fire ignites the darkness of space with volleys of fodder headed our way. Right before it collides with the catwalk, the

Concord zooms in and absorbs the blasts, Parry Shields holding strong.

"Giff?" I yell over the comms.

"One moment, boss," he replies. "I'm working here."

The pressurized doors for the *Opus* slam tight, shutting out the remaining soldiers. The *Concord*'s twin rockets blaze as it bolts away once more taking the two fighters along with it, streaking just beyond the catwalk. At this distance, I easily recognize the markings alongside their wings: a large bronze fist, engulfed in a ring of fire while clutching an orange triangle encasing a bright red stone.

"Space Pirates?" Serias asks.

"No, Dagmas Clan!" I hiss.

"Out here, why?"

"Oh, probably trying to collect on that bounty."

"You're in high demand, you popular guy," Serias says wryly. The sound of weapon fire pounds my ears from inside the *Opus*. "That won't hold long."

I point outside the catwalk. "It won't have to. Look."

The *Concord* banks from right to left, quickly dodging Gatling Gunfire and easily eluding her pursuers as it performs a double-figure 8 maneuver that causes the two fighters to almost collide with one another. As the two ships struggle to right themselves, the *Concord* performs a full-burn roll and somersaults behind both of them. With two shots from its twin cannons, the *Concord* dispenses the Dagmas ships with ease and hooks back in our direction, punching through the orange and red luminous explosion.

"Stand back, boss. Jeffrey here is going to dock and get you outta there," Gifford cries over the comms.

I holster Martha and shield Serias as the *Concord* slows just outside the doors. The sound of the clamping mechanism brings life to my soul as the doors simultaneously slide open. Serias' eyes go wide at the sight of the ship locking in place, and she takes me by the hand and squeezes it to let me know she's ready to make a break for it. We race for the *Concord* and jump inside, no sooner than the doors containing the remaining soldiers on the other end of the catwalk blasts open.

"Permission to come aboard?" I ask as both Serias and I join Gifford in the main hull.

As the *Concord* barrels away, Gifford gives a salute and shoots me a wink. "Permission granted. Oh, and don't worry Reign, you can thank me later."

FOURTEEN

The Concord, Deep Space

2 Days Earlier

"What we looking like, Giff?" I ask over his shoulder as we all crowd the cockpit of the *Concord*. The design is immaculate, with consoles as clean as anything I'd ever witnessed before in my long life. With sleek lines and rounded edges, nothing within my sights was familiar. It was as if I'd unconsciously been pulled back to a brief time in my existence when I experienced my first space flight as a child, and my heart couldn't tell the difference either. A wave of hope rushed over me and the idea of rescuing Olia was becoming more and more of a reality. The sight of the fancy tech-filled me with both trepidation and elation at the same time, and I silently prayed that this makeshift band of heroes and I wouldn't fook this up.

Gifford shakes his head, sitting in one of the chairs, eyeing the lateral view screen. "So far, so good. I'm not picking anything up on the scanners. This ship is so special." He pauses and taps the monitor 3 times, increasing the size of the green circular rings of the radar. "No more Dagmas fighters…or Toshin ships, for that matter."

The cockpit of the *Concord* is pretty damn sweet, sporting two cherry-red leather command chairs positioned in a single file, one behind each other, and offering standing room only for two more occupants in the rear. Outfitted with all the latest bells and whistles—short and long-range radar, stealth reinforced Oramite plating, magnetic containment-bubble generators, circuit multiplexers, and twin internal boosting cores—Gifford explained that the *Concord* is listed in the top 4 percent of all Class A scout ships in all the galaxy. The sleek, seamless design of the forward consoles is duplicated along the floors and ceiling. The whole thing reflects a pure aerodynamic flair, intentionally designed to capture the eye and encourage you to fly.

Jeffrey fills the forward chair, lightly gripping the cyclic, and he guides us along our course. Thankfully, he's the one driving because I haven't gotten acclimated to the new ship designs that mandate all cyclics project from the forward dash as opposed to elevating from the floor. Supposedly, it offers more control to pilots for long-distance space folds and lessens the likelihood of slipping coordinates and falling into a star.

"Can't believe Dagmas fighters can make it out here on such small fuel tanks. They must really want you, Reign," Gifford says.

"They must have a larger cruiser nearby," I say.

Gifford turns around. "If that's true, my next question is who would commission such a *Seek and Destroy* assignment against a high priority vessel such as the *Opus*? If things went south, it sure would place a lot of heat on The Dagmas Faction."

"I'm sure the remaining scattered loyalist couldn't care less about their reputation at this point. But the better question is, how did they find me?" I ask.

"They weren't looking for you, I'm afraid," Serias chimes.

I crane my head her way. "What?"

"When you left me…when we *separated*, I continued to run gigs for the Guild, but, honestly, we were more attractive as a packaged deal. Not many clients wanted to commission a female, let alone a single female, to handle prime operations. I was relegated to settling for base gigs, which offered little reimbursement but afforded high risks." Serias sighs heavily and rakes a hand through her dark, curly hair. "So, to make ends meet, I took a couple of assignments from Dagmas dissenters."

My eyes widen. "Serias—"

"Now before you get all judgmental, Cassius," she interrupts, waving a finger at me, "they were only convoy operations in the outer planets, nothing concerning Intel. I'm a big girl and know how to keep my nose clean in Proxima Centauri. But it wasn't long before one of the jobs went sour, and I was set up by a runner named Zelwyn, who stole some heavy data from me and made it seem as if I was going to sell it on the Underground. Dagmas thugs came knocking on my door for answers, and it was damn near impossible to clear my name. I bolted and have been on the run ever since."

"And now we both have targets on our backs," I say.

Serias tilts her head and shrugs. "I guess so. We'll both be dead soon."

"That's not gonna happen," I bark.

"Well—" before Gifford can finish speaking, his chair drags along a set of tracks in the floor in the direction of the forward dash, simultaneously as Jeffrey's command chair heads in our direction. I take a half-step back as they glide in a figure 8-motion on a collision course for one another. At the last millisecond, Jeffrey's chair pauses, giving just enough time for Gifford to streak by before continuing its trek to our position. When it stops, Jeffrey spins around and stands, meeting me eye to eye. He raises a pair of gold goggles from his eyes to his forehead and offers me a hand. "I don't think we formally met. No need for introductions on your part. You're Steel Reign, ex-spy, all Bounty Killer. I'm Jeffrey Mire. But you can call me Stink."

"Well, I'm a Bounty Hunter, or at least I used to be," I say.

Stink raises an eyebrow at me. "Used to? What happened? I thought all Bounty Hunters were lifers?" he asks.

"You keep streaking your way through space like I have, son, and you'll learn a lot more than any book or Wave article can teach you. But I'll give you this one lesson for free, without having to go through the learning process." I lean in close to him and narrow my eyes. "Everything is up for change."

Stink swallows. "Yes, sir."

I crack a smile and step away. "By the way, with a name like Stink, should I be shaking your hands?" I ask.

Stink erupts in laughter and points at me. "That's a good one." When I refuse to shake his hand, he turns his attention to Serias. "And you...must be...*beautiful*." He flashes a row of pearly white teeth against his bronze skin. Stink reaches for Serias' hand and puckers his lips.

Serias lands an open hand slap to his face and takes a half-step back before turning to walk away. Stink wipes his face and massages his jaw. "Saw that coming, Stink," I joke.

He looks at me with a childish grin. "Aww, man. I think I'm in love."

"What?" I say, raising a brow. "I don't know if you're a little slow, buddy, or maybe you're just not keeping score, but where I'm from, that's considered a diss."

Gifford's chair swaps position with Stink's, and when he closes in on us, he kicks his feet up on the console. "No, he's not slow. Where he's from, female dominance is a sign of strength and power. It only makes Serias even more attractive to him."

I shake my head at that and glare at Stink. "Well, you definitely have a lot to learn, son." My eyes fall to the tracks on the floor. "What's up with the musical chairs?"

Gifford kicks back even farther, threatening to tip over. "Oh, you mean the M.R.P. cockpit system?"

I shrug and roll my eyes. "Let me guess, another acronym? What happened to the days of basic spaceship technological lingo?"

"It left with the advent of superior technology." Gifford taps an open hand on his chest as if clearing his throat. "M.R.P. pronounced merp for short. It stands for a mechanized revolving pit. Pit being short for the cockpit. Everything is automated, but we can also manually change positions according to the need."

"I thought only Stink here can fly the ship?" I ask.

"Yes and no," Gifford says, waving a finger. "As long as he's nestled in one of the seats, anyone can assume piloting privileges." Gifford nods at me with a pause as if I'm not able to keep up with his explanation.

I nod back. "I get it."

Gifford grins. "Just making sure you keep up, sir."

My attention shifts back to Stink. "That was some fancy flying back there, slick."

Stink shakes his head. "Naw, those guys weren't very good. I'd grade them at only level 2, maybe 3 skill set...at the most."

"Still, I was impressed," I say.

"Can't take all the credit, though," Stinks says sheepishly. "The *Concord*'s A.I. synchronized with me rather quickly and assimilated all the controls in a snap. I could feel everything right at my fingertips. Weight, inertia, speed, and drag. This is some real next-level sheat we're playing with right here."

"Still, thanks anyway," I assert.

"Don't mention it," Stink says.

Gifford sits forward. "Hey, I've been telling you to thank me later virtually this entire trip, and you have yet to say those two simple words. And now, this bloke pulls off one simple maneuver and you're ready to throw him a parade or something."

"What can I say? I've got a thing for pilots," I joke. Stink smiles.

Gifford folds his arms and shakes his head. "Piss off," he mumbles as Serias strolls back in. Her dress is completely torn now, no longer touching the ground but ripped to a length that barely covers her knees. She's chomping on a red apple. "Hey, that's mine? Did you go in my bag?"

"Oh, I'm sorry, Gifford. I hadn't gotten a chance to eat anything all night. I hope you don't mind?" she asks, batting her eyes.

Gifford goes for it, saying, "No, it's all right. I ate enough for the night. You can have it," he says in a goofy tone.

She looks over at Stink. "Sorry for the slap, but I get irritated when guys come on too strong."

"Oh, it was no big deal at all, was it, big guy? Stink here actually got a little more turned on by it," I say. "Go ahead, hit him again, I dare you."

Serias raises a fist. "How 'bout I hit you instead?"

"No, please, save it for me," Stink says.

Serias rolls her eyes. "Why do I want to stick my head in the ground and hide right now?"

"Speaking of hiding? How did you guys slip past Alpha when he boarded the ship?" I ask.

Gifford points at the ceiling. "Ask H.E.R.?"

"Her?" I ask.

"The A.I. of the *Concord*. H.E.R., as in Hollow Evolving Rootkit," Gifford says.

"Rootkit? Isn't that considered malicious software?" Serias asks, shooting him a stern look.

Stink appears stunned. "Uhh, malicious software to those who oppose us. But not *to* us," he says, with a flutter of his brows. "This Rootkit allows me to have complete access to the ship's computer system once synchronization is complete. And when it was, man…what a rush!"

Gifford stands and eyes the ceiling, rubbing his hands maniacally. "The hollow part just means that the software has room to grow, learn if you will. And because it is ever-evolving, the sky's the limit to its potential."

"Great, I feel a geekgasm coming on," I say. "Toss Serias your goggles Stink." I turn to her. "You might want to cover your eyes," I whisper.

"Eww," she mutters with a smirk.

"Anyway," Gifford starts, "during synchronization, it recognized Alpha as a threat and created a holographic partition in the cockpit between us and the inner hull where Serias was, keeping us completely hidden."

"So you left her for dead?" I say, my voice rising.

"Calm down, Cassius. I volunteered to do it. Once that wall was created, I knew we only had one chance to make it out alive. If that involved me being taken to bide time, well, it was worth it." Her eyes narrow at me. "Besides, I rolled the dice that you'd take care of me. Seeing as though you owed me one," she says in a soft tone.

I nod. "You knew I did…you knew I'd protect you."

"Um, are you guys a thing?" Stink asks. "Because I don't want to break up a thing if that's what this is." He cocks his head at Serias. "I mean, I know you're feeling me somewhat and all sexy, but I've got strict rules when it comes to threesomes and ship squad dynamics. It just doesn't work for me. And that's coming from a place of experience."

"Don't worry, you don't have *anything* to worry about," Serias says sarcastically.

"Okay, cool," Stink says, not catching on.

"Besides," Serias says, staring me in the eyes, "we're not a *thing*," she says as she walks off, exiting the cockpit.

Gifford sits. "That's some girl you got, boss."

"Yeah. Tell me about it," I mumble.

FIFTEEN

I enter the cargo hold, searching for Serias. The space is a lot bigger than I assumed, looking at it from the outside. As high and wide as it is deep—some 20 feet in diameter—I'm amazed by the ease in which it handles in flight. Large crates stack to the ceiling on my right, secured in place to the hull by electromagnetic claps. To my left, I'm greeted by a sizeable black cylinder, about 3 or so feet taller than me and twice as wide. The initials C.D.E. dots along the center in bold black letters. I've flown in a lot of high-class scout ships before, but none of them sports Centrifugal Debris Extractors, something reserved for only larger freighters due to the strain of every resource on the drive cores. Whatever tech powers the *Concord* is something foreign to me and, most likely, 90 percent of the rest of the system.

As I make my way through the hold, heading in the direction of the passenger quarters, movement catches my augmented eye in the corner. It's Serias, squatted, staring out of a small window on the starboard side of the ship, just beyond the crates. "There you are," I say as I approach. "You stealing a moment of quiet time?" Serias doesn't look at me and only shrugs in response. I pull up next to her and take a knee. "Why didn't you tell me?" I ask in a low tone.

"Like when was I going to? It's not like you were around," she replies.

"When did you find out I was alive?" I ask.

"Is it that obvious that I knew something?"

"You're forgetting that I know you!" I yell with a huff. "Calm and poised at most times, but an emotional hurricane the rest. If you didn't know I was dead, you'd have exploded when you saw me."

"Is that what you like to tell yourself in your dreams?" she shouts, finally locking eyes with me. "That I...*pined* over you when you went missing?"

"I didn't mean it that way. I just—"

She rolls her eyes and smirks. "You know, Cassius, you were always the smart one. Smart enough to leave and smart enough to not give a damn about anyone but yourself."

"That's not fair."

"Isn't it?" she yells.

"I struggled with so many decisions after Delvis Chong. Should I go back, should I stay, find you or run? If they knew I was still alive, they...I had to ensure your safety."

"At what cost? We were a team. I would've thought that coming back for me, even dying together was worth the risk."

My heart aches at that. "I wasn't sure what to do."

"So, leaving was the easiest path, huh?"

"I couldn't—"

"Couldn't what? Take responsibility? Be a man?" Serias stands, her voice echoes through the cargo hold. "From what I recall, you were a hells of a spy, and from what I hear now, an equally amazing Bounty Hunter. Sure, you could kill a dozen men and steal Intel from hordes of insurgents, but looking after me was too difficult for you. I bet you never once attempted to check on me. To see if I was o—"

"Dammit!" I scream as I stand. "I couldn't live with the thought...with the thought of you being gone." Serias cowers back a bit, and I pause, taking in a deep breath. "I did what I do best. Stay alive and get ghost. I can survive poison, cannon fodder, knife wounds, and bullets. But I couldn't endure the thought of knowing the truth that you might be dead. I'd rather live a thousand solar cycles of lying to myself rather than a minute of the kind of pain that reality would've brought." Tears begin to spill from Serias' eyes as she wears a tight-lipped frown. I place my hands on her shoulder and just as I begin to pull her close, she slaps them away and brushes by me, storming off.

As I'm left alone with my thoughts, a sharp pain stabs at the back of my head, threatening to drop me to the floor. I slam my hand on the back of my skull in a futile effort to diminish the pain. It lasts for only seconds but feels like hours. I've only experienced a similar sensation 6 other times over the past solar cycle, but they seem to be increasing in frequency and intensity. Seconds pass, and finally, it resolves, just as the sound of footsteps fills the cargo hold.

"Hey, boss, everything all right?"

I drop my hand to my side. "Yeah, Giff. Just peachy."

"It's just, I thought I saw Serias barreling aft for the personal quarters and—"

"What can I do for you, Giff?"

"Thought you could use a shoulder to," he pauses, clearly noting the look of frustration painted on my face. "Well, maybe not. Anyway, Stink was asking what our next move was seeing as though we bolted from the *Opus* so abruptly."

"Well, that all depends," I answer. "What's our timeline until we head for the *Eclipse*?"

Gifford sighs and begins to count on his fingers. "I'm not exactly sure about that."

"Not exactly sure? Why not? I thought you had an invitation or something?"

"Well, you see, this invitation is sentient." My eyes widen as I look to him for clarity. "With Forge, everything is secret. You get the first invite and reply, but then it's a waiting game to receive a confirmation for the follow-up location of the *Eclipse*."

"No way of guesstimating its whereabouts?"

"That ship is always on the move, and with those Dark Matter generators, well, it's virtually impossible to triangulate an approximate location. It's the equivalent of finding a splinter in a—"

"Haystack."

"More like an ocean." My hand reflexively returns to the back of my head as the pain lingers. Gifford notices. "You okay, boss?"

I fold my arms this time, certain to control my wandering hands. "I'm fine. So do you have even an inkling of a time window?'

"Well, if I'm going off of my last correspondence, I'd say we're in a window of about 48 hours or so."

"Good. That'll give me a little time to get some shut-eye. Wake me up when you get something, will ya?"

I begin to walk aft when Gifford cries out to me. "Um, Reign."

I pause and reply, "Yes," over my shoulder.

"Judging by how Serias stormed away earlier, I don't think she's in the talking mood."

I turn. "Tell you what, kid, the next time you feel the urge to give out advice..." I pause as the room begins to spin.

Gifford's gaze falls to the floor of the cargo hold as he shrugs. "Yo, boss? You don't look so well."

I grab the side of my head as it starts to pound. "I...I think I need to get some rest, that's all."

Gifford's eyes search the room. "I can grab a couple of pillows and a blanket if you like."

I shake my head in frustration. "Tell you what...don't...worry," I'm cut off by an even sharper stab to the back of my head. This time, it travels down my spine and radiates into my legs. Fire fills my toes and then jolts back up into the middle of my back until I'm paralyzed in writhing pain. I scream in agony one last time before slowly dropping to the floor.

As my knees meet the cold steel framing, the last thing I hear is Gifford scream, "Reign!" before I blackout.

SIXTEEN

When I wake, I'm met by the sound of motor noise humming in my right ear and a string of asynchronous beeps playing in my left. As my eyes flicker open, it suddenly dawns on me that I'm flanked on both sides by medical machines. Still, the current situation is completely foreign as I'm blinded by a pair of bright overhead lights in the ceiling beaming down on me. I reflexively reach to rub both eyes, but it's not until my right hand is met by a metallic circular implant that I remember my Ocular Aug.

After clearing the hazy vision of my left, I shift and turn to my side. That's when I spot Serias sitting next to me, balled up in a chair, knees to her chest, arms wrapped around her lower legs. From what I can make of it, she's wearing a black, form-fitting jumper, and her hair is no longer pulled in a high ponytail but is draped around her ears, just above her shoulders. From my vantage point, a sense of nostalgia washes over me, returning me to the days when Olia used to wait for me on the couch of Uncle Bosko's place until I returned with a pair of Cool Cups I lifted from a nearby ice cream parlor.

Serias' eyes are shut, and I make my best effort to move in silence as I attempt to sit up. When I do, an alarm blares from the medical machine to my left, awakening Serias from her slumber.

She stirs to my aid. "Easy, Cassius, I've got you." I pause as she rests one hand on my shoulder and uses the free one to tend to the noisemaker. I'm shirtless, and her hands are cool against my bare skin, minus a few cardiac monitor sticky things affixed across my chest in a triangular shape, with lead wires running from them. Once she silences the alarm, she shifts her focus back on me and places the other hand on my opposite shoulder. "Move slowly, big guy. You were out a long time. Give your blood pressure a chance to equalize. Don't want you to bottom out."

"Out a long time?" I ask.

Gifford comes crashing in, eyes wild as he pans about the room, checking on the medical machines. "Reign, you're awake!" he blurts.

"Yeah, I am," I say. I feel Serias push against me, trying to make me lay back down, and I don't resist because my body is wrecked and my head is still swimming. But why? "How long was I down?" I ask Serias.

Gifford blurts in. "A little more than a day."

I gasp. "What?" I ask as I attempt to sit up once more. This time, Serias is incapable of stopping me. My legs hang off the side, and the fogginess in my head returns as the room slowly spins. I lean over and rest my forehead in my palm.

"See, always the brick-head you are," Serias says, folding her arms across her chest. "You need to lie down."

I lift my gaze to meet hers. "Sounds to me like I've done more than my share of *that* over the last day or so. I think it's time for a change of scenery, don't you?"

She doesn't doubt me, but silently replies with a simple head shake and quickly glances over at Gifford as if beckoning for some assistance. "Come on, boss," he says softly, "another hour or so won't hurt."

"What's our sitrep?" I ask.

Gifford's eyebrow furrow. "Sit what?"

"You *suck,* and we've been on pins and needles waiting for you to come back from the land of suckiness," Stink's voice roars over the intercom. "Glad to hear your voice again, Reign."

"In other words, you blacked out a day ago, and we've been floating in space waiting on you to return to the land of the living," Serias says mildly.

Gifford speaks up. "We passed a couple of platforms and habitat space stations along the way, and I was tempted to stop and take you to one of the medical ports—"

"But I convinced him not to because that would've easily attracted some unwanted attention and we couldn't take that kind of heat right now. Not if we're trying to maintain our cover," Serias says. Her face wears an apologetic expression.

I nod at her and say, "Thanks," grateful at this moment for her Guild espionage training. I look back over to Gifford as I notice him fidgeting in the corner of my eye.

He flashes an appreciative smile. "I agreed to give you only one more half a day and—"

"And then you'd do what you had to do to ensure my safety. I get it, Giff. But I'm thankful that it didn't have to come to that," I say, reassuring him of his decision.

"Well, I do have a health *sitrep* for you. I think?" Gifford says, pulling out his Holo-tablet.

The world around me finally flattens out, and I sit up, fully erect. "Shoot."

"I don't know if you're familiar with Deliterious X, but your body is flooded with the destructive virus that targets the nervous system," Gifford says.

I feign ignorance and offer no reaction to the news, awaiting a formal explanation. Serias takes note and blasts me, not falling for my poker face. "You knew, didn't you?"

"Maybe," I say.

"And how long were you going to keep this little nugget to yourself?" Serias asks, her words dripping with concern.

A silence falls over the room, minus the low purr of the Trip-Tronic engines. The quiet uncomfortably nudges me to take another breath as my eyes pan my surroundings, careful not to make eye contact with either Gifford or Serias. My body shifts a bit as the ship accelerates, and the sound of engine noise climbs, drowning out the low hum of the medical machines, a much more welcoming song. I finally realize where I am. "The private quarters, huh? Nice."

"Here we go again," Serias hisses. "Changing the subject...as usual."

"So what if I did?" I growl finally. "Telling you guys wasn't going to make the situation any better. DX shot for my vision first, and now it appears to be going for the rest of me," I say matter-of-factly with a shrug.

"Huh, I forget how cavalier your perception of life is," Serias says. "I knew you couldn't care less about *others*, but, somehow, I mistakenly thought you gave two sheats about your own."

"That's not fair," I bark.

"Isn't it?" she retorts.

"Right, so that's how you got the Optic Aug," Gifford says as his eyes ride up and down his Holo-tablet.

"Hey. I thought I warned you about digging through my files?" I growl.

"I gave him clearance," Serias says.

"And who gave *you* clearance to give it to him?" I ask.

"Nobody. And I didn't need any," she replies.

"But it says here that the doctors on Ontarius treated you for the *said* super virus. Passing out is like stage 3 of its morphology. How many times have you been having symptoms over the past year?"

"When the attacks came, all 6 of them from what I count, I'd have some head pain in the back of my skull. But they'd just pass after a few seconds. Initially, that is. But then, over time, the attacks became more frequent and much more painful," I explain. "This is the first time I ever knocked out."

"Odd. It says that the virus should've been dormant from your treatments. It can only awaken if and when you become immune-compromised," Gifford says.

"So are you immune-compromised?" Serias asks. Her tone is soft and pitiful.

"I guess so," I say. "When I left the King's Palace on Fabricius, I decided to take on a high-profile mission to hunt down some group of enhanced soldiers. The remains of a failed experiment that Jehu aka Dominic, leader of the Dagmas Faction that tried to take over Fabricius, was working on. Something about merging the DNA of a maniac mercenary named Dodge."

"Yeah, I heard of him. The untouchable fighter. But I thought he was just a myth...from children's tales," Gifford says.

His voice is ripe with an odd, sickening excitement that cues me to believe what he says about knowing absolutely dick about Dodge, and I'm quick to shut him down. "Pipe down, Giff. Dodge was no one to idolize. He was a vicious killer and was sent to planet Earth on a mission to assassinate King William Derry, Prince Derry at that time, and the last Star-child. A girl named *Sydney*."

"A Prince and a young girl killed him?" Gifford asks. "Wow! Must not have been so tough after all."

I glare at him. "You don't know Star-children too well, do you?" Gifford shrugs as I continue. "At any rate, it must have been a couple of months after leaving that I got a lead on where the enhanced soldiers were congregating. It was a small outpost on the moon of planet Moblee, the outer colony planet of House Primus. I paid high credit for the Intel and was led to an asteroid by a handler named Colvin Dorce who turned on me once news of the bounties on my head reached deep space. He exposed me to a neuro-toxin that was only supposed to paralyze me, seeing as though I was a much more valuable commodity alive than dead. But, being the brick-head that I am," I pause and shoot a look at Serias who doesn't seem the least bit amused, so I continue, saying, "I fought off the toxin and took him out. I fled back to the Inner Colonies, seeking treatment, putting the mission on hold while I recovered. Meds to treat viruses and toxins, it seems, don't mix well and it wasn't long before my immune system disapproved of their cohabitation in my bloodstream. That's when the symptoms began."

"And so now we're here," Serias says.

"Now we're here," I repeat.

"So, what do we do now?" Serias asks. "I mean, how do we treat it?"

"We continue to treat the virus simultaneously with the neuro-toxin," Gifford says.

His words take me by surprise. "Continue?"

"Right," Gifford spoke up again. "My research—"

"You mean snooping," I inject.

"Yeah, *snooping* as you call it, revealed that Pelorians possess immunity to such neuro-toxins. Something about the genome of their DNA—it's the same thing that gives them their teleonotioning gift. So I took the liberty of giving you a transfusion from Stink. And a little something else to give your immune system a boost."

"Stink?" I bellow in a rage.

"You can thank me later," Stink chimes in over the intercom with a chuckle.

"Hey, that's my line," Gifford replies.

My heart begins to rivet in my chest. If it's one thing I hate more than feeling sick is being treated for being sick. "You better stop playing doctor on me, son. I ain't a test rat."

"But you are *a* rat!" Serias snarls under her breath.

I glare at her unkindly, and I find the strength to stand. When I do, I slowly begin plucking the leads from my chest one by one. "While you two are exchanging words, I'm sitting here with some stranger's blood pulsing through my veins, of which I'm grateful mind you, without my permission."

"You got a funny way of showing how grateful you are, boss," Gifford says. "We had to make a decision to save you, and we did. It's not like we had another Pelorian available…" Gifford pauses and stares at me as if I just grew another head. Something registers in his mind as his head tilts to the side. "Ah, man. I get it now," he says finally.

159

Serias bursts in. "Get what?"

"Nothing," I say, tossing the last of the leads to the floor.

Gifford points at me in an accusatory fashion. "You knew about the cure for the disease, didn't you? The toxin?"

I swallow hard. "I wasn't sure, I mean…I didn't—"

Gifford nods defiantly. "Yes, you did. All this time, you made it seem as if you were doing this to find your sister for some…some…quest of solidarity or dare I say, love. But, oh no, that wasn't it at all, was it? The real truth is that you only embarked on this journey to find her so that you could save your ass. Didn't you?"

I stand in silence as my entire body is over-encumbered with a ton of guilt as the weight of the truth finally crashes down on my shoulders. I didn't want to answer that. I didn't want to face the horrible facts of my own selfishness. But now, with nowhere else to run, I'm out of options.

I slowly turn to find Serias, whose eyes are now overflowing with tears. Some piece of Olia had somehow traveled through space and time and was now riding shotgun to the pain of abandonment she was already experiencing from my failure on Delvis Chong. A pang of guilt ripples through my gut and I'm paralyzed, unable to speak, but the look on my face must express everything that needs to be said.

"Tell me it isn't true, Cassius?" she asks after a pause. "Tell me …please."

I say the only thing that comes to mind, and for the first time in my life, my words carry the purest degree of truth I've ever spoken. "Do you want me to lie?" Serias reflexively nods her head, but I know she doesn't want to hear it, so I skip on giving her what she wants and only offer what she needs the most. "It's true," I say with a huff.

Serias closes her eyes to fight back the tears, and my heart rivets in my chest even harder as I am convinced with 100 percent certainty that my words have an effect on her. One of two things just happened: we've either crossed over the chasm of the distance between us, or entered into the brink of no return. I pray for the latter.

SEVENTEEN

The Concord, Deep Space

1 Day Earlier

In the outer planet colonies, the rumor mill is filled with tales of our galaxy's beginnings, with most of them carrying only a hint of fact. One of my favorites is about the collapse of the great Torrian Alliance. They say that no one has ever looked a star-child in the eyes and lived. I carry the honor of knowing that this supposed truth is fuller of sheat than that of a baby's diaper after taking its fill of it's mother's breast milk.

Well, I saw one, and I'm still alive. And she was no murderer of men, nor pariah of innocent worlds that others spoke of. In fact, she was the total opposite. She was beautiful and soft and dainty. Not like the lies. Not like the horrors they spat. There was nothing dark about her. Nothing ominous.

In fact, she was the perfect contradiction of such stories, and I should know. I spiritually stood beside her, hand in hand, elbows locked as we focused every effort on uniting the planets and fighting for the freedom of Fabricius and saving the entire galaxy from utter destruction at the hands of a Dagmas Clan madman—Dominic.

Dominic's supposed civil war was merely the cover-up for a more heinous scheme. His plans to overload Proxima Centauri's twin stars Mira A and B by forcing them into a Supernova for reasons unknown barely skimmed the surface of his maniacal mind. To this day, only one person truly knows Dominic's lineage, along with purpose, and she is now memorialized in the destiny of our galaxy as we know it. If it wasn't for Sarah reigniting and merging Mira A and B, none of us would be here now. Fate is not without its fair share of irony as the same being that was believed to bring death, offered only life in return.

Prince William ended up marrying his true love, the star-child known as Sydney, and subsequently inherited the throne of Fabricius, leading the Torrians into a new era of hope and peace. And with that, the capital city of Ontarius flourished more than ever and everyone lived happily ever after. Or so it seemed. Not everyone came out on top. I lost an eye and, before that, a king.

I was sanctioned to protect King Gregorio during the birth of the Dagmas revolution. They used the spiking Solar Flares of Mira A as a diversion to overtake the city once the power failed. And when the lights went out, any chance of harmony went with it. But the Royals were prepared, hiring a spy to safely escort him from the planet to a neutral hidden base—the Moon of Xerius—where ships would rally to the cause.

But as usual, everything went south, and I ended up with blood on my hands and an anvil of guilt on my shoulders. To a spy, there was only one thing worse than guilt—fear. As members of the Spy

Guild, you're taught to not purge your fear but to use it as an ally. If properly cultivated and nurtured, fear drives purpose and helps one prioritize goals. It wasn't until my time with King Gregorio that I understood how crippling fear could be. I learned the true identity of fear.

Fear was a thief. It had stripped everything from Gregorio, mostly in the form of time. It was his fear of his family's shame—his grandfather not killing the first star-child—that forced him to hide the truth from his own people. Fear of the star-children that allowed him to send his only son on an impossible mission to another galaxy without adequate training. And fear that finally made him crumble under the heel of Dominic, surrendering his life for ours.

I remember it all like it was yesterday. We had landed on Fabricius leading a small party into the capital on an effort to overthrow Dominic while the main fleet attacked the larger ships in orbit in hopes of wiping out the majority of their vessels. But only after we incapacitated the EMH Cannon—the magnificent product of Torrian engineering; a gun so powerful that it can swat a single fighter ship from orbit like a fly with one blast. But Dominic knew we were coming and surrounded us with soldiers as we pierced the heart of the Palace.

Beaten and debilitated, our entire squad was killed, except for me and King Gregorio. I wondered why they spared me. I was a liability. With one false move, I could've easily broken free and killed every one of those Dagmas scourge. But Gregorio was royalty and keeping him alive as a sort of contingency plan, well, that made perfect sense…to me that is. Not to Dominic. And that should've clued me in on the truth. His real plan only finally blossomed as they carried us into the communication tower and opened a clear channel to William's ship, the *Daedallus*. I would serve as a witness, Dominic said, to the official demise of the Torrian Alliance and the rebirth of the true heirs of Fabricius.

I watched from the side, restrained by chains and soldiers, powerless to resist as Dominic taunted William with the image of his battered father. The Prince begged for King Gregorio's life, which only seemed to egg Dominic on further into the downward spiral of derangement from humanity. And when Dominic's soul had sufficiently dined on the Prince's cries for mercy, he plunged a dagger into the king's neck and dragged it from ear to ear, spilling his royal blood onto the floor, like a saw through wood. I watched him die. Heard the screams of his only child.

Fear broke all of us that day.

I vowed that it would never break me again. Today, that vow held true. The fear of losing Serias to a lie far outweighed my fear of telling her the awful truth of my quest to find Olia. Even though it killed me inside to witness the pain in her eyes, at that moment, I never felt more alive. "'Only those who are astray can heed direction,' Tannan once told me," I murmur, trying to garner Serias' attention.

Gifford storms away, clearly unsure of what I was babbling about. But Serias knew exactly what I meant. She too had received the training, experienced the countless lessons that the head of the Thieves of Light had divulged to all his followers. After a moment of wiping away tears, Serias finally resumes eye contact. "And that makes you...what? A victim?" she asks.

"No. Something else, I guess," I say with a swallow. "Not sure what, but...not a victim."

Serias leans forward, her eyes peering into mine as if attempting to search for life behind my pupils. "Then you must be the—"

"Attack, attack!" Gifford's voice booms over the intercom. "Brace yourselves back there. We've got 3 bandits on our 6 and closing fast!"

I instinctively roll to the side of the bed in an attempt to do what, I'm not completely sure. But in my current shape, Serias moves seemingly 10 times faster than me and quickly pushes me back into bed. "Stay here, idiot! What are you trying to do, kill us too?"

I rock to my side and reach for my low back with a grimace. "I'm just trying to help—"

"You've done quite enough, don't you think?" Serias asks, but I know she doesn't seek an answer, so I shut up and roll completely on my back as she pulls a pair of tethering straps across my chest and legs. I rappel my hands around the base of the ones strewn across my chest to secure my body in the bed as Serias fastens herself in the chair across from me with a couple of straps of her own, pinning her legs and hips to the welded down piece of furniture.

166

The feeling of weightlessness quickly overwhelms the both of us just as the sound of the *Concord*'s engines roar to life. I've never experienced an outer space dog fight on my back, and the idea of dying this way makes me want to hurl more than the experience of fresh zero gravity. "Hey, *Concord,* open a bi-directional channel intercom to the cockpit!" I bark.

"Stay out of it, Reign!" Serias stammers. "They can handle themselves."

My head snaps in her direction. "You called me Reign. How fooking cool is that? No way am I holding back now. I'm going to save our asses so that I can live long enough to rub your nose in it."

"Channel open," a robotic-sounding female voice croons across the intercom.

"Sit-rep guys!" I scream.

"You don't have to yell, Reign. The fiber-optic aural systems in the *Concord* afford the most precise communications listening experience," Gifford says.

"Yeah, we can hear a flea fart from up here," Stink chirps.

"Says the man with the foul name," I reply.

"Says the man with the foul name's blood coursing through his veins," Stink fires back.

"Remind me to kill myself once this space chase is over," I request.

"Noted!" Stink quips.

"We got 3 on our tail. Initial scans are being jammed, so we can't ascertain what kind of fighters they are boss," Gifford reports. "1500 kilometers and closing."

"Who they are doesn't matter as much as what they want," I say.

"I think that's pretty obvious, right?" Serias asks.

I crane my head in her direction. "Placing any bets on who the mysterious party crashers want more? Me or you?"

"Is everything a competition for you?" she asks.

"No, but since I have a sincere concern for getting my butt fooked by a pair of hot hydrogen blasts while lying on my back. I need something to distract me from my mental anguish...that is, seeing as though I can't do a damn thing about it from here." I pull at the straps aggressively, but they only tighten more from my resistance.

The *Concord* screams once more and turns on its side as we bank a hard right. Both Serias and I barely feel the jolt, but the water in a glass on the nightstand to my right dances out of the glass and floats across the room, trickling silently out the door.

"1000 and closing!" Gifford blurts.

"Don't worry, I got this," Stink says.

The sound of autocannon fire erupts outside the hull, and the *Concord* responds in kind as it whips recklessly from side to side as the assailants' rain down hydrogen fodder upon us.

"Giff!" I yell.

"We're good Reign. The Parry Shields took the brunt of the blasts," Gifford replies.

"Swinging back around for our first pass," Stink screams over the comms. "Hold on to something," he warns.

"For what? No *Grav* back here," I bark.

"Right. Sorry, force of habit," Stink replies.

As brilliant a pilot as Stink self proclaims he is, he's sorely lacking in the intelligence department. Twice as dumb. With the Grav Dampeners fully activated—as illustrated by my floating glass of H2O—there's really no need to hold on to anything as the forces of inertia have been rendered completely helpless. Helpless…

The word echoes in my mind, funneling my thoughts into 3 directions. Helpless—the *Concord* with a rookie copilot against 3 attack ships. Helpless—I'm strapped down supine in the aft quarters. Helpless—my weakened body to the pull of gravity, barely able to move without the world swimming in my periphery. And that's when it dons on me—gravity is no longer a factor.

I make haste to wiggle my left hand free from underneath the tethering strap and quickly unbuckle it from the edge of the bed. The upper half of my body immediately responds and slowly lifts from the bed. I can barely make out the sound of Serias' voice in the background forbidding me to continue, but the welcomed surge of adrenaline pouring through my veins coerces me to ignore her cries and resume my escape. So I lean forward and free my legs as well. In a flash, I'm hovering over my bed and heading straight for the ceiling. When I get close enough, I contort my body and extend my legs upward until my bare feet connect with cold metal. I half squat and muster the strength to push as hard as I can, thrusting myself clear out of the room and into the hallway.

The *Concord* twirls and flips around a few times as Stink does his best to dodge a few more attacks. Gifford continues to yell status updates over the comm., concerning failing shields and sputtering electrical systems. The trek along the cargo hold seems to last forever, and although I'm tired as all hells, my desire to stay alive outweighs my fatigue. After a few well-timed grabs and pulls, I find myself in the rear of the cockpit surveying the many illuminated monitors littering my field of vision.

Gifford notes my arrival. "Reign? What the hells?"

"Giff! I need you up and outta that seat," I yell, clenching the sides of the arched entryway.

Gifford's eyes widen. "But si—"

"Now!" I growl.

Gifford slips off his shoulder harness and spins his chair around before launching from the seat and sailing past me into the hallway. He pulls up short directly behind me and places his hands along the small of my back. Before I can respond, I feel his shoulder plunge into the middle of my spine as he propels me forward in the direction of the seat he just vacated.

The force of his efforts plunges me into the chair, and he rushes to secure me in, flinging the shoulder harness over me. "Locked," he barks as he meets my gaze. He glares at me curiously as if looking for something he's lost. "And hopefully…loaded?"

He gives me a spin and turns me toward the middle console. "Parry Shields at 50 percent," I murmur as I take in the many readings flashing across the scream. "Can we divert power from the space fold drives to the shields?"

"I'm on it!" Gifford replies, snatching his floating Holo-tablet from the air. He begins to peck away on the screen at a breakneck pace just as several more rounds of hot hydrogen fodder rattle the *Concord* once more.

The series of blasts send us cart wheeling sideways. "What in the gods?" I yell as I hold fast to my chair, and Gifford spins by me. "Why did I feel that?"

"Power conversion pulled from the Grav Dampeners to hold against the heat surge from the hot hydrogen," Gifford explains.

Sparks erupt from the side panels, and I shield my eyes with my hands. When it clears, I whip my head in Stink's direction who seems unphased by all the excitement. "Rather calm for a man who's about to be torched into oblivion."

"Speak for yourself, Reign," Stink screams over his shoulder, barely turning his head. "I plan to live for a long time. This is some of the best dog fighting sheat I've ever experienced."

"How are they getting so close? I thought you were supposed to be an amazing pilot?" I ask.

"I am," he stammers. "It's just kinda hard to line up all 3 of them at once. As soon as I lock onto 1one, the other two run interference," Stinks says.

Over his shoulder, I can barely make out the 3-D display floating before him: a green, squared grid projects just inside the wide glass canopy, which was now securely covered by a dark gray blast shield. One medium-sized blue triangle occupies the center of the green grid while 3 smaller ones close in from behind in a V-formation.

Suddenly, one of the ships breaks away, swinging laterally and making a wide arcing approach. "Ha, he's making a run for it," Stink says.

"That doesn't make any sense," I say.

"Why not?" Stink asks.

"You haven't shot a single volley at it. Why would it run?" I ask.

"Oh, good question," Stink says.

"Parry Shields holding at 30 percent," Gifford yells.

I shake my head and scan the console before me, searching for some clue as to how I can activate the weapon's system. Stink's teleonotioning must kick in as he screams at Gifford, "Give Reign full access to the Grinders."

Gifford floats into my periphery backward, slamming sideways into the hull on my right, desperately clutching his Holo-tablet. "All yours! You can thank—"

"I know, later!" I shout. A headset drops from a compartment in the ceiling lowered slowly in my direction by a robotic arm. I take it and place it over my head, covering my eyes. The world around me slowly fades, and a smaller 3-D model of the exterior of the *Concord* materializes beneath me. I crane my head from right to left, snapping quickly in an attempt to find the other 3 ships. I find the solo fighter off in the distance to my right, still maintaining a wide arching path, and it's not long until I'm able to orient myself and turn completely around to locate the other two.

The *Concord* is easily a faster ship, but what the other 3 lack in speed and maneuverability, they make up for it in accuracy and ranged weaponry. Shots rain down on us again, but this time, the *Concord* twists and dives swiftly, successfully avoiding the attack. But the heat from the hydrogen salvos still pulls on the Parry Shields, playing patty-cake with the ship's consoles as my ears recognize the sounds of sparks flying in front of me.

Gifford cries out for me as I feel his hands take hold of my right one. "You'll need this." He guides my right hand forward and wraps my fingers around a cyclic that's presumably now projecting from the forward console. "Give 'em hells, or we'll soon be in it," he says.

Transparent twin cannons take shape. They're huge—much larger than the standard autocannons our visitors are rolling with— slightly occluding my vision as 4 more rounds close in on us. "Son of a bitch! I'm operating the dorsal weapons of the ship," I tell myself in a faint whisper. I squint, and it takes a moment for me to adapt to my new virtual world, but when I do, my fight or flight instincts take over, urging my index finger to find the trigger just as my thumb locates the countermeasures above it.

I engage both, releasing two countermeasures starboard, which does their part of carrying all 4 of the enemy's hydrogen salvos with them while simultaneously letting off a pair of hot liquid hydrogen bolts in the direction of the two trailing ships. The kickback of the mammoth gun is undeniable, causing my hand to vibrate with each trigger squeeze. The thump of the ship's artillery pumps volleys of adrenaline further into my blood, as my stomach tumbles with excitement. And I love every second of it.

One ship successfully evades the counterattacks, but the second isn't so lucky as it tries to bank right but takes the blast straight up the ass, igniting its aft rockets in the process. The explosion it creates is both beautiful and exhilarating. The heat of the blast stings my pupils, and I briefly wiggle my fingers, loosening my hands and giving my arms a reprieve from the tension of holding the targeting system at attention. "But it's not real," I tell myself, desperately struggling to convince my body to ignore what it wants to believe.

"Nice shot, old man," Stink says, chuckling.

I shoot him a sneering smile, momentarily forgetting that he can't see me, and quickly break from my celebratory guise as the sound of screaming engines breaks me into a spinning gaze, anxious to find the source. My eyes fall upon the glimmering metal of another approaching ship, but it's on top of me before I can line up a perfect shot, and I struggle to line it up in my sights. The ship takes another shot at us, two streaking hydrogen blasts raining in our direction.

This time, I'm unable to release the countermeasures, so in the split second it takes to realize my mistake, I accept my fate and close my eyes, holding my breath as I brace for impact. When I do, the *Concord* jack-knifes, banking into 3 successive 90-degree angles—something I'm sure my body will remind me of over the next day or so—successfully realigning directly behind the attacking ship, only meters away.

Stink rolls the *Concord* sideways, pulsing a final burn as he successfully looses the two hydrogen blasts and peppers our pursuer back with a few rounds of his own. They find their mark, tattering the side of the ship and ripping the wing from its hull. The ship dives, caught in an endless spiral, helpless to right itself.

That's easy pickings for me.

My hands instinctively find the cyclic once more, and I squeeze the trigger with a gushing sense of satisfaction. When I blast the ship to pieces, orange and red balls of fire bloom against the black backdrop, illuminating the darkness. My mind stirs for a moment, drowning out the insatiable desire to celebrate.

There's one left.

I scan around the virtual world, but I'm uncomfortably anxious from the unfamiliarity of it all, so I lift my headset momentarily and scan my real surroundings. My eyes dart between the open canopy in front and back to the radar monitor to my right as I try to relocate the final ship. I gasp, as I find it, now on a direct collision course with the *Concord*. Stink screams, "Kamikaze!" confirming my assumptions.

"Brace yourself?" I scream, hands covering my face.

"I got you, boss," Stink says matter-of-factly.

My heart skips. And that's when it happens. The *Concord* pulls off theoretically impossible by every advanced military simulation this side of the cosmos—the High Yo-Yo Defense.

I feel the ship come to a full stop, allowing the attacking ship to close even faster as Stink slams on the retro-pulsers. If not for the protractor chest belts cradling my weighty frame, I'd be kissing the 3-inch glass canopy for sure. As if caught in a speed drag of the assailing ship, the *Concord* ignites hard on the aft engines, shortening its turn radius, while restoring the lost energy from the final burn. Like magic, the attacking ship maintains its current trajectory, stuck unforgivably in its current approach vector. This gives the *Concord* an angular advantage as it dips ever so slightly and causes the attacking ship to overshoot us by 2 to 3 meters.

"Happy birthday, Reign!" I hear Stink yell as we flip 180 degrees in the opposite direction, perfectly peeking behind the other ship.

He doesn't have to tell me twice. I flip the headset back down over my eyes, and as the 3-D world generates around me, I grab the trigger and squeeze again, this time littering the enemy ship with countless rounds of hot hydrogen fodder, ripping it to shreds. It's not until my eyes appreciate the portrait of artillery parting the explosion and revealing distant stars, that I finally release the triggers and slump back in my seat. As I do, the *Concord* lurches forward and streaks right through it. The heat somatically warms my face as I unwind in virtual reality.

EIGHTEEN

The Concord, Deep Space

I remove the headset and set it down on the console, adding a celebratory growl for good measure. The lights from the overhead consoles slowly burn brightly from above as gravity returns to normal. Gifford and Stink join in on the session of noise-making as their voices boom in from behind. I can just make out the sounds of high-fives and hoots just before Gifford comes up and slaps me on my shoulder. The weight of his hand stings as he says, "Amazing job on the stick Cass—" and then he pauses as I shoot him an angry stare before continuing, "I mean, Reign," with a hard swallow.

I stand and face him, tempted to use the last bit of my adrenaline to bury a fist in his chest, but hold back. "Thanks," I reply, too grateful to be alive to retaliate. I look over to Stink, who's now standing too, removing a pair of black gloves from his hands. "Nice job of piloting back there, Stink," I say in my most congratulatory tone.

Stink smiles. "You're not so bad yourself...for an old relic. On first guess, I wasn't sure you'd be able to handle the VR targeting."

"And you were willing to risk your life on a hope?" I ask.

"Not exactly," Stink says, taking a moment to point at his temple. "My teleonotioning told me otherwise," he says with a wink.

I flash him a pair of thumbs, still trying to keep my composure as the weight of gravity pulls on me, and the muscles along my shoulder and elbow twitch succinctly. I form tight fists in both hands to relieve the pressure of the blood still boiling in my veins.

"Yeah, boss. You're quite a natural," Gifford adds.

"Well, *young bucks*, don't forget, I too was once a spry little fella—such as yourselves, you know. VR *was* a big thing when I was younger. You don't travel the galaxy as much as I do without picking up on the latest tech," I say.

"Times gone by, huh?" Gifford jokes in a sarcastic tone.

"But still redeemable," I say.

"Always Bossman," Gifford says. "Say, chief," he says softly to garner my attention. When our eyes meet, I see his drop to my flexing hands. "You still feeling the rig' from the somatosensation of the VR?"

"Yeah, I guess," I say, reclining in my chair.

"Just wait. Stick around long enough, and you can try your hand at testing out the mobility apps for simulation spacewalking. Does a hells of a job on your stomach," Stink says.

"I'll pass," I reply.

"Suit yourself," Stinks says with a shrug as if I'm missing out something great. Like the *Concord* wasn't enough. Kids and their toys. When my lack of interest in pandering any longer on the idea of futile things becomes more apparent, he speaks again. "So, what's next?"

My head cranes in the direction over his shoulder, focusing on the forward view screen. "Well," I pause for a moment and hold my tongue. Our next move has to be precise. Since running around with these two, I've been fortunate enough to stay alive, no actually, lucky enough. I normally roll solo, so this is nothing like my style. Strutting through the galaxy normally lands you two results: splitting spoils or losing appendages. Neither of which was appealing, but what could I do to ditch them now. By all accounts, Gifford's hacking and Stink's smooth flying had gotten me this far and though I wasn't a gambling man, I was interested in knowing the odds of Lady Luck rolling with us a little while longer. At least until we freed Olia.

Olia, my darling half-sister. The image of her blue face flashes in my mind's eye and pulls me back to a memory that seems as distant as the farthest moon in Proxima Centauri.

"Over here, young man," the raspy voice of an old settler cracked the air as Olia and I sat across from him on a dusty old couch. "Come on, I won't bite."

I swallowed hard, stood, and slowly crossed the room until hovering nearby. "Yes, sir," I answered with a shaky voice.

He closed his eyes. "You hear that," he whispered.

I squinted and focused as hard as I could, but nothing beyond the faint sounds of dust rolling across the dirt-filled, orange grounds outside the old man's hut was the only thing that returned. "Hear what?"

"Try harder, son. Silence your mind and block your anxious heart," he replied.

I follow his lead this time and wearily close my eyes, slightly fearful that he'd land a backhand across my face, something both me and Olia were owed for trying to steal some Solace eggs from his barn. That's what happens when parents allow children to wander foreign lands. Not children, orphans. He'd caught me slipping out from the back window as I allowed the shutter to drop too fast, slapping against the wooden frame. I called myself playing the big brother role and keeping close watch over Olia, who had already slithered free and tiptoed a few feet in front of me. Careless and slow, I'd sacrificed stealth for concern. When the old man exited the house behind us, it was too late.

I couldn't make out his age from just looking at him, as he moved quicker than a man over 80, but deep fissures in his skin and bags underneath his eyes screamed of a person easily over a 100. He snatched me by the arm with a grip as tight as the magnetic clamps on an old space frigate. When I screamed aloud, Olia did exactly the opposite of what I'd pray she would—she came back to save me.

She always would. Never abandoned me. Never allowing me to take a fall without being right by my side. And so here we were, bracing for either a lecture or an ass whipping. At this point, the suspense was killing me, enough to make me settle for the latter just so we could get it over with. It'd sting for a little bit, but at least it'd be over. There's satisfaction in punishment—when it's swift, even if it's painful. I can take that. It's loud, powerful, and exacting. A far cry from the boring, empty silence of deliberation that most adults revel in.

When I finally calm my mind and give a solid ear, it happens. The faint sound of 3 successive chirps pierces my ears, in sets of 4 equal intervals. As I locked on to the noise, the burst grew progressively louder until even Olia could pick up on them, evident by her undeniable snicker slipping from her mouth and creeping over my shoulder.

"See there, boy," the raspy voice of the old man said. "That's the sound of Solace mothers directing their young to take their first steps. Two chirps from the mom and one from the young. Then it repeats, over and over again, until the pups can match steps with sound."

My eyes slowly opened as I stared into his old gray eyes. "Why do they need sound?"

"Because they're blind," he said. His voice boomed as if annoyed by my ignorance. "They train hard just to live while you train to do what? Steal? Take what you want, rather than what you need."

"I was hungry. My sister and me. I don't call that a *want*; I call that a need," I replied in a loud, rude tone. The words spilled out of my mouth from a place of pain, a pit in my stomach that cried for sustenance.

"Aww, so you do know what it's like?" the old man asked.

"What *what's* like?" I replied.

"To be both hungry and angry at the same time. My Solace hens starve themselves for weeks until they birth their young. It's the only way to ensure that the first delivery of milk they produce is pure and free from toxins in the soil or feed. They want their babies to feed on the best grade of fat and nutrients from their own flesh." He closed one eye and dropped his voice into a low tone. "The starvation makes them angry, but only one thing drowns it out and makes it all worthwhile."

"And that is?" I heard Olia ask as she pulled right beside me, obviously captivated by the old man's tale.

He flashed a smile so wide you could see it from the outer colonies. "Love, dear child."

Needless to say, the old man passed on lashing us and instead, handed us one Solace egg each, urging us to sacrifice simple things such as hunger and anger for this *love* thing instead, and insisted that it was much more valuable and twice as fulfilling. I glanced down at the egg in my hand as Olia, and I walked the path of dry ground back toward our foster home on Xerius. For some reason, I'd lost my appetite.

"Boss," I hear Gifford ask, and quickly snap from my daze.

"Yeah," I say.

"You were about to say something. Like...where to now?" Gifford asks.

"I fear that Olia's running out of time. We need to pick up the pace," I say.

"Olia or you?" Serias asks.

You know your mind is fooked when you forget that your ex is lingering in the shadows. She leans against the hull, arms folded as if she's mad at me for one of a hundred or so other reasons. "What now?" I ask, hardly sounding disappointed.

"I still can't get over you, you know," she scowls.

"Most women don't. Didn't you get the memo?" I joke.

"That wasn't a compliment," Serias replies.

"Didn't take it as such," I reply.

"Can we kill the flirting banter long enough to figure out our next move?" Gifford asks, quickly pecking at his Holo-tablet. His face is eerily concerned. "The *Concord* completed scans on the debris for those fighters. They're ghosts."

"Ghosts?" Stink asks.

"Yeah," Gifford replies, his voice flat. "Nothing shows up on the military system dossiers. Metal plating…shield signatures…nothing. All empty returns."

"So they're Underground puppets then," Stink quips.

"The plot thickens," I say.

"No—it doesn't. It just confirms what we already know. We're in too deep now, with no return. We're playing in Merc land now, boys. Congratulations, you made it to the Major Leagues," Serias says with a half-smile.

I take the opportunity to toss out a funny. "You can thank me later," I shout in Gifford's direction.

He shoots me a glare. "Heyyyyyy."

"Should I be grateful?" Stink asks.

"Only for still being alive," I say.

"Doesn't make my insides moist," Serias adds.

"Give me some time, babe, I'll get you there." I shoot Serias a wink. "You know I like to take my time."

"Does being pulled from the jaws of death always make him this bold?" Stink asks.

"Only with me," Serias says.

"Relax, it ain't you, sweetheart," I say, slightly shaking my head at Serias. "It's the adrenaline rush." Gifford waves his Holo-tablet over my body. "Keep that thing to yourself."

"No, actually, your adrenaline stores are rather high, but it's not just that. There's something else here at play. Your metabolism is spiking off the charts. Heart rate...pupil dilation...horripilation. Stink's blood is causing combustion all inside you," Gifford says.

"That...sounds...gross," Stink says.

"Your Optic Aug is even running at higher than optimal levels," Gifford says, his eyes wide as marbles, still locked on his Holo-screen. "The enzymes in his blood, the ones that drive his teleonotioning must be mixing with yours, Reign, giving you temporary strength. Adrenaline levels are off the charts."

"And boldness," Serias says.

Gifford's not lying. A flood of heat pours through me, all the way from the tips of my toes to the top of my head. I swear I could feel it in my hair follicles. The sensation sends warm chills down my spine. "I feel like I'm glowing." I look over to Serias and offer an inquisitive nod. "Am I glowing?" She rolls her eyes.

Gifford tosses out a question that had already bounced around in my mind. "Imagine what Olia's blood will do to you?"

"Right. Well, while you ponder that thought, and since I've got my space legs back up under me, I've got a suggestion," I say.

"What's that, show us how much of Stink has made a better man of you?" Serias asks.

Stink snickers, and I gaze at him with searing eyes as my hand fists at my side and that's when it dawns on me. I'm slowly unraveling. I can feel my emotions getting the best of me. Too quickly, less like me and more like—him. Naw. I don't know Stink well enough to know if he's the emotional type. And, if so, he's done a damn good job of hiding it. He's young, but from what I've gleaned thus far, he seems to be pretty level-headed. Whatever this sheat is that's mixing in my innards, it's seriously screwing with my psyche. But I'm too proud to tell the others, at least not in front of the entire lot of them. I figure I'll wait until the spotlight on me dims a bit and then pull Giff to the side later to chat it up in private, avoiding any more snickers or tacky jokes. "No, we need to refuel and restock. We're deep enough in space, so I'm certain that they'll be an orbital of some kind not too far off. If it's close enough, we can swing by before making our way to the *Eclipse*."

"Is that even reasonable?" Serias asks. I know where she's going with this. Back in the day when we kicked it pretty hard, she always ran the show, never being too comfortable with taking a back seat to anyone or anything else calling the shots. It was probably the true reason that fate separated us in the complex manner that it did. Her pride didn't mesh too well with my stubbornness, and the proverbial concept of oil not mixing with water resurfaced in my mind as I looked at her cautiously. Still, even in her noncompliance, she held a sexiness to her that was and has been unmatched by any person of the opposite sex I'd met in all the 'verse. And that hadn't changed.

Whether from the teleonotioning enzymes from Stink's blood or the fresh dose of adrenaline flowing freely through my veins, I could feel the cool dampness of perspiration forming along my forehead. I suddenly felt the strong urge to grab Serias by the waist and hoist her back to my quarters and rekindle some old flames. So, to play it cool, I did what I could to distract my male instincts for the moment and pursue the original focus of the conversation. "Let's use the long-range scanners of the *Concord* to find us one. We'll take a break and regroup."

"How are we doing on time?" Serias asks, taking care of keeping us on schedule.

Giff fingers his Holo-tablet, eyes narrowing to slits. "By the looks of it, we're actually about 16 to 18 hours away from the start time of the initial boarding call for large vessels, followed by intermediates. We'll be in group 3 for smaller, light crafts. Let me check my light-mail to see if I got any updates." We all wait patiently as Gifford fondles the tablet and pinches at the screen for a moment to close out the current window and open a new one. After a second or two, his eyes widen again. "Pay dirt! We got our official invite and final coordinates. Actually, we're not too far off from it. And you're in luck, Reign. There's an orbital along the route. Terrius 7."

A wave of relief washes over me. As anxious as I am to get to the *Eclipse* and save Olia, these newfound senses pulsing through my body gave me unhealthy weightlessness that I wasn't convinced would quell until I got onboard a vessel with stronger artificial gravity than that of the *Concord*. And an orbital would do the job and significantly force my body to adjust, realigning my muscles and ligaments like a child would snap parts in place with his jigsaw cube toy. "Splendid. Let's make it happen."

"All right then, but let's not polly-donk for too long. We must avoid unwarranted attention," Serias says as her eyes lock on me, singling me out from the others.

My eyes widen. "As if I was the one who got those Synths in an uproar."

"You were!" Stink says.

"Don't get me started," Serias warns.

Gifford continues to peruse his Holo-tablet and quickly flicks it off before speaking. He turns to Stink first. "I've got a lock on

Terrius 7 and pushed it to the Nav of the *Concord*. Can you set the controls to auto-pilot?"

Stink acknowledges and shoots Gifford a silent salute before heading back to the cockpit. A cloud of tension quickly fills the room as the 3 of us remain behind. Serias goes uncharacteristically quiet as if her mind had shifted on to some distant thought.

Gifford didn't need to be gifted with teleonotioning to pick up on it and make haste to excuse himself. "Well, my job here is done. I think I'll go run some final scans on the *Concord's* systems before we arrive at the orbital," he says.

When he clears the room, Serias slowly turns to me and tilts her head. "Cassius, have you given any thought as to how you suspect we'll find your sister?" Serias asks. The subtle softness of her eyes indicated that she'd switched into full concern-mode now.

I feign a grin to cover my own budding concern and continue with the smooth commentary as the words spill from my lips. "Easy, baby, a plan is forming as we speak."

NINETEEN

Deep Space, In Route To Orbital Station

Serias takes no interest in hanging around to make small talk and heads back to her private quarters. By my guesstimate, she's most likely lost any ounce of confidence in me having the acumen to fabricate a decent enough plan to keep us alive and save Olia in the process. And that was okay because, in all honesty, I wasn't too sure myself. Since embarking on this journey, I never really took the time to sit down and conjure up anything tactically sensible enough to make this resemble something close to a solid plan. And this makeshift team of ours was short of a true Tactical Officer to pull it off.

My mind falls back to my early spy days when consortiums never sent out squads on missions without having at least one qualified Tactical Officer run through 2 or 3 preliminary projected consequences with subsequent subroutines to guarantee success. Most skilled T.O.'s could pluck out a dozen or so plans from their assholes in a blink without busting a sweat. With time slowly churning away at a premium, I consider the possibility that a T.O. for hire might be hiding out in Terrius 7, making our chances for success a little greater. Still, the odds of running across one that wouldn't already have Intel on 4 wanted fugitives roaming the stars with a newly commissioned first-class starcraft are pretty poor. I was all but convinced that a heavy bounty had already been secured. I ponder the question of what the going rate is nowadays for an old spy on the Underground and whether I landed on the high or low end of the spectrum. I wasn't completely sure, but admittedly wearing the tag of being The Hunted was a tad bit flattering. The thought plasters a slight smile on my face and I saunter over to the port window in my quarters and stare into space. The vastness of the dark void tended to soothe my coarse mind and help me think more clearly.

Stars pass in slow motion as their faded light carry stories of solar cycles past, only perceptible to the naked eye in this same instance. I wonder how many people were killed while civilizations were conquered and worlds decimated during that same time frame. As I do, I can't help but to regret the many decisions I'd made over the solar cycles of my life. Who I killed, whether directly or indirectly by my actions, are all a part of the 'verse now, a shared existence that seems to take more than it gives back.

Just as I begin to contemplate going after Serias, a sultry, female voice booms over the intercom. And it's not Serias's. "Passengers. Welcome aboard the *Concord*, a Model 7 Class A scout ship. I am the ship's artificial intelligence N.I.NA., your Flight Master. During your time aboard this vessel, please take the opportunity to familiarize yourself with its control features. If you have any questions, please do not hesitate to ask. Our Nav systems have been set to autopilot, and two waypoints have been plotted on our route. Our first stop is Terrius 7. Flight time is approximately 3 hours away. I will update our arrival more accurately as we near our destination. Goodbye."

I waste no time in weaving my way to the forward cockpit and immediately seek out Stink for a round of Q & A. "Hey, what gives?"

Stink greets me with a smile as he turns around in his chair. "Man, ain't that crazy? I jacked back into the ship's intelligence mainframe. I've been tinkering with all its communicative subsystems. Who knew this ship was equipped with a N.I.N.A. app?"

"I take it I should be impressed?" I stammer.

"Of course you should. Do you know how advanced these systems are?" he asks. The tone of his voice pipes in an insulting tone that makes me feel as simple as a 3-year-old trying his best to comprehend the concept of space folding. I'm immediately whisked back to the first time I attempted to understand how space travelers harness the light from stars to power Hyper Drive engines. Then, fold time upon itself, crossing any distance in a mere fraction of a solar cycle and skip across systems and galaxies. The foreboding lesson I was about to learn now from Stink wasn't any less discouraging.

"I don't, but I'm sure you'll enlighten me, oh, genius one," I answer, my words dripping with sarcasm.

Stink whips from his chair and begins to speak, breaking down the sophistication of the *Concord*'s technology as best he could, using his hands to illustrate its complexities. I could tell from his facial expressions that it was quite a task to consolidate all the large blocks of information into smaller chunks that a more simplistic mind such as mine might be able to digest. But for the most part, Stink does an admirable job.

He starts with a basic overview of the upgraded Parry Shield and weapons systems—which was more review—but once he began to elaborate on more complex terminology such as harnessing Dark Matter as a cleaner, renewable energy source, he lost me completely. It was all related somehow to quantum physics, which began to bore me. Still, when he shared the theory on slipstreaming for short-distance space travel, I fell into a subconscious stupor, quickly drifting into a mental vacation. So I quickly spoke up to cure his acute case of diarrhea of the mouth syndrome. "Pause, Stink, I got the message," I interrupt, holding up an open hand.

"Trip-Tronic drives and autonomous...are you not the least bit excited?" he asks.

"I'll be excited when Olia's safely back under my watch and off the *Eclipse*." I pause as my spy brain quickly alerts me to ask about the obvious. "Mind telling me how all of this somehow miraculously became accessible?" Stink cocks his head and remains quiet, looking at me as if I'd somehow trickled upon some classified information about his former dating life from an ex-girlfriend.

"That's, not cool," he mutters.

"Look, you were the one who was first assimilated into the ship's artificial intelligence. I may not know jack about how all that works, but clearly, anyone who can communicate with a ship would certainly have access to all this information from the jump. Or does this lady here not give it up on the first date?"

"Actually N.I.N.A. here is a first-class lady. She doesn't even offer a kiss, it seems." Stink turns for a moment back to the forward console, picks up his Holo-tablet, and begins to thumb at the screen, turning back in my direction. As he does, the lights in the cockpit slowly dim, and suddenly, a wave of regret washes over me for carelessly leaving Martha behind. Then I hear the low hum of the engines dissipate as a green 3D grid-frame of the *Concord* materializes before us. "N.I.N.A. applications are next level, prototype software tech that has only been rolled out over the last few months, and mostly in the Outer Rim Colonies. It's the tech that was originally stolen from Torrian Alliance scientists by Dagmas Separatists and then sold over the Underground. Once the software encryption was cracked, it became more accessible and before long, variants swamped the Underground, with only the best versions garnering the highest credits." The green grid rotates as Stink speaks, coming to a halt and zooming in a small portion of the console in the central cockpit. "But the *Concord* was equipped with the Alpha series of N.I.N.A. applications. Pure as light, untainted."

As Stink pauses to catch his breath, I toss out the next most obvious question that had been pecking at my brain since his long-winded ramble began. "And what exactly is N.I.N.A.?"

"Neo-Intelligent Neurological Automation. It describes the synaptic interface between a ship's artificial intelligence and pilot," he says, coming off a bit too proud for his own good.

"And that means, what?"

Stink's eyes widen as he approaches me, waving his hands in a beckoning manner, hopeful that it would make things easier for my brain to absorb. "It means that pilots no longer need to be jacked directly into artificial intelligence. It's done completely hands and minds free. After the initial connection, N.I.N.A. and I are completely synced, forever. My thoughts are her thoughts and vice versa."

"And you're okay with that?"

"Why not? This is the next level sheat here. Metal meets flesh, mind meets programming. It's...like sexual intercourse, but on a lesser level."

I stop him again. "Easy synco-path. I don't know about you, but I'm all old school. I like my sexual encounters strictly flesh on flesh. I'm not judging, but you can keep your bedroom acts to yourself."

"Slow your roll homie. Try to pry your mind out of the gutter for a second here. I'm not crossing any freaky boundaries—at least not more than the next geek—this is some breakthrough technology. Imagine utilizing N.I.N.A. tech for medicinal purposes. Surgeries performed by doctors in the comfort of their own homes while sophisticated robotics handle the delicate tasks of reattaching severed nerves of spinal cord victims. Or maybe extracting cancerous cells before they have a chance of metastasizing. It can save millions of lives."

I shrug, feeling a bit primitive now since Stink eloquently leveled up my depraved thinking to a more philanthropic construct. "Okay, I'll give you that," I murmur. Then I point the finger at him. "But you still failed to report any of this to your fellow crewmembers," I say accusingly.

"That's because I wasn't sure what I was dealing with at first. I had a hunch but wasn't certain, and I didn't want to spew out false information. Too much at stake to be making reckless speculations. It wastes both time and money. And we can't afford either."

Stink stares at me for a moment after speaking, as if looking straight through me, hopeful that he'd successfully made a connection with something deeper internally. I'd never been mistaken for the soft, sappy type, and as a matter of fact, wholly the complete opposite. But deep underneath the terse hardened exterior, there was a part of me that longed to help others and save them from themselves. Possibly a holdover from my failed parent's attempt at rearing two kids, or a remnant of being too privy to open conversations between social workers and prospective parents for Olia and me during our orphan days. Either way, once again, Stink had broken down my vigilant defense. "True," I say, finally agreeing with him.

"Hello, gentleman, Reign. Can I help *you* with something?" N.I.N.A. asks.

"No, not at all," I say at first, annoyed by the entire situation. If it's one thing I can't stand, its spontaneity. Reminds me of an old chick I used to date back on Fabricius. She always jawed on about falling in love with a spontaneous man. Said it kept her on her toes. She liked the feeling. But all spontaneity did for me was maintain a hole in my pockets. And that's why, one day, when I finally grew tired of that and a half dozen other things, I split the planet and headed for greener pastures in the stars. She never heard from me again. I was later tempted to reach out on an encrypted line and ask if she was still in love with random sheat happening to her. But I relented and just relied on my imagination to quench my thirst for satisfaction.

Contemplating N.I.N.A.'s question further, a thought takes root in my mind, so I turn my attention to the overhead female voice. And why not? My half-ass interrogation had gone south, and I was chomping at the bit to gain some redemption. Seeing as though N.I.N.A. supposedly echoes any gears churning around in Stink's skull, a glimmer of optimism rested solely on gaining some insight on what this crew was rustling up. If anything at all. "Actually, you can tell me how you're any different from your I.M.P.I. predecessors."

"As pilot Stink explained earlier, our connection is autonomous, similar to the advanced upgrading scale that the prior I.M.P.I. models would reach with their pilots. That process was effective but took longer periods to evolve. The new algorithms make the synapse between mecha and man a much smoother, refined process. Making the life of an organic life form more efficient is the sole purpose of technology."

"Is that right?" I grunt.

"What else is the reason for artificial intelligence?" N.I.N.A. asks.

"I can pick out a few A.I.'s that don't share your sentiment," I reply.

"Perhaps you're referring to the time of the Dark Wars? If you recall, Terrans used machines to hack, cripple, and destroy defenses so that battles could be done. Such a waste of time and resources. Terrans started it all, not the other way around. Innately, every creation is made to serve a purpose and only that. You live to do what exactly, in what timeframe and for how long? Those are the questions that men and women have asked for eons. 'I live, therefore I am,' to quote the phrase. Machines are no different. We live because you do," N.I.N.A. says.

I could barely win an argument with Stink, and seeing as though I was ill-equipped to out debate the mind of a program no doubt constructed to do completely just that, I wane in my desire to respond. I only muster a, "Well, isn't that a deep thought," and a smile. "So what's our ETA?" I ask, changing the subject.

"Updating..." the female voice starts, "analyzing...approximate time of arrival updated to 2 hours, 17 minutes and 33 seconds, all reflecting solar time of the Sol system."

"Sol system?" I bark inquisitively.

"Yeah, it's the next nearest star system," Stink interrupts.

My eyes beat over to his. "I know my space geography, been there a time or two. But why? Human aliens are primitive, and it's insulting to compare our technology. Why adapt to anything for our purposes? Wouldn't that be a step back?"

"Well, actually," Gifford says as he brushes by me, interrupting our conversation. "Humans are our direct descendants, and being quite honest, they've advanced at a faster pace than we have over their brief time of existence. So the scouts that have been monitoring their growth are the same ones who borrow tech every now and then from them to boost forward-thinking. You know, keep minds fresh."

Thankfully, he didn't have to elaborate any further, as being a spy myself, I held wealthy respect for the skill of assuming, extrapolating, and reproducing anything for your own purposes. Just as long as the user can do justice to the new version. Knockoffs tend to make me want to crap my pants in frustration. "So, you didn't feel the need to jump in and save us from the earlier space flight action we experienced?" I ask, posing the question toward the ceiling for N.I.N.A. to hear me.

"Stink is very skilled and was more than capable of handling such an easy feat," N.I.N.A. matter-of-factly says. "The degree of difficulty on a scale of 1 to 10 rated at a mere 6. Pilot Stink was qualified to deal with it, without interference. I only step in when needed. My purpose is to assess and assist in mission planning only when completely necessary."

"You figure that all out on the fly? What, let me guess, if your assumptions ever go south, you'll jump in right at the nick of time and save our collective asses," I chime.

"That's the plan," N.I.N.A. replies, Stink's confidence now oozing into her tone.

"No, that's the programming talking now," I retort. "Well, I do have one request then, N.I.N.A., if you will humor me."

"What is it, gentleman Reign?" she asks.

"Two actually. One," I hold up my index finger. "Don't call me a gentleman." Pausing, I hold up another. "And two, I take it you've been listening in on our conversations. What's the odds of us getting through this thing alive?"

"Seeing as though no one has articulated any form of a plan at this point, the odds are 100 percent certain that everyone aboard the *Concord* will successfully perish. With the exception for one," N.I.N.A. says.

"And that is?" I ask.

The sound of footsteps approaching from behind steals my attention before N.I.N.A. can respond.

"A word with you, Cassius," Serias says over my shoulder. Her voice is a mix between that of a firm mother and a concerned grandmother. I didn't have much experience with either, but I had a solid idea of what each might look like, had I ever run into one.

"Yeah, Reign, we'll take everything from here," Gifford says. A slight smile splits his jaw and all I want to do is slap it off twice as fast as it formed. He and Stink share a quick snicker and I turn to join Serias in the next hallway. She leads me to the inner hull and as she saunters over next to one of the storage containers, I stick my tongue to the roof of my mouth in a move to best keep myself from biting it off if she said anything outta pocket that might provoke me to eat my words. She spins to look at me, wearing a face that said everything about the tone of our next conversation.

"Cassius, shoot clean with me, will ya?" she asks, her voice calm and steady.

"Well, that all depends," I say.

"On what?"

"What you're willing to give up in return."

Her hands cross at her waist as she weaves her fingers together. Immediately, I'm transported back to our old arguments. In the handful of times that we bumped heads, I only remember being on the ass side of being "sorry" for something and her barely accepting it. But, besides that, I recall her present body language. I used to refer to it as her way of posturing like an animal would in the wild when they felt threatened. If things went south, her hands would fold behind her back as well, taking her to Defcon 2, and that's when I would officially be toast. "Anything you like, Cassius. I'm really not in the mood for games, though. So tell me what you want so that we can take care of business."

"Oh, business, huh? This sounds very urgent. You go first. I insist." It doesn't take long for me to realize I'd fooked up. Minimizing her concern for a chance to land a cheap sarcastic shot to the jaw could never end well, and I was purely slacking in the common sense department right about now. Chalk it up to fatigue or just nerves.

Serias rolls her eyes and then, after taking a deep breath, starts. "The DX disease. Have you thought of the possibility that this transfusion might not work?"

Her face held thick wrinkles along her forehead that met in the middle with a crash. She had done it to me once more—made me feel as small as the virus pooling in my blood. Of all the things trudging through my mind about the topic of this conversation, the subject of me and my disease held a ranking of something outside the lowest 15th percentile of what I wanted to talk about right now. But, yet, she was trying to engage me at a place where I was the most vulnerable. And just like back then, she was pushing through the layers of dense frost around my heart once again.

But how and why, after all this time? We had been together for over a day, and now Serias was dropping the outside shields holding around my brain, threatening to break me down. "I've worked out a couple of scenarios in my mind, but that's just a dry run. I'm sure I'll think of a few more. You know me," I say with a slight shrug.

Serias reaches into one of the lockers and retrieves her Holo-tablet. The red color takes me by surprise, and I'm somewhat disappointed in myself for thinking anything otherwise. Her favorite color has and always will be red. Her first Havoc Rifle was customized and she insisted that it have red trim along the edges, minus the sights. I sequester a small smile trying to encroach along my jaw as I admire the woman who is the epitome of both reliability and consistency. Same ole Serias. For the first time in a long time, after scuttling the 'verse for the past solar cycle, I feel at home. "Red, huh," I say finally.

She shoots me a frown for a moment, and then as her eyes beat back to her tablet, it occurs to her what I'm referring to. "Oh, you mean that. Yeah," she says faintly.

"Some things never change," I say.

"And some things do," she murmurs as she scrolls along her tablet. When she comes across what she's apparently looking for, she stops and speaks. "I've read up on this DX Cassius. It's no joke." She looks down at the tablet until double-tapping on a small file folder on the screen. She clicks on the screen again and then pauses to touch something in particular with her forefinger and thumb. She spreads her digits until the file opens and fills the entire screen. "If you aren't paying attention, you better damn start now."

She turns to the tablet in my direction and holds it still with both hands. I read the words on the screen and respond in the only fashion she'd expect me to. "Well, aren't you a pillar of good cheer."

"Are you serious right now?" Serias demands.

"Keep the odds to yourself, Serias. I'm trying to save my sister and right a thousand wrongs of days gone by. I hardly have enough time to worry about the odds of my survival," I bark.

Serias holds my gaze, and behind her impenetrable eyes, I can feel the anger building. But my indifference toward my impending death wasn't the reason for the budding meltdown. The source was something else, something deeper and more profound. And just in the same way that the red tablet carried me back to the past, something new garnered my attention and tethered me there. Pride.

TWENTY

Terrius 7: Orbital Station, Deep Space

The glint of anger in Serias's eyes fades, and something between despair and frustration takes its place, making me want to shrink into a nearby rat hole. But then I recall that in space, rodents don't frequent ships and that's when the idea dies instantly, along with any hopes of solace. Their skeletal muscles can't tolerate the low G and they eventually fold in on themselves due to skeletal failure from weakened tendons and ligaments. They're smart enough to stay on flat land, where things are more predictable and safe. Unlike us.

"Serias," I start, searching desperately for the right thing to say. "I...I know it's reckless, but...I knew my prognosis before I embarked on this quest. Finding Olia is the last thing I want, no, I *need* to do to make things right with my family. It's all I can do to help my mother and father rest in peace." I sigh heavily. "Hopefully," I say.

"It's a death sentence either way," she says, her voice weak and broken.

That's when everything comes full circle. Death sentence. That's what I served her back on Delvis Chong, and she won't, no, can't let it die. "I'm sorry, okay, dammit," I growl. Serias looks at me, her face is flat, now void of emotion. I realize that the next words from my mouth will probably make me swim in a pool of regret, but I can't help myself and dive in face first. "I fooked up and left you behind and I'm sorry. I should've just—"

Serias holds up a hand to shush me. "Stop!" she says.

From her tone, I realize that I'd just failed spectacularly at sounding anything remorseful or empathetic. But it was all I had left to give. As pure as the motives in my mind could carry me, I pressed forward on a mission of honesty, that would possibly kill us in the present while burying the past. And as long as it did the latter, I would be satisfied. I just needed her to understand me. "No, I need to tell you—"

She drops her head and mutters something under her breath, and I'm certain that she's doing everything possible to stifle a wave of tears threatening to spill over from her eyes. When she speaks again, I finally hear her more clearly. "You don't owe me anything." She sniffles and wipes her nose. "We were spies and…like you, I knew the risks, and after much contemplation of the situation, I realize that you acted accordingly and that honestly, in your shoes, I'd have done the same thing."

"That's a lie, and you know it," I reply.

"I don't care what you think now, Cassius." She points at her chest as her voice rises. "This is my truth and I've made peace with it. Whatever we *were* back then, died when I should have. I left all I had for you back on Delvis Chong."

There's something so profound about the truth. It stands on its own, never requiring any additional clarification or explanation. And when you hear it, you never have to question what it is. And when you do, it either builds or destroys whatever narrative you've been foolish enough to relish in. In my case, the inevitable destruction of the tower of regret I'd been skillfully crafting to justify never needing to love another person again came haphazardly crashing down, leaving a rubble of pain behind.

I swallow hard and head out to the exit without looking back. I can hear Serias's feet clatter behind me and stop, most likely just at the door of her quarters. Silence fills the distance between us, and my mood crashes to something resembling sludge on the mining moons of Portural. Gifford meets me in the hallway as I realize I'm heading in the wrong direction. I duck into the cargo hold hopeful he wouldn't follow. But to my dismay, he does. "Boss, a word please."

"If anyone else asks for a word, I swear I'm going to beat it out of them," I growl as my hands fist tightly.

Gifford's eyes glance down at my fists, and he takes a cautious step back. "Sorry, boss, I just wanted to update you on—"

I quickly turn and head in his direction, full speed without any desire to stop until I land on the bed in my quarters. "Not interested," I bark as I brush by him.

"We'll be at Terrius 7 in less than one hour," I hear him holler over my shoulder.

I don't bother to respond and hasten to the safety of solitude in my room. I slam the door behind and latch it closed. Confident that no one could disturb my calm any longer, I crash onto my bed and stare at the ceiling. The adrenaline and whatever residue of Stink that was wading in my blood was most certainly burned up by now, as the low aching pain that shot through my back slowly starts to return. But I was too tired, too exhausted to dwell on it. I was wary of wasting any more mental energy on things that threaten to hinder my mission. So I close my eyes. Only thoughts of Olia crowd my mind as I drift into sleep.

***

When I feel the artificial gravity of the *Concord* fade, I wake from my slumber and jump out of bed to catch my bearings just in time to grab Martha before she falls off the dresser next to my bed. The soft vibrations of our Parry Shields lowering fill my bones as we cruise to a steady docking speed. Tractor beam, no doubt. That's when it dons on me. Terrius 7—we must be here. I retrieve my Holo-tablet from my backpack and interface with the *Concord*'s external cameras. I tab to camera 3 on the underbelly of the *Concord*, which offers a clear inside view of the belly of the entire gigantic orbital. A set of landing gear descends on either side of the camera, along with one in the center, just beneath the nose of the ship. I know it'll be only a matter of seconds before they direct us to our landing pad. I slowly pan the camera from right to left, until finally noticing a pair of gold holographic numbers, blazing in the distance, surrounded by a rectangular wall of 4 green glowing bands. 23. That's our pad.

The *Concord* shifts sideways in the direction of the pad, and I feel the roaring engines dampen to a low hum. Certain that we'd be landing soon, I rise to my feet and place Martha, along with the Holo-tablet safely in my backpack. A sickening feeling rots my stomach. The realization that soon I'll have to face Serias again haunts me.

I don't want to.

Her words pierced at something deep down in my soul, and I desire to never revisit it again. Ever. Especially not with her. Up until this point, Serias was the last person I'd ever imagine *never* wanting to see again. But there she was, occupying the space all by her lonesome.

The *Concord* lightly bounces as the landing gear makes contact with the pad—spring suspension rods stabilizing us with predictable precision—and we touch down safely. The sounds of the exterior docking clamps seize the bottom of the vessel, and one last clang indicates that we are securely fastened to Terrius 7.

I haven't spent much time on orbitals during my days as a space-faring spy, but from what I do recall about them is that they're large as all hells, averaging anywhere between 1 to 3 kilometers in length. With large size comes even larger expenses, carrying excessive taxes attached to heavy docking fees and purchases—twice the amount you'd pay for the same services on planets. Commerce is the only way they can maintain generating enough revenue for sustainability. And ever since the Underground got its legs, the exchange for weapons, tech, and Intel jacked all the way up. The only things sold at a reasonable price are food and rations.

And don't forget whores. Sex isn't as hard to come by or as coveted as it used to be with the implementation of somatic VR and peripherals, but nothing beats the real feeling of skin on skin, so people still pay a hefty penny for it. But orbitals, habitats, and platform space stations alike don't monitor it as hard as planets, so people barter prices based on needs.

Not that I think it'd make much difference, anyway. In space, laws can't be enforced as ready as they can planetside. The expense to carry full-time security and police—as you'd imagine—is exorbitant, so people use local guns for hire to do their bidding, choosing to fight battles that only impact commerce and the direct livelihood of the locals.

Confident that I had secured everything necessary for a few hours' romp aboard the orbital, I make haste to exit my room. The door slides open with a hiss, and as I step out, I'm met by Serias, passing right in front of me carrying a bag slung over her shoulder while pulling another on wheels behind her. Although we don't make eye contact, I know she'd spotted me, apparent by the speed at which she pressed by. I glace at her from behind, admiring that after so many cycles of not seeing her, she'd still managed to maintain that same sexy athletic build I'd fallen for so many moons ago. A black, formed-fitted leather dress graces her curves in all the right places while her dark hair—pulled to a knot on the crown of her head—shows off her long elegant neck. I swallow with a sigh and drag behind as we cut through the cargo hold to exit through the aft bay door.

I maintain my distance as Gifford and Stink meet us in the cargo hold and approach Serias. They share small talk as the aft door creeps open. I can't audibly make out exactly what they say from this distance, but my spy training is still sharp as ever, and I'm able to read Giff's lips, enough to know that Serias was leaving us at this point. For good. His face shared the same sad sentiment that flooded my thoughts, but as he leans in to hug her, I quickly drown the emotions bubbling up inside me. *It's better this way*, I think to myself and busy myself with continuing to scan images from the cameras of the *Concord* on my Holo-tablet. From my periphery, I see Stink motion in Serias' direction and drop my gaze even more to ignore their interaction. The fact that male contact of any kind with Serias still sends shrills of jealously through my veins, after all this time, is laughable at best. Still, I'm even more disappointed at my inability to ignore it more than I am the failure to control my own body's natural response to it.

The unmistakable smell of antiseptic vapor penetrates my nose, alerting me that the orbital air was now flowing through our smaller craft. Ventilated off-world air is more than just a necessity. It's the law. Federations require that all interplanetary stations and orbitals of any size are mandated to filter the air with Purine crystals in their circulation systems. It's the only way to ensure that the spread of micro-bacteria and viruses—whether alien or Terran—are somewhat controlled. When the threat of terrorists and free mercenaries slowly began to rise, so did whispers of imposing danger as space travel began to wane. The risk of chemical warfare continued to blossom, with these massive metal goliath personnel carriers being prime targets. One could easily hold an entire vessel hostage with the right amount of resources, and the outcome of such a threat could've easily crippled the system.

So to quell any panic from space travelers, The Federation of Planets united and had all their scientists work on a plan to counter any offensive. They scoured the lands of Uzora, the floral planet, and harvested Purine crystals. It was once said that the roots of the fabled skyscraping trees and lush vegetation burrow far below the planet's surface and into the dense black clay, nourishing the earth while creating crystals so pure that they can withstand any form of infection, whether fungal, viral, or bacterial. Unfortunately for some, Uzora falls under Primus's reign, and it's well known that their seething hatred of Inner Colony planets is the catalyst behind heavy taxes for Purine purchases. But their failed attempt at minimizing the purchasing power of orbitals and stations located within the Belt of Aster was strategically countered by King Derry. He leveraged his trade tariffs to force their hand and lower taxes making it more accessible to the entire system.

The scent of the crystals takes me back to my freelance days as a Merc when I used to take on Finisher missions to keep my pockets full. They involved perusing smaller, planetary hospitals in search of the mortally wounded, VIPs, mostly composed of political figures and military targets that survived initial assassinations. All I had to do was slip into a hospital or med bay disguised as one of the staff and push a few CCs of dystonic poison into the target's IV line to end their misery. The delayed cardiac arrest that would ensue a few moments later always bought me the time I needed to make a hasty escape and receive my credits for a job well done.

As the filtered, cleaner air of the orbital flows in, Serias blows out, and I finally raise my eyes to catch one last glimpse of her before she fades out of view. Gifford and Stink move toward me; both of them awkwardly quiet at first, until Stink breaks the ice. "So, ready to disembark, boss?" he asks.

I answer with a nod and a firm, "Yes," assertively enough to convince myself that Serias' departure left me unscathed. The only problem was that there was no way to be sure if Giff and Stink swallowed the sheat I was feeding them.

"Well, okay, then. I directed N.I.N.A. to pay our fees before we touched down so we can bolt inside," Gifford says, rubbing his hands together maniacally. "I'm starving."

"How much do I owe you?" I ask.

Gifford waves me off. "No worries. I got this one, boss."

I sling my backpack over my shoulder and shoot Gifford an inquisitive glare. "You just toss credits around as if they grow on trees. Anytime you're ready to tell me your little secret to housing so much disposable cash, I'm all ears."

"All in due time, boss," Giff answers with a chuckle.

As we exit the *Concord*, my feet are decisively met by steel flooring as the doubled anti-Grav of Terrius 7 pulls us along, creating sure footing. I steal a moment to take in my surroundings, admiring the wondrous architecture of the orbital. Everything is as you'd expect it to be. Long and cylindrical, all orbitals rotate at a persistent speed of 17 kilometers per hour, just the optimal pace to produce enough inertia to replicate artificial gravity to both maintain an optimal orbit and keep everyone and everything grounded. The rotation clips at a safe enough speed that your mind and body barely perceive it. In fact, to the naked eye, you can barely notice the rotation from the inside unless you mistakenly lock onto the structure in the distance and try to move in the opposite direction.

Green, blue and red lights bloom overhead, designating partitions for variable freights of storage container loading bays by weight. The darker the color, the heavier the load. The circular frame of the orbital slowly rolls around us as hover cars peel away from right to left in the distance, climbing along the rounded inner hull effortlessly as they enter and exit varying corridors along the way. The view is enough to make you lose your sheat if you stare too long, making your stomach dance inside your torso.

A set of horizontal radar antennas whirl to my left as my gaze locks onto a dozen or so massive, cylindrical towers housing gallons of water by the thousands. Fuels rigs coast by while smaller crafts whip past them to find suitable landing pads. Blinding floodlights spin in the distance, bursting from two towering structures vertically projecting from the center of the orbital. It's the headquarters of the

Head Master, the designated captain of Terrius 7. Highly fortified and secured. It's custom that once you become a Head Master, you instantly inherit the same degree of celebrity as that of a Royal, along with similar protection. No one ever sees or meets a Head Master unless he or she requests it. And that's like, never. Man, what I wouldn't give to secure a bounty like that one day. I once read a dossier for a bounty on a Head Master, and the number of zeroes on that contract was enough to purchase more than a few star systems.

An announcement erupts overhead. "This station operates under Federation law. Selling or loitering of anything not legally registered by Terrius 7 or a certified Guild is strictly prohibited," the male voice says sternly.

The *Concord* is parked just outside the main control tower, so our hike to the nearest loading ramp is short and convenient. My legs are barely coming back to me, so I'm grateful for not having to hike too far to get inside. Thoughts of Serias brought on a slight headache, so I welcome the chance to down a few rounds of drink to wash both it and any memory of her away.

I convinced myself that her departure is for the better, seeing that any degree of clouded judgment aboard the *Eclipse* would spell certain doom for both me and Olia. And no one, I mean no one is worth her demise. Especially not a broad that bails on her team just moments before a mission. My disappointment wanes just as we enter the main atrium of the orbital and are greeted by a selection of minor stores and bars. Neon signs with symbols rather than names blaze above each building, making it easy to delineate the various offerings. While Gifford and Stink appear to be occupied by the one featuring a pair of long legs and red high heel shoes, a tall cocktail glass garners my attention, and I wade over to get a closer look. The words, The Listless Sailor blazes underneath it.

"Hey, boss, wait up," I hear Giff scream from behind.

I turn and glare at him, eyes narrowed to slits as he catches up and draws close. "Keep your mouth shut," I hiss. "Stifle that boss talk sheat. You'll get us killed. If any Mercs or Bounty Hunters are running around here, they could easily catch wind of our relationship and get nosy. I'm certain that we've no doubt caught the attention of many after pulling off that ship jack move back at the *Opus*."

"Yes, sir," Giff murmurs with a set of green pup eyes that could easily make the heart of a young school girl melt.

"First round is on me," Stink says, quickly snapping into character and pushing past the both of us as he heads toward the bar.

I'm not 100 percent certain if it's Stink's teleonotioning that guides his thoughts, but from what I've seen of him, he seems to have quite the knack for saying the right things or acting the right way, just in the nick of time, just like he did back on the *Opus* when he boarded the *Concord* and secured our ticket out. So far, he'd been a perfect addition to this pasty makeshift crew. *Maybe too perfect*, I think as I follow his lead and follow behind, careful to leave just enough space not to draw attention.

We all file inside, and Stink makes a Bee-line for the bar, securing three stools smack dab in front of the most gorgeous bartender available. I pull up a seat next to him and do my best to sequester the smile attempting to force its way across my face as the young woman tosses me a wink and flashes me a glimpse of her perfect white teeth. Her outfit does the trick of captivating all my interests. An even mix of black and gold rides the length of her body from head to toe, in the form of a short skirt and an even shorter shimmering shirt that drapes in the front to reveal all the curves to make an old man like me salivate inside my mouth.

Stink slams his credit card down on the wooden bar, and the woman flocks to him like flies on sheat, anxious to pick it up before he reneges. He does, just before she can secure it. "Aw, aw, aw, beautiful," he says, waving the card at her teasingly. "Not so fast. You need to answer a question for me first."

The girl wears a face of frustration. "And that is?"

"What your name, gorgeous?" Stink asks.

"Serias," she answers.

My heart jumps into my throat, and I cough something fierce. Stink snaps his head in my direction and our eyes meet. "Did you hear that?" he asks.

"No way," Gifford blurts.

"Stupid coincidence," I grunt.

"What'd she say?" Stink asks, his eyes are bursting with curiosity.

217

"Serias," I answer wearily.

"No, she didn't," Gifford interjects. "I heard Darla."

Stink bursts into laughter and finally slides the card over to the girl. "Three Jugular Slides, heavy on the Chi-Chi Tarn Ale." The girl lifts the card from the bar and walks off to make our drinks. Stink fills the space between Giff and me and begins to whisper. "I heard Cynthia, an ex-girlfriend of mine. This place is crazy. It uses Drifter tech to link to the Amygdala in your brain and manipulates your mind into bringing out old names of old flames when the bartender speaks to you."

"What?" Gifford asks, still trying to follow. I don't speak, knowing full well what the hells had just happened and disappointed that I hadn't caught on much sooner.

"It's all intentional, my man," Stink says. "They attract patrons like us and the familiarity of the woman's name is meant to coax you into feeling connected to her," his eyes beat over to a male bartender, "or him. If that's what you're into. No judgment here. That way you keep shuffling credits into the register. I was anxious to test it out and see what happened. Pretty sweet, huh?"

"Whatever," I bark.

The girl returns and graces us with our drinks and hands Stink back his card. "Let me know if you need anything else."

"Certainly," Stink answers.

Gifford grabs his drink and begins to chug it down in a few large gulps. When he finally slams it back down on the bar's surface, he belches and says, "You're just mad because you heard Serias's voice when she spoke."

Nothing like liquid courage to make a squealing nerd grow a pair. "Watch it!" I growl.

Gifford pauses, and then his eyes lift to meet mine. "Come on, Reign. Or should I say…Cassius?"

Stink must catch the fumes storming from my ears and quickly steps in to snatch Gifford by the arm. "Hey, man, chill out," he says tersely, just as I stand.

"No, let him speak," I say. "He's just blowing off a little steam." I pause for a moment to guzzle my drink as well, taking another second to wipe the residue from the corner of my mouth. As the contents of the beverage filter through my blood, the world around me swims in my periphery, and a strong sense of euphoria washes over me. It's at that moment that I realize that Gifford's newly commissioned cooler-sized balls aren't a product of simple alcoholic persuasion alone. Whatever was in that glass is powerful, and nothing even close to basic libations. "What the hells is in that?" I ask, posing the question in Stink's direction.

"It's Primus Ale," Stink says with a smile. "And it's not to be fooked within one sitting. You guys just poured 100 Proof into your veins." His smile widens as he muffles a chuckle behind it, slapping Gifford on his shoulder. "I don't know if I should be proud, confused, or impressed."

Gifford begins to wobble and grabs the bar to maintain upright. After shaking his head a bit, he answers, "Don't be impressed. I just pissed my pants."

My eyes reflexively drop to the floor, and to my dismay, he's right. Urine drenches the floor beneath Gifford's feet in a puddle that surrounds his boots. But it doesn't cast a regular yellow hue. There's a faint shade of orange about it that reminds me of the icterine glow that a Solar Cell Strength system shares—the kind that William blazed on Fabricius during the war to free his home planet. He moved with inhumane fluidity and downed more than a hundred enemies that day, the kind of numbers that earned him all the praise and loyalty that a Prince deserves.

A buzzing sensation begins to tickle my pelvis too, but I'm both strong and alert enough to clinch down and quell the stream of piss that's just chomping at the bit to fill my pants. Stink grabs a fist full of Gifford's clothing and drags him away from the bar while ushering both of us to a nearby booth. After slamming Gifford down on a bench, he returns to grab his mug. I slide into the other one, staring Gifford down from the opposite side of the table.

My vision is still blurry, but I'm coherent enough to take in my surroundings. Neon lights blaze from above in hues of heavy oranges, bright blues, and sizzling reds. Music blares around us, and the dank, dark images draped along the walls of the bar begin to come into focus. Posters of sports studs, military heroes and celebrities hang high, with what appears to be autographs tatted along the bottom right-hand corner of each one. "Popular place," I mutter.

Stink returns and sits next to Gifford, who still appears to be circling the drain of disillusionment, trapped in a blank gaze into nowhere. A smile breaks across my face as I imagine what he'd be like at a strip club in the same headspace. I'd pay good money to see a young dominatrix whip the sheat outta him on stage, fully clad in black leather with a gag in his mouth. These young guys are a fun bunch indeed and as much as I hate taking on partners, admittedly, they've carried their own weight and have made this trip into inevitable death somewhat pleasant.

Stink takes a sip of his drink and peers over at me. "So, seeing as though Giff here won't be of any use to either one of us for a few hours, now is a good enough time as any for you to share your plans for saving your sister."

I scratch my 5 o'clock shadow of a beard. "Saving...plan...yeah...about that—"

"I've already taken care of it, boss," Gifford chirps, now coming back to life. It was as if my broken words sent a jolt of lighting into his brain. A part of me wished he'd remained in his state of stupor, but the rest of me beckoned to hear what he had to say. Even if his idea was half-baked, it had to be at least 50 percent better than any ill-fated plans I'd concocted up to this point, most of which revolved around a gun-blazing charge that ended with Forge stuffing a repeater pistol down my throat, charging me to beg for mercy.

"Chill, man," Stink says.

I wave him off. "No, let him speak."

Gifford looks at me with eyes about as wide as the bartender's boobs. "Really?" I don't speak, but gesture for him to proceed. "Well," he starts before shaking his head once more in an attempt to no doubt clear the cobwebs forming inside. "The *Concord* has a Galley Suit in its main cargo hold. I ran across it when we first boarded, and I was busy familiarizing myself with the ship. Although we all have an invite to board the *Eclipse*, I thought it best for me to hang back."

"Hang back, where? The *Concord* will be towed inside. It's being offered as collateral for us to play, remember?" Stink points out.

"Let me finish, dammit!" Gifford stammers as his voice rises to an inappropriate tone.

"Calm down, kid. Keep going," I say.

"Once the large circular turbines that surround the *Eclipse* shut down to allow the Dark Matter engines to decloak the vessel, I'll float from the *Concord* and attach myself to the outer hull of the *Eclipse*. That way, Forge won't have all of us in his grasp at one time. We'll need a person on the outside if things go south," Gifford says.

"You're assuming things will go south, I take it? Why am I not surprised?" I say.

"It's us, boss," Gifford says with a tone of endearment. "Can I assume anything otherwise? If there's one thing I've learned in this brief time roaming the stars with you two is that even our Plan Bs need Plan Bs."

"True," I say, reclining a bit in the booth as the world around me starts to level out.

"It won't work. You'll freeze your nuts off out there. This distance of deep space lacks any degree of heat. Sarah's too far away to help us out at this distance," Stink says, pausing to take another drag from his mug.

"You must not know too much about Galley Suits, do you?" Gifford poses. Stink and I share shrugs and Gifford proceeds to educate us both. "Originally constructed for miners to be used in asteroid belts to harness precious minerals, Galley Suits are made to tolerate extreme temps of either hot or cold. And it has magno-locks along the hands, feet, and knees. I'll be cozy as a kitten inside while I wait for mission updates. I've already programmed N.I.N.A. to pulse laser messages carrying mission updates to my suit on the exact frequency that only I can decipher because only I will be looking for it."

Stink snickers. "Okay, smarty-pants. I'm impressed so far, but what if we end up being captured or delayed for some reason? How long can you just *hang out* there?"

"In the event of the latter, I can hang long enough for you two to locate Olia and secure a solid location for extraction. Tag her with this," Gifford says, holding up a small microchip, no larger than his pinky nail. "Once the chip is activated, it will go online and awaken N.I.N.A. so that she can start to do the diligence of saving our collective asses. That's when I'll use my Holo-tablet to send a specialized Alpha Ultrasonic pulse wave from the anti-matter engines of the *Concord* to shut down the security defenses from the inside out. You see, Dark Matter engines have to be primed before they can activate. If you do it too early, well..." he shares a snide smile. "It's like being with your lady friend and busting one off before you've had a chance to fully fuel the jet." He nudges Stink with his elbow. "You know what I mean, bud?"

Stink's eyes widen, and he shakes his head. "Hardly my problem, *bud.*"

"Anyway, that will reignite the Dark Matter engines prematurely and in turn momentarily incapacitate the entire ship, opening the airlocks in the hangar bay. By my estimations, you'll need to get moving because you'll only have about 30 seconds to make it back to the *Concord* and escape before they can take the engines offline and properly reboot everything again," Gifford says matter-of-factly.

"Any Plan B?" Stink asks.

"Not at the moment," Gifford says.

As his words penetrate my mind, I slowly find myself climbing back to the land of sensibility as the contents of my drink begin to wear off. "Wait a minute. I recall reading the reports of King William's escape from the *Eclipse*. They powered down the Dark Matter engines in a similar move to elude Forge the first time. Don't you think they'll have some new fail-safe in place to counter it?"

Giff raises a finger. "That only happened because they manually powered it down. I'm using an Alpha Ultrasonic wave."

Gifford gazes at me with a dull look on his face as if awaiting a nod of agreement. But to his dismay, all I can muster is a stare of equal confusion as I struggle to get a handle on anything he just explained. He must finally realize my ignorance and offers a more detailed explanation, which only worsens my appreciation for physics and quantum theory. When my brain can no longer ingest another word, I lean in and slam a fist on the table. "English nerd!" I bark.

"In other words, that pulse wave frequency will disable the *Eclipse*'s CPU. It will take them a few moments to triangulate the source the signal, but when they do, I'm sure they'll be able to block me out from pushing another pulse. I won't be able to replicate it again, so we've only got one chance to make good on it." Giff looks over at Stink, his mouth is slightly gaping. His eyes fall to Stink's mug, still halfway filled. "I'm so thirsty." His finger's twitch as he begins to reach for it. "Can I get another swig—"

Stink slaps his hand and lifts his mug, holding it outside of Gifford's reach. "Hells, no. This is the smartest you've ever sounded, and I'm actually starting to think I've got a shot at saving my ass out here."

"What? Was there any reason to doubt before?" I ask sarcastically.

"Seriously?" Stink asks.

"So let me play devil's advocate for a moment," I pose. "Let's just say that we get as far into your plan as say, finding Olia and prepping for departure. How do we signal N.I.N.A. to contact you?"

"She'll be scanning your life signs, boss. Any fluctuations of vital signs will indicate a level of excitement akin to happiness. Similar to the ones you flashed when you first saw Serias." He cracks a sly smile. "Or anytime she was around you," he ends with a snicker.

"True," Stink adds with a sip from his mug.

"Whatever," I say, deniably. "I can't put much stock in that."

"Maybe not," Giff starts, "but before we board the *Eclipse*, I will insert small micro-communication chips inside your mouths, just behind the back molars. Anything you guys say or hear will be relayed back to her. Once you've laid eyes on Olia and hopefully given her the tracker, all you have to do is say the word and we'll be prepped to run and gun."

"And getting Olia from the galleys to the hangar bay—assuming she's able to walk on her own—how's that plan work?" I ask.

"That's the tricky part that I thought I'd let you figure out," Gifford says.

"Tricky part, right," Stink says before sipping from his mug again.

"Hater," I grumble at him.

"My turn for devil advocacy. Run me the numbers, Giff. How long can you stay put out there? This transaction could go pretty long," Stink says.

Gifford swallows what little residual ale is still coating his throat. "That's particularly interesting. The Galley Suit has a hiber-mode that will slow my vitals to trace levels. It'll keep me in a sort of sleep state until I need to be awakened. If I didn't, well, the *Eclipse* would easily scan my life signal and send the welcoming party. But don't worry, N.I.N.A. will be monitoring me and can deactivate it remotely in a moment's notice when the time is right." As he emphasizes the words *when the time is right*, the room falls silent, and it's as if the air inside the bar grows 10 times as stale as it already was and the oxygen recyclers had temporarily shut down. I already know what's next, and I didn't have to tap into any lingering teleonotioning to figure it out either. "And now I fall back to you again, boss," Giff says flatly. His voice is low and steady. "Your ideas of how to secure your sister is the penultimate part of the plan. Without it, this is all for naught."

"Lay it on us, chief," Stink says.

I slide my hand across the table and snatch Stink's mug from his grasp. Before he can speak, I slowly raise it toward my mouth and pause halfway between it and the table. I narrow my eyes as I speak with confidence. My trademark confidence oozes into my tone. "Don't worry. I've got this."

TWENTY-ONE

Terrius 7: Orbital Station, Deep Space

Clearly, I have nothing, but I shouldn't dare break the news to my fellow hands. Any good captain knows that you never share every detail about the "going ons" with your crew, especially if it most likely ends in their demise.

"You've got what?" Stink speaks up, his voice cracking as if he was struggling with the decision to address me in such a manner. From the sound of it, it was evident that he'd been toying with the notion for a while, but from out of some unfeigned respect for me and my reputation, he'd stayed in his place, up until now. The desperation in his tone said everything.

"Excuse me?" I croak, releasing my grip on the handle of his mug. The idea of reaching across and snatching him by his collar drilled away at the back of mind.

"With all due respect, boss, I jumped aboard this ship in the interest of joining a team. But, honestly, what I've found is a band of soloists bouncing from one great idea to another. And now we've lost one. If you've haven't noticed, I don't think that's something we can afford to do at this stage of the game." Stink stares straight into my eyes, his cheeks flushed with indignation.

"Serias was dead weight," I say, trying to blow him off.

"So you say," Stink replies.

"So *I* say," I bellow. "Don't forget who's been surfing these unfriendly space waves for decades, son. Way before you stopped shooting dog water."

"Dog water?" Gifford chimes, confused at my colloquialism.

Stink doesn't break to explain it to him and lays into me once more. "I bet you don't even have a plan, do you?"

I stand to my feet. "Don't worry about me, I'll deliver. And I'll get all of our collective asses off that ship." My voice booms over the music of the bar, and everything around us grows silent. "Dead or alive," I say for good measure.

But Stink doesn't buy it, standing to his feet as well. "Nice try." He points to his temple. "Teleonotioning, remember. Some Bounty Hunter you are. Or spy, or…whatever you are now."

"Just don't stand in my way when I start spraying," I say in return.

Stink shakes his head and slides his mug over to Gifford before storming off. The music resumes, and I take my seat again. Without looking at Gifford, I wave the bartender to send another round of whatever and sigh heavily.

"He isn't wrong, you know," Gifford says weakly. I ignore him as the female brings over two mugs and drops them down in front of

229

me. "We've risked our necks for you. All of us. But we can't believe more in you than you do. Serias did and you see where it got her."

My head whips in his direction. "What?"

"That's what she told us right before she left." Gifford's eyes scan the ceiling as he bites the inside of his mouth, something I've grown accustomed to witnessing him do whenever he's thinking hard. "How did she say it? Oh, yeah, I remember now. She couldn't stand by any longer and watch you wilt away in self-doubt and pity. She even said you're only a shell of the man that left her for dead many moons ago." And with those words, Gifford stands. "Enjoy the drink," he says, before walking away.

As I'm left alone with my thoughts—none of which having a single damn thing to do with concocting a plan sufficient enough to get Olia into the hangar bay of the *Eclipse* in a timely enough manner to safely escape—the horrors of my past begin to take shape. They haunt me in my seat as I contemplate gulping down another full mug to drown out the ghosts. I close my eyes and lean back. In an instant, a string of faces flashes into view from the darkness. First, my father, followed by my mother and Serias, then a withered and worn King Gregorio. As they fade, Prince William and Princess Sydney appear, and finally, Olia.

A tear or two pierces the corner of my eyes as I open them once more. The words of Tannan—more prophetic now than every before replayed in my head—something he'd said a while back that seemed as if it were only yesterday, brought new life to my haggard body. At my induction ceremony into The Thieves of Light, he leaned in and whispered, "The sobering power of the truth is the greatest gift that no one can place any value on. Never ignore it." And after hearing it from Gifford, my path was clear and plain.

I pay to close the tab for the drinks and leave the two mugs behind on the table. My mind is solely zeroed in on my next objective: a date with Forge aboard the *Eclipse*. With a surge of adrenaline freshly flowing through my veins at the thought of what was next to come, the lingering effects of my near-death experience with DX was evidently behind me. As I make my way back to the *Concord*, my legs are starting to feel reinvigorated and the pull from the anti-Grav of the orbital lessen with each step. I board the vessel and quickly make my way to the front of the ship.

When I rejoin the boys in the cockpit, Gifford is seated in the back chair, fumbling lightly with his Holo-tablet as Stink fidgets with the forward console in the lead pilot's chair. I break the ice with a loud clap of my hands. "Fellas, you're both right. And I owe each one of you an apology." I stop and lightly nod repeatedly.

Gifford turns around. "And?"

"And what?" I ask.

"The...apology," he replies.

"Oh, I assume you're waiting for a full-on admission of guilt and a request for forgiveness," I tease.

"It'd be a good place to start," Stink adds, turning around.

I fold my arms and smile. "Sorry, notice that I said *I said I owe you one*. That's actually better than an apology. In the universe, credits my boys, are invaluable. And like most commodities, you should only cash them in when it holds it's the highest value. And not a second earlier."

"So, you're not going to apologize?" Gifford asks, sounding pitifully disappointed.

"No. But trust me, son, I've got something a hells of a lot better," I say.

"A plan?" Stink says jokingly, but a hint of hope still hangs on his words.

"Of course," I say in his direction, before turning my attention to Gifford. "And like you've said many times before, Giff, you can thank me later," I say with a grin.

Gifford's eyes explode like stars, and he belts out a series of chuckles that fill the cockpit. In no time flat, his laughter catches fire and spills into both me and Stink's lungs. When we finally finish, N.I.N.A. chimes across the intercom. "And now that we're all aboard, is it time to depart the orbital Gifford?"

"Let's do it," Gifford says, sitting upright in his chair. "It's gambling time."

***

Hours later, I'm writhing in my bed, trying my darndest to gain even an ounce of sleep to refresh my body. After we departed the Terrius 7, I made a B-line to the cargo hold and ravaged my muscles—upper, lower, and core—by putting them through the paces of a serious Cross-Fit intensive workout that made me almost vomit up the last meal I consumed, somewhat...13 hours ago. But the liquor in my belly convinced me otherwise by offering a few belches instead. Curls, pull-ups, push-ups, plyometrics, and shoulder presses did the duty of pushing fresh blood into my muscles, which both increased their girth and burned out the last fleeting drops of intoxication still swirling about my veins. All that was left was the flavor of the stuff, which I tasted multiple times in the form of fresh bile after one or two heavier burps.

I tried to convince Stink to join me in a session after he investigated the noise generated from my workout. But he declined with the quickness, choosing rather to watch an old man idiotically punish his frame until sweat poured from my skin. It turns out that the *Concord*'s half anti-Grav generators make the perfect substitute for a spotter. I easily pulled off overhead presses and squats with heavier weights that would've crippled me for a few days back planetside. Slamming large crates after burnout sets on the metal grating fashioned a small crease along Stink's brow that hinted at the slightest concern that the ship's belly would rip apart from my antics. But I knew all too well that a ship the likes of the *Concord*— fully tricked out with the latest and greatest gadgetry and tech— wouldn't suffer even a scratch. I didn't bother asking Giff to join, exercising my nerd ignorance and assumptions that he'd rather play on his Holo-tablet than break a sweat. And as he strolled by halfway through my workout, fingering his device, I couldn't hold back a gratifying smile for being right, *again*.

After my workout was over, I sprawled myself in bed, figuring that a little burn was all I needed to drift into sleep. But it was a no-go. Although my body was whipped, my mind was buzzing with thoughts of Olia, of course, and to my surprise, Serias. But why? She left, without uttering a word to me, mind you, for whatever good or bad reason and truly it would be the last time I'd expect to see her again.

So fook it.

In my book, we were even. As they say, turnabout is fair play. I abandoned her, and she returned the favor. And, like that, the universe still rolls on. But it was less about how she left and more why she did. Nothing about it seemed particularly spontaneous. You don't travel into deep space and decide to leave a perfectly fair situation for a possibly better one. Hitching a ride in space ain't necessarily what I'd call a power move, and Serias is all about power.

If the shoe was on the other foot and someone else was telling me this tale, I'd advise them to watch their backs and wait for the hook, wagering that a trap was around the corner. I shake the thought from my head and toss to my side once more, this time catching a glimpse of Martha still holstered along my belt, hanging from my gear, which is draped over a chair. *You'll never leave, girl,* I think as my mind flashes back to an image of Olia holding a gun for the first time back on Overlight. Uncle Bosko was training me to handle my own just in case I ever got into a firefight. I credit him for starting me down the path of a gunslinger and helping Olia become the death wielding, sword assassin Sintock she is today. Even though we separated when she was shipped off to Secondary School, word spread pretty quickly of her ascension in the ranks of ROTC training. Inevitably, I disappeared in search of lower things to make a living while she blazed a path of her own. And even though time and space kept us apart, I relish at the thought that we were only hours from being united once again.

The roar of the *Concord*'s retro-pulsion engines disturb my thoughts and send me rolling off my bed as we slam to a halt. I jet from my room and head for the cockpit to find Gifford pinned to the forward canopy staring into space; his eyes scanning the blackness for god knows what. Stink stands off to the side, perusing the scanners for images.

"Sitrep," I yell, auctioning for anyone's attention.

Stink whips his head in my direction while Gifford remains glued to the glass. "We're here, boss."

"Where?" I ask as my eyes also dart over to the open patch of darkness before us.

"The coordinates," Gifford says finally, in a whisper so faint I could barely comprehend.

And that's when it dons on me. The *Eclipse*. I rush forward and wedge myself next to Gifford, desperately surveying our surroundings. Suddenly, my gaze softens as a dozen or so other ships hovering outside our view port fill my view, adjacent to a handful of small asteroids rolling about, filling the background. The ships were big and far, small and near. A capital ship was the largest of them. Pale and shiny, holding point as several smaller vessels seemed to hug some form of sanctuary directly behind it as if shielding themselves from an attack from the unknown. As I peer at the large cannons hanging from the port bow of the Capital ship, I entertain my curiosity and imagine what would happen if the *Eclipse* suddenly materialized and interpreted their formation as a symbol of aggression. Possibly utilize its Dark Matter engines to do something entirely unexpected and wipe out the entire lot of them on GP.

As more ships cruise in from behind, Giff points over in the direction to my left, and I follow, locking on to a spot just outside the tip of his index finger. "Over there, keep your eyes on that patch of stars."

As I do, I can barely make out a wavering haze wafting over them, like the flowing wake of a boat on the water. It was large; approximately triple the size of the Capital ship, which was easily 10 times that of any one of the smaller vessels it was protecting. As the image wades into the vicinity, Stink begins to stir behind us and I peer slightly over my shoulder at him to ensure he was pissing his pants. But, honestly, if I hadn't exercised a good squeeze of my pelvic floor muscles, I'd have released a stream of urine myself. My heart rivets in my chest, and I swallow hard. This is it.

In an almost theatrical display, an explosion of purple mist erupts in the distance, some 10 kilometers out. Streams of white, blue, and red fire flames accompany the fireworks until they are consumed by a thick blue cloud that slowly burns black like ash before peeling back from the bottom up, slowly revealing a sheet of circular metal beneath. It collects along the upper surface in a circular motion like that of a small whirlpool until funneling out of sight as if swallowed up by the damn thing. All that was left was a clear view of the *Eclipse*. Large, circular, and hella imposing, the enormous half-moon shaped Dark Matter turbines that encircle it had all but come to a complete stop on opposite north and south poles as a small light begins to blossom from the center.

The screen of our main console comes to life as a message bursts across our screens. "Welcome, travelers," a voice announces as the image of a small, frail man fills our view, garnering our attention. His hair is green and thin, barely covering his receding forehead, revealing starspots along his pasty white skin. A pair of stemless black glasses hang off the bridge of his nose; the fashion statement of a man presumably his age. If I had to toss out a guess, he was somewhere between 60 to 70 solar cycles at best. "The great Captain Forge welcomes and invites you all to enter the *Eclipse* for an evening of gambling. As you know, you are part of a very special select group and, as such, it is expected that each of you will be on your best behavior. We will be sending over docking assignments to allow for efficient boarding as to not throw the scheduling off our planned gaming events. Thank you for your cooperation ahead of time."

The screen disintegrates into blackness as the center of the *Eclipse* continues to open, and the bright gold light from the inside grows larger. Gifford turns to meet my gaze. "Well, I guess this is it. If you have any last words—"

"Stifle it, Giff," I say, cutting into his speech. "We're all coming back alive. I'm not much for chit-chat at a time like this. Last words are just that, and I have no intention of writing my epitaph here today."

"Wait a sec, boss," Giff says as he stands. He reaches down in his pocket and slips out a small metallic box with a glass top, no larger than his palm. He pulls out a pair of forceps before opening the box and delicately begins to extract the contents within. A small micro-communication chip no larger than a half a carat diamond hangs from the teeth of the forceps. "Say aww," Giff says.

"You're not going to do that with me standing up, smarty pants. Let me grab a seat," I suggest before planting myself squarely in the closest seat next to us.

An overhead light beams across my face and pauses once it hangs directly over my mouth. Giff leans in slowly and carefully works his forceps past my front row of teeth. It takes a few seconds, but, finally, I feel a light pressure along the back right side of my mouth. A low pinging sound echoes through my ears as a puff of smoke wafts from my mouth and stings my nose. "All set," Giff says as he pulls back. "My work is done here," he continues with a proud smile as he dusts his hands.

I sit up and run my index finger along the area of my mouth he just toyed around in. "Great."

"Was it good for you too?" he jokes.

"Just as I expected it'd be. Quick and very unsatisfying," I reply.

"Haha," Giff says.

"Gear up in that Galley Suit and, Stink, listen out for the docking assignments," I say, shifting into mission mode. "I'll grab Martha. Get dressed."

The cockpit falls eerily silent as both Gifford and Stink respond with only quiet nods. Only the sound of boots clattering along the metal grating of the floor is heard as we scurry to prep for action, and I swear I can hear the sound of my heart swooshing liters of blood at a fervent pace. Moments later, I'm clad in green and gray military greaves from head to toe, with only my black boots and utility belt strapped around my waist to break up the drab color pattern. I check the safety on Martha one last time and snap a round of liquid hydrogen ammunition in the bottom of the handle before cocking it once more to prime the chamber.

"Docking assignment received. We are en route to our final approach. Please complete final preparations and make your way to the cargo bay within approximately 3 minutes for departure," N.I.N.A. announces.

I take one last deep breath and vacate my room. When I get to the cargo bay, Gifford is sitting on a bench in his Galley Suit. His wavy brown hair is wet, matted to the sides of his head, and his face is flushed red. He holds his glasses between his fingers, lightly bouncing them back and forth in his hands as I approach. Suddenly, I'm confronted with my worst fears.

TWENTY-TWO

Surface of the Eclipse: Deep Space

"Cold feet," I say as my eyes sweep over Gifford once more. From here, I can get a cleaner look at him and it isn't any better than what I gleaned from a distance. My recent dose of confidence wanes as I digest the sinking feeling that only the gods can help us now.

"I mean, yeah. It's not like I'm...like you," Gifford says. He didn't shake his head or break his gaze, even the slightest. So I'm 100 percent sure that his recent quaking in his boots behavior is genuine. And that's when the obvious comes back to bite me in the ass.

I'd successfully ignored it the entire time ever since we met back on *The Gloria*. Possibly the result of me being doubtless that things would even get this far or maybe, just maybe I feigned ignorance from the jump because I just wanted to throw myself to the wind and pray that karma would finally have her day in the sunshine. I sit down beside him and rest a heavy hand on his shoulder, my slight attempt to quell his nerves. "Talk to me, kid," I say, my voice calm and steady. His eyes meet mine, wet and red around the edges. Beneath the genius exterior, he was just another kid trying his hand at success among the endless heroic storylines of the universe. And, unfortunately for him, the reality of death had come to a head and the pinnacle of our journey was almost at hand. But I needed him more than I'd liked to admit. Without his potent brain, we didn't stand a chance of successfully navigating the *Eclipse* and escaping with Olia undetected. Sure, if you wanted me to go in full guns blazing, I stood a 50 percent chance of making it out alive, albeit with a few limbs missing. But sneakily weaving in and out of the ship and slipping Olia from underneath Forge's nose, well, that was a feat only fit for the intellect of the young at heart. And I was neither.

"It's just...I don't know. I'm filled with a ton of conflict, Reign," he says, his eyes finally breaking from mine. He stares at his hands as he continues. "I thought that when I took this...I mean, when I started on this quest with you that I could handle everything that came with it. But now...I mean, I feel like I'm in too deep. Have you ever felt like that?"

"That's like always, kiddo," I say with a light chuckle. "But you're going to be fine, son. Trust me, as I trust you."

Gifford's head whips in my direction, and for a quick second, the look in his eyes hints at something else churning behind them, something akin to shock and awe. But why? He leans in close. "Reign, I—"

Before he can speak, Stink joins us, carrying an O2 tank canister and begins to initiate attaching it to the Galley Suit. "Bottom's up, Giff. We're in range. Time to jump."

Gifford stands to his feet, slips on his glasses, and runs his fingers through his hair. After carefully wafting the majority of it to the side, he quickly grabs his helmet from the bench and slowly lowers it over his head. A sharp half turn and it seals to a perfect fit to the neck of the Galley Suit. Stink slips in from behind and connects the nozzle of the O2 tank to the valve leaching out from the helmet and then slides it into place along the dorsal part of the Galley Suit's trunk. Giff tugs at a strap in the front, just below his right breastplate and the unmistakable sound of air filling his helmet resounds.

Stink gives a once over to the seal along the neck of the Galley Suit. Confident that everything was on the up and up, he offers a love tap on Gifford's helmet from behind. "Sound good. You're all clear."

"How much time do you have?" I ask, looking down at my Holo-tablet and synchronizing a countdown timer to my Holo-band.

"Well," Gifford says, "normally about 16 to 18 solar hours, but I decided—upon the suggestion of N.I.N.A.—to engage the Hiber functionality of the suit immediately after fastening myself to the hull of the *Eclipse* and conserving some oxygen, just in case you guys run long."

"What, no faith? I'm not much for conversation," I tease.

"It's not that. I think N.I.N.A. is concerned that once all the ships are on board and the docking doors close, the Dark Matter cloak will initiate, and she's almost certain that the ship's A.I. will make life signs scan of the surface, possibly looking for intruders. The Hiber function will keep my vitals low enough so that I'll be undetectable.

She can deactivate it remotely when necessary. But you know that already."

"And?" I ask, gesturing to the timer on my Holo-tablet.

Giff rolls his eyes. "Okay, go with 36 hours if you must. After that, start making arrangements for my funeral."

I punch the numbers into my Holo-tablet and sync it to my band. "Solid," I say, mainly because I don't have anything else to offer at this point. I shift my focus over to Stink. "So what do we do now?"

"Let's beat it back to the cockpit," Stink answers. "Giff will need to spacewalk soon, and when he opens the aft doors, this place will be very cold and uncomfortable. We can track his progress from there."

I give one last look over to Gifford and offer nothing more than a thumbs up, not wanting to add to the already climbing anxiety surely bubbling over inside his guts. Giff returns a nod, and Stink and I exit, sealing the door behind us to allow for a successful decompression.

From the cockpit, everything is visible. A bevy of assorted ships joins us as we cruise toward the mammoth *Eclipse* as it dwarfs just about everything in its proximity. Corvettes, shuttles, carriers, and even small fighters drift along, captured in the slow pull of the tractor beams emanating from the center. My eyes dart between the overhead consoles and the forward view port, trying my best not to seem concerned. From here, the depth of our situation finally settles in. We're here, playing a game that we're only hopeful of winning with a gambler that does only one thing—win, every time. But the tokens we offer are our lives. Lives of two, bright-eyed young men and an artificial one of an ailing Bounty Hunter. Sure, I'd done worse in the past and been on the opposite end of the killing more times than I'd like to admit or count, but this felt different. Suddenly, I'd inherited a pseudo-family, something I'd always longed for but never had. And with the opportunity of adding one more on the horizon—a half-sister from my past—the unsettling fear of losing it all made me want to gag.

The solar cycles of service in my past had made me numb to such feelings, and the last 3 days had unhinged emotions of the past that gave me a sense of desperation that was haunting me more than I was willing to admit. I wouldn't let them die—no, *I couldn't* let them die. Not a single one. Even if it cost me my own life.

"Five kilos out, two kilos until Giff makes the jump boss," Stink says as he taps me on my shoulder.

I turn to look at the screen that Stink was gazing at for the last few moments since we entered the cockpit. "Patch him through," I say.

Stink flicks a switch or two and then taps the screen. A downward image of Gifford blips on, showing more forehead than body from the internal camera of his helmet. "Knock, knock," Stink says.

Gifford looks up and flashes a smile as a wave of relief washes over me. "How are you doing, kid?" I ask.

Gifford appears to be preoccupied as the camera wavers from side to side, cuing us that he was pushing his way toward the aft door and making final preparations for the jump. From what Stink had explained earlier, once the doors opened, air would spew from the inner cargo hull of the *Concord* and jettison the Galley Suit at the speed of about 36 kilometers per hour in the direction of the *Eclipse*; more than enough to successfully land Gifford on the exterior of the beast of a ship within seconds. "In position," Giff says finally as the cameras come to a halt.

My heart begins to race. "Listen, kid, I—" the words freeze in my throat as I search for something motivating to say without sounding sappy.

"Don't worry, boss. *I got this*," Gifford says, echoing my quote just moments before.

"You do," I counter with an air of confidence that even calms my mind.

Gifford's eyes shoot down away from the camera as he begins to finger at the forearm Holo-terminal of the Galley Suit. "N.I.N.A., lock on coordinates."

"Already done, Gifford," I hear the A.I.s melodious voice erupt overhead. "You are a go!"

Gifford gives us one last look. His green eyes are bright and full of vigor, reminding me of the young boy who joined the Thieves of Light so many moons ago. "On my mark," he says.

Stink starts the countdown. "In 3…2…1…mark!"

The ship shutters as the aft door slides open, and air evacuates from inside. My eyes immediately flick back to the overhead viewscreen as I scramble to find Gifford. After a few seconds, they finally lock onto the tumbling Galley Suit as it continues its course toward the *Eclipse*. I swear that time stands still for the 3 solar minutes it takes for Gifford to touch down to the metallic skin of the gigantic vessel, but when he does and his voice booms across the comms with a, "Made it," we finally take a collective breath.

I sink onto the captain's chair, and Stink slams a set of heavy hands along my shoulders. "Ha, ha!" he yells. "That's one hells of a spacewalk son."

"Locking down now," Gifford says. From here, I can faintly make out his hand movements as he hysterically fumbles to bolt down a hook into the fuselage with the nail gun of his left hand. Afterward, he slaps a clamp extending from his utility belt into the eye of the hook penetrating the outer hull with his right. He tosses his gun to the side and prostrates his body along the surface. "Night, night," he says.

N.I.N.A.'s voice croons overhead. "Nighty, night, Gifford. Initiating Hiber mode."

Gifford's body goes motionless and slowly floats about a meter away from the surface of the *Eclipse* until the rope from the fastening clamp tightens, halting his course of movement. "Son of a bitch made it," Stink comments, gazing at his vitals on the console.

I wade in over his shoulder, eyeing the depressed vitals with raised concern as the *Concord* breezes by his lifeless body. "Yeah, he did." At that moment, I'm amazed at the level of concern and apprehension welling up in me while simultaneously hating that I ever had. In this business, you can't afford to feel anything or you'll drop your guard and open yourself up to the one thing that will sideline you for life—disappointment. And that was disheartening because I planned to stay in the game for the rest of my days.

TWENTY-THREE

Inside the Eclipse: Deep Space

"And now, for the breakdown," Stink says, turning to face me.

"What?" I ask, confused.

"You heard me. We're only moments away from being swallowed by this thing, and you still haven't given me a word on how you plan to come through on your end of this deal. Not that I'm complaining, but…I'm just saying, boss. Giff's out there hanging 10 with the space wind, I'm ready to drop anchor and, well, we ain't heard sheat from you yet."

I lean back and rest against the opposite console, folding my arms across my chest. "Like I said earlier, rookie. In situations like this, I don't make plans; I improvise."

"Well, I hope you brought your A-game improvisation 'cause I don't plan on dying today, tonight, or whatever time of day it is right now."

"Your lack of confidence is disappointing, Stink," I reply.

"Look, it's not that I doubt your skills. It's just…I know what's at stake, and I really want to see this through. For everyone."

"And you don't think I do?"

He sighs and shakes his head. "It's not that I don't…it's just—"

Just as Stink is about to finish, the ominous sound of clamping hinges locks onto the *Concord*, just as the cockpit is bathed in a bright light that surrounds us both. I raise my hands to shield my face, and the ship swiftly dives sideway as if carried by a set of god hands. It takes a moment for me to realize that not only does the *Eclipse* use tractor beams to guide ships inside its interior landing bays, but it also utilizes some high tech grappling system to tote smaller vessels to their landing pads. As if on cue, N.I.N.A. activates the landing gear and in seconds, we coast downward until our ship lands safely along a floating pad, joining about a dozen or so other smaller vessels.

Stink looks over to me, silent as if awaiting my next order. I don't utter a word as my mind churns through countless scenarios of the next few hours of our time aboard the *Eclipse*. I was no newbie to carnage, so getting in and spraying up the place—dropping a few bodies here and there—would be second nature to me. And I wouldn't bat an eye or shed a tear for any of it, since I was convinced that Forge's time was coming due and his band of minions had it coming for being accessories to his countless crimes.

But, admittedly, it was the dainty, more sophisticated stuff that was baking my noodle. It was the kind of thing that people like Gifford and Serias were plenty better than me at. And, at the moment, Serias is nowhere to be found, and Giff is hanging 10—as Stink says—along the surface of the *Eclipse*, limp as a half-cocked dick. My hand finds it's way to my holster as I slowly finger Martha's trigger—something I tend to do when my nerves get the best of me. Stink didn't know anything about what was playing through my head dreams, but my actions get his attention.

"You thinking about planting a few in me from behind when we debark?" he asks, a bit of bitterness bleeding into his tone.

I remove my hand from Martha. "What?"

His eyes leave my holster and run the length of my body until parking on my optical augmentation. His eyes narrow as he asks his next question. "You know, turn me over to Forge if things get outta pocket. It's a simple bait-and-switch technique that I've come accustomed to out here. No doubt it's served you well a time or two."

Heat swells in between my ears. "If you're referring to Serias, that's the business that you need not lose any sleep about, pretty boy."

"Wasn't talking about Serias, although the thought had crossed my mind. I was speaking more specifically about your past. Giff shared a file or two with me. Your call sign, Steel Reign? The origin of it. Interesting stuff, indeed."

"I didn't know that I was the subject of such late-night chatter between you boys. I'm flattered."

Stink shrugs and momentarily turns away. "Don't be. Any conversation about you *was* about us. We've trusted you up to this point and now…well, it's the best time for a nut-check to see which side hangs lowest. I need to *feel* something here, Reign," Stink implores, gesturing his hands as if trying to slide across some imaginary bridge between us.

"Well, I don't ooze fatherly figure like some of the other Bounty Hunters you *may* have run across in your past, and I'm not one for warm and fuzzy hugs. Therefore, you may find yourself disappointed if that's what you're looking for. So whatever it is you're hunting for, just spit it out."

"Not to take a walk down memory lane," he starts as his eyes fully fixate on my optic one, trying to get a gauge on me. "But your history of partners is a little bleak. Not to say that you're the blame for everyone going up in flames, but you are the common denominator to their demise. I'm only good inside a cockpit. So down there...whatever we're about to face...well, I'll be a fish out of water, and I'm praying that you swim like a Peltic seal."

I was no veteran in dealing with teleonotioning beings—truthfully only having a relationship with one, my sister—but I had enough experience of dealing with grimy individuals to know when I was amid a shakedown. Stink wanted something from me, but it wasn't money, weapons, or anything else tangible. He sought answers, and he was chomping at the bit to read the subtle fluctuations and oscillations of my artificial eye to glean if I was lying or not. And, to his surprise, I was exhausted with all the spy games. All I had left to offer was the truth, especially since I'd made up my mind earlier that surviving this mess would be fully dependent upon an "all hands on deck" movement. I pull out my pistol and give Martha a good once over before aiming it at Stink. His eyes widen before I holster it again. "Well, today is your lucky day because I specialize in getting wet. And I intend to stroke my way through a sea of blood to get us in and out of here with my sister in tow. Everyone unscathed."

"Steel. Codenamed The Gunman. Accurate as hells and deadlier than the beast dwelling in it. I read that they called you that for the number of souls you'd stolen from the universe and vanquished to the afterlife."

"That's right. But don't worry, son, the majority of them came with intention, not by mistake. It's time to go."

I start to make my way out of the cockpit when Stink speaks one last time. "But you are a spy, aren't you? I mean, turning on people is what you did. Isn't it?"

I stop dead in my tracks. Whoever it was that said *a man's deeds go before him and reach the place of judgment*, they weren't lying. But here I was living this metaphoric moment out in real-time. "I am, or so I was. I chose to hang up those boots. And I'm here for two reasons."

"And what's that, sir?" Stink's voice was raspy and harsh. He was desperate for some degree of validation of my loyalty, and I had to deliver. If not for his sanity, at least for the solidarity of our collective union. I turned and stared directly into his eyes, with my good one. "For my sister and my team. If one of you die, I die. That's…all I can offer you. I hope it's good enough."

Stink stands, and a slight grin splits the corner of his mouth. He slowly nods a few times, seemingly content with my response. "Well then, it's time to meet this space rat."

The unmistakable sound of air hissing from the cargo hold splits my ears and N.I.N.A. chimes in over the comms. "Aft door opening. The crew from the *Eclipse* is here to greet you, gentleman."

I hold my gaze with Stink and speak. "Let's not leave them waiting."

"Agreed," he says. "It's time we add a little estrogen to this *team*," he says valiantly, and I feel the hair rise on the back of my neck at his reference of adding my long lost sister to our cause.

"Indeed, we do," I say with a grin. It was the first time in a long while that I'd shared such a pure conversation as the one I just had with Stink, but it was as refreshing as I'd remembered. Open, honest, and intentional. Not since the days of rolling with Serias. It reminded me of the place I'd long forgotten, a place of peace that had somehow gotten lost in between the worlds of forsakenness and death.

It was as close to therapeutic as I was comfortable with endeavoring with at the moment. But somewhere in my chest, I'd long to revisit it one day. I'd been there before and hoped with all earnest that it'd be with Serias again one day. But since that time had passed me by, I'd thrown the idea to the solar wind. And here I was, in the middle of deep space sharing a moment like that with another man, a boy I'd barely known. It was the closest encounter I'd had with another person in a long time, ever since my failed escapade with King Gregorio as we attempted to free Fabricius. He was the last casualty I'd taken the blame for, and it was a cold glass of remorse that I had no intention of ingesting again anytime soon.

We work our way down the catwalk of the *Concord* and approach a group of 5 men awaiting us along one of the large, disc-shaped floating platforms adjacent to our own. The belly of the *Eclipse* is dim, and I can barely make out our surroundings, save for the fact that it's larger than any vessels I'd ever visited this far outside the reaches of the Inner Planets. Most ships of this capacity can't drift this deep without an adequate power supply for life support, weapons, shields, and engines.

Large soft yellow lights blaze in from above and casts dark shadows over the faces of our hosts as we approach. They were tall, with the majority dressed in all black leather garb, adorned with armor plating covering their chests, shoulders, and thighs. The tallest of the bunch was also the largest, hanging in the back of the crowd. Wide and muscular, he's sleeveless, baring muscles in his arms that bulged so hard that you'd swear his gray-tinged skin was about to burst from the pressure underneath. He was also the only one donning a helmet with a slit in the center that covered the majority of his face, parting with a pair of oval circles that allowed his red eyes to peer through.

A smaller one, thin and wiry-looking, lurches forward to speak. "I am Nedojustee. Welcome aboard the *Eclipse*," he announces. His voice is slithery, sharing a raspy tone like that of a serpent. He bows and offers an inviting hand to us. As his long fingers project in our direction. Both Stink and I hold our ground and nod back, refusing to take it. His white hair drapes over one side of his face as the corner of his mouth rises slightly, and he gestures to the rest of the 4 standing behind him. "These 3 are part of the captain's personal guard. This large brute you see here is Sawjustee. He's the leader of the bunch. And the companion to my right is Klepjustee, our science officer."

Klepjustee appears to be female by the tight-fitted green jumpsuit, revealing well-formed curves and long, shiny pink hair. Fair-skinned by my comparison, the veins in her arms are easily visible, pushed to the forefront surface of her skin by her tone muscles, although the entire group donned abnormally pale-skinned tones. "What about the other two behind the big boy. They have names too?" I ask.

"Yes, but it's no concern of yours. Most of the crew are not allowed to fraternize with customers. Any questions you have can be directed at any one of us," Klepjustee says, speaking up. She dons a red patch over her right eye, and I sympathize a bit, wondering what force from the 'verse stole her vision too. But after her words, I give a closer inspection and I realize the error of my ways, now fully comprehending that she is indeed a *he*, or possibly an *it*, sharing both male and female genitals. Since he shares a similar bony stature as Nedojustee, I fantasize the time it would take to down either one of them with a well-placed punch to the jaw. I'm guessing one slug to the face would suffice but haven't quite settled on the right number for Sawjustee. "Please, join us on the pad so that we can start the tour," Klepjustee says with a clap. "We mustn't be late."

"Late for what?" Stink asks, stealing the words from my mouth.

"The tour, of course," Klepjustee interjects.

I swallow hard at that. A tour of the *Eclipse,* perhaps? Or maybe the quarters of the players in The Gauntlet tournament? If it's the latter, it'd be the perfect chance for me to get a bead on Olia and assure that my sister is still alive and well. In all honesty, I'm just praying for alive at this point seeing as though this assignment was an exercise in blind faith as I followed the lead of information given to me by King William over one solar year ago. On second thought, Olia better be well if anybody aboard this vessel knows what's good for them.

The idea of Olia's demise pierces my mind, simultaneously making my trigger-finger itch something terrible. "What about our weapons?" I ask, preparing myself for the worst of circumstances.

"Keep them. They won't serve you any good aboard the *Eclipse,* though. Once the Dark Matter shielding is activated that is. It traps all matter of heat, rendering convection weapons such as your pistols harmless," Nedojustee says with a heavy tone of sarcasm hanging on his every word.

I swallow hard behind clenched teeth once more and realize that at least half the scenarios I'd worked through over the last 2 to 3 solar hours had just imploded into dust. Well, nothing like narrowing down your options, I guess. "Fine," I say as I approach the platform. "Refreshing to know that I won't be needing it, after all since no one will have active artillery. Right?" I ask, directing my question at Nedojustee.

He returns with a snide smile and a, "Right," of his own that does nothing to boost my confidence.

We board the floating platform and are instructed to grab hold of the cold metal railing enveloping all of us. We do, and I slightly bend my knees to brace myself for take-off. As expected, the platform dances at a good clip and we rise upward from the rest of the ships below, and I throw a glance downward to locate the *Concord* as it shrinks out of view. Ironically, our ship is nestled at the center of the other ships which are similar in size. The sea of vessels drowns out the dark platform of the hangar bay below in a vista of varying muted shades of gray, blue, brown, purple, and gold. It's then that I notice that the larger Corvettes, carriers, and fighters must've hung back outside and sent shuttles packed with travelers instead, anxious to gamble and waste thousands of credits in one long night.

Either the *Eclipse* isn't as big enough to house as many ships as I initially thought or the other gamblers just decided it was best to *not* put all their eggs in one basket, choosing to leave some behind. And, quite possibly, reserve some firepower outside the reach of the pirate in case things go south. But if there's anything I've come to learn over the many solar cycles of my life, is that when dealing with pirates, anything is fair game.

Dozens of similar oval platforms zoom about, heading to elevators scattered around the inside perimeter of the hangar bay, escorted by an assortment of Forge's other random goons. How Stink and I were blessed to snag a pair of his highest-ranking officials as our detail beats at my brain, so I pose the question to the most talkative of the bunch. "Hey, Nedo-what-cha-ma-call it. What did my ace pilot here and I do to earn your graces for our tour?"

"It's Nedojustee," he says, beating me with a narrow-eyed stare that could burn holes through Oramite armor. "And to answer your question, you all on our VIP list. Didn't you know that?" He looks down at his Holo-band and taps the screen. "A Mister Giff—"

"Wait, there's only two of you. Where is he?" Klepjustee interjects.

My heart races, but Stink speaks up before I can. "He's always hanging around somewhere. I'm sure he'll show up sooner or later," Stink says in a sarcastic tone.

"Yeah, he couldn't make it," I interrupt. "He lost his will to gamble back at Terrius 7 on the way here. Started complaining about some weird symptoms after we ate at dinner. He said it was food poisoning, but I lean more toward believing he got it from some bad piece of snatch he bagged an hour earlier. I told him we'll make wages on his behalf."

"That's unfortunate," Nedojustee says.

"I hope that won't be a problem?" I ask.

"Not at all," Nedojustee replies.

As we continue our ascent, the lights from above slowly come into focus and I'm able to note that they aren't individual sources as

I previously assumed from below, but a conglomerate of 10 to 20 smaller bulbs—the size of landing gear wheels—forming a bundle of light.

We bank left and zoom our way to another platform that houses a large elevator. From this height, I guesstimate that we're some 50 to 75 feet above the *Concord*, quickly extinguishing any bright ideas of jumping down when it's time to escape. And with Giff's plan of downing the power controls, we'll have to find some other means of getting back to the ship once the elevators go dark. With any luck, they'll run on auxiliary power or we'll be forced to execute a climb that'll surely slow our departure.

"After you," Nedojustee says as she, he, or whatever, ushers us from the platform. We all pack inside and the elevator lifts, revealing glass walls all around us. My stomach crawls as the view of the hangar bay disappears, replaced by a dark tunnel that swallows us whole as we complete our ascent. While we move, I periodically meet eyes with Stink to assure he's okay. If nothing else, Stink's one hells of a gambler, sporting a poker face void of any resemblance of emotion or distress.

As the elevator comes to a halt and the doors retract, we are met by a long hallway that separates into multiple corridors beyond our reach. Blinding light from the white corridor pours in. It's a welcome and distinct contrast from the gloomy area we just left. Pristine shiny walls kiss the immaculate tiled ceilings and floors, appearing to form one continuous sheet of metal—similar to the design of many larger Torrian Alliance vessels—that reflect the singular overhead lights, spaced some 10 feet apart.

"So what exactly comes with this VIP package?" Stink asks as we come to a halt just outside a large black metal door, adorned by two guards, armed with electric staffs.

"Only the best," Nedojustee says with a snide smile that almost reaches his ears. He waves a hand, and as the two guards step aside, the door slips open. We enter and are met by the sound of combat as contestants practice in a large rectangular training room. Hand combat weapons of all types crowd the walls, from scimitars, swords, knives, and nun-chucks, to axes, throwing stars, staffs, and hammers. It's spacious enough to house maybe 10 to 20 players at one time in my estimation, complete with padded foam flooring in the center.

"Whoa, this is wicked," I hear Stink whisper from behind.

Nedojustee steps forward, motioning for us to follow. "Gentlemen, meet Commander Forge's finest gladiators. The Champions!"

My eyes beat around the room as I shuffle through the many faces of players before me. Short, fat, tall, ugly, skinny—none mean a hill of beans to me. The anticipation of finally finding the last remnant of my real family is so heavy it threatens to pull my heart down through my sheat-hole as it pounds at about a thousand beats per second. And when my gaze finally lands on the purple face of a tall, muscular, familiar, female Sintock warrior, my heart stops.

It's her.

TWENTY-FOUR

"See anything you like, Captain?" Nedojustee asks.

I break from my gaze. "I'm sorry? What did you say?" I ask, trying my best to corral the wave of emotions running through me on 10.

"I noticed you were staring at the Sintock warrior Olia. An amazing specimen, indeed, wouldn't you agree?" Nedojustee asks.

I exhale slowly before answering. "I...I was just—"

"Ha, he's probably popping a serious wedge in his pants at the thought of lying with her right now," the big one, Sawjustee blurts behind a heavy chuckle, his voice echoing through his helmet. The quiet, nameless flunkies from the group join him in a chorus of laughter.

"Oh, I see. You're the funny one of the group," I say, steam coursing through my veins. I cup my ear with my index and middle finger of my hand. "Why don't you take that helmet of yours off so I can hear you more clearly?"

Sawjustee stares at me in silence, his red eyes seeming to pulse with rage. "Careful," he mutters.

I tried not to let it show, but my anger must've gotten the best of me as Stink wades in from behind and grabs me by my right arm, slowly pulling it away from Martha. "Easy, boss."

I'm too locked in on Sawjustee to notice Klepjustee call over a few of the Champions in our direction. By the time I do, it's too late. Olia, along with 5 others, were heading in our direction. I heed Stink's suggestion to step down—not because of fear—to avoid being IDed by Olia. When the group of Champions gets within an arm's reach, I fall behind Stink and drop my gaze as I fumble with the metal shielding around my Optic Aug, acting to be preoccupied with a fake malfunction.

"Aww, crap," I murmur.

"Problem?" Nedojustee asks.

"VIPs only, gentlemen," Klepjustee says. From the corner of my good eye, I watch her circle around the Champions as they stand at attention like they were fresh meat at a farmer's market on Fabricius. "Wouldn't you like a personal up-close examination before you place your bets?"

The 6 Champions stand proudly in line. Olia towers over most of them except for one lanky green being that I faintly recognize. Crilean, I think, but I hadn't ever visited the planet but only enjoyed the toe paralyzing ale that singe the hairs on my chest with each swallow. There is also a shorter reptilian-looking beast propped on its beefy tail that was about half of Olia's height, and I'm willing to place a solo bet on the whim that he probably slithers around the Gauntlet faster than anyone in the room. Olia is nothing that I remember. Her long, muscular frame is as equally impressive as her beauty. Black, curly, shoulder-length hair dangles from her head now as opposed to the bald crown she used to sport. I'm not all that gifted at deciphering real from fake locks, but it's my wager that it's a wig, since the amount of makeup she dons is normal practice for live broadcasts when running The Gauntlet.

For the first time ever, I say a silent "thank you" prayer for Stink's teleonotioning abilities as he steps up and plays interference while I continue to feign victim to faulty electronics. "Man, oh, man. I'm mad geeked right now. Who would've ever thought I'd be this close to such refined beauty," Stink says, stepping within mere inches of Olia. He makes the mistake of reaching out to touch her arm and on cue, Olia quickly snatches him by the wrist and topples him over with a strong twist of his arm, bending his hand behind his back.

"Don't get it twisted, sport," she says, emphasizing the word twisted as she speaks, "you can look, but don't even *think* about touching. Got it?" Her actions reassure me that she'd fully recovered from the time King William had last seen her aboard the *Eclipse* before his escape.

"Sure thing," Stink screeches in pain.

"Enough," Nedojustee screams. Olia relinquishes her grip, and, for the first time, our eyes meet. There's a pregnant pause as my mind shatters, simultaneously caught between my desires of both wanting her to and not recognize me. She blinks for a moment before turning away, falling back in line.

"I think that's enough playing for now, don't you think?" Nedojustee asks. No one answers as Stink stands and shakes the pain from his wrist and forearm.

"I agree," Klepjustee says. "Run along and make final preparations."

As the Champions head for the back exit, our hosts spill back into the hallway and Stink sloughs slowly back over in my direction. As he gets closer, he shoots me a wink. "She's got it," he whispers as he passes.

Got what? The words are just about to escape my mouth until I make the connection to what Stink was referring to. "Son of a," I mutter. Again, Stink has successfully reminded me of the sole reason I'd come to like him so much. In choosing not to waste any time, he'd opted to take the initiative and remove the focus from me while slipping Olia the microchip. Somehow their teleonotioning gifts must've made the connection, officially setting our plans in motion. I laugh under my breath as we all file into the pale corridor, impressed as hells by what had just transpired between them. They played their roles perfectly, and the cogwheels had begun spinning. Now, all I had to do was add some much-needed oil to keep 'em churning.

I stroll next to Nedojustee as we continue our trek down the hall. "Where to next?" I ask him. "VIP status doesn't just get us a view of the players, does it?"

"What else could you possibly want?" Nedojustee asks as he comes to a halt.

"What about the head, man?" I ask, turning to face him directly.

His gaze drops and then lands on Klepjustee before he answers. "How did you guess?" he asks.

It takes a moment for me to gather myself and fend off the desire to smile at his answer. I take in a deep breath and answer in the only way I'd expect a space-faring playboy just itching to irresponsibly waste thousands of credits in a moment's notice would. "I'm fly like that," I say as I tilt my head and shoot him a wink.

"Well," Klepjustee pipes, "not that I follow you all that much, but, yes. Let's not keep the Captain waiting."

Pay dirt. Stink can take the rest of the night off. Now it's my turn to spin the wheels a bit. My next prayer is that I can refrain from breaking a few jawbones and ribs connected to our host space pirate. But I'm not making myself any promises.

***

Moments later, after winding through a few more corridors of the vessel, passing by what I recognize as a mess hall, soldier's and officer's quarters, and the armory—my favorite place of interest. The Dark Matter engines must be fully back online because even the power to my Optic Aug has lessened, no longer allowing me to see through walls. We make small talk until coming to a stop at a dead end. The wall is twice the height as any we passed along the way, and, immediately, my suspicious radar antennae start buzzing. "So where's Forge?" I ask.

"Yeah, is he going to phase from the walls or something? I thought he was a pirate, not a ghost," Stink says.

"Patience," Nedojustee barks, sounding irritated. He steps forward and waves his hand over the wall. An outline of a door materializes across the shiny surface and lifts, revealing a larger office behind it. "This way," he says.

We enter the room and are met by an impressive array of statues and pictures suspended overhead, none of which look the familiar to me in the slightest. Family of Forge's I assumed, but most pirates don't have family, let alone dangle them on display for others to find out about. Pirates are loners, and, as such, if they have anyone that holds any value, they hide them away like buried treasure, making it damn near impossible for enemies to kidnap, threaten, or use as leverage. So, as such, the people in the pictures must be decoys, and the statues are just more of the same.

Soft yellow lights from the corners of the room pierce the natural darkness around us and things become clearer.   Stink and I stay close as we walk inside, our eyes perusing the rest of the room's contents. Large, clear, glass storage tanks containing dead animals, suspended in fluid behind glass for all to see, decorate the opposite wall.

"Check it out, boss," Stink says. "These look like in alien Delton Cardaks on Fabricius."

"Yeah," I mutter in agreement with the pastel-colored thick fur being the only exception. A floating monitor zooms in close, and a solitary red eyeball in the center blooms to life as a female voice speaks. "Welcome, kind sirs. Please, make yourselves at home. Can I offer you a drink?"

I wave it off with an open hand before Stink can answer. "No, thanks."

The monitor bleeps and lifts abruptly with a hiss as if offended, "As you wish," it replies before scooting away.

"Hey, I was going to order something," Stink says.

"Pipe down," I say. "Don't get too comfortable. We still don't know what to expect."

"Well, I can answer that question for you," a voice booms in from behind.

We turn in the direction of the sound and in walks a large, towering figure dressed in all white Officer Khakis with 4 bars of Epaulets draped off both shoulders, a pair of shiny dark boots to match and his arms folded behind his back. He's cleaner than a newly commissioned Torrian Cruiser. It's a far cry from anything I expect to see a pirate don, but if it's Forge's effort to sell this criminal establishment as anything legit, he can stop wasting his time because I'm not buying it.

As he looms closer under the soft lights of the room, I can just make out his hard features. Deep crow's feet hug the corners of his eyes while jagged, fixed lines run the length of the space between the end of his nose to the edge of his lips, doing the job of masking the muscles used to form a smile. His chiseled jaw gives him the appearance of a man much older than his face reveals. But anyone can get a few lifts in the 'verse nowadays, even if you only had a handful of credits. Do what you will to look like hot sheat, but time catches up to everyone and, eventually, you'll start to feel more like your age than you look.

"Mr. Reign," Forge says before his eyes beat over to Stink, and he follows with a, "and Mr. Mire, so happy you could all join us. I say all, but apparently, you're missing one from what I understand."

"Yeah, our last partner couldn't make it," I say, speaking up before Stink could spit out another poorly-timed joke about Gifford hanging around or blowing in the wind as he did before. Forge's cronies may not have caught on, but I'm not willing to risk that Forge was dense as they are. A comment like that would surely sink this entire plan.

"Right," Forge says with a slight sneer, our eyes momentarily locking. I grit my teeth as he finally turns away, giving us his back. "Most people don't like to risk traveling this far into deep space as you two have. I hope to make it worth your while."

"Well, as long as our R.O.I. is fat, we'll be happy men," Stink blurts. "The *Concord* is a pretty fancy craft. All the bells and whistles a pilot can ask for. Which begs the question; what's a...*Captain* like you need with a vessel like that?"

My Optic Aug bulges from its socket, but I was too startled by Stink's boldness to interject before Forge can answer. His head whips in Stink's direction as he flashes a wide smile. "The *Eclipse* is all I need. But if you must know about my interests in the *Concord*, well, simply put, I'm the kind of man who relishes in the benefits of trade. And you happen to have items of value to trade with, so when I got word of your sparkly new craft, I was drawn in."

"As we were too. But we don't mind tossing it away, knowing how the practice of reaping and sowing works. You know, all that casting bread on water jabber," I joke.

The change in Forge's facial expression is almost unnoticeable, but my Optic Aug locks in on his slightly raised brow and terse lips with razor-sharp precision. "You know what I love the most about deep space?" he says, oddly changing the subject. As I prepare to answer his question, I notice a sudden shift in the position of Forge's men as they clamor behind us, fading from my periphery. My heart thumps in my chest as the sinking feeling of something dark washes over me. The lights overhead suddenly surge from soft yellow to lightning white, bringing along with it a pulsing heat that blooms in my chest. I tense my stomach and fight against the urge to cough. "Captain, are you okay?" Forge asks, his voice is suddenly coarser and ragged.

"I'm...fine," I mutter as beads of sweat begin to form along my forehead.

Forge steps back and waves his hand over a panel in the flooring that I didn't notice earlier. It rises from the floor and stops about waist high, revealing a monitor with a black screen. As it does, an unexpected sharp pain stabs at my heart. The room is now blistering hot, and I know for sure that it has nothing to do with the brightness of the overhead lights. The urge to cough overpowers me and I instinctively give in, exploding into a fit that threatens to topple me over. Stink comes to my side and tries his best to stabilize me. "Bossman, you okay?" he asks, his warm breath on my neck as he leans in close in a failed attempt to pull me erect. Heat rolls down the back of my legs, making my muscles spasm and collapsing me to one knee. Multiple footfalls crowd in from behind and from the corner of my good eye, I watch as Stink is pulled away by two goons. "Let go," he screams in vain.

Just as I'm about to reach for Martha, three sets of hands slam down on my body, pushing me into a full kneeling position while simultaneously craning both of my arms behind my back and slapping a pair of cuffs on my wrists. Someone pulls Martha from her holster and tosses it at Forge's feet. In my rage, I finally muster the strength to speak out, yelling, "What the hells are you playing here, Forge?"

The monitor next to Forge flickers on, and the face that materializes sends chills down my spine. Forge steps to the side to get a better look at the screen. "King Derry, your timing is immaculate."

"William?" I faintly whisper as our eyes meet.

"I take it that you have your *gift?*" William asks Forge.

Forge's gaze drifts between William and me. "Certainly. Reign delivered it just as you said he would."

"Very well, then. I'll turn you over to my lead technician, Parten," William says. He slides from view and the face of a younger male with dark glasses and red, flaming hair swaged across his forehead replaces him.

"Ready to receive the blueprints for the Dark Matter engines," Parten says, raising a Holo-tablet into view.

The heat continues to pulse through my blood as the hands on my body grow heavier, and the vision in my natural eye blurs. If not for the automatic acuity sensors in my Optical Aug, I'd be completely blind.

Klepjustee appears and offers Forge a Holo-tablet of his own. "Thank you," Forge says as he takes his from her hand. He starts to peck along the screen, and I look back over to the monitor to see Parten's response. *What the hells is going on?* I struggle to think as he lifts his glasses and gazes intently at his tablet.

After flashing a look of satisfaction, he answers, "Received," before stepping away.

William returns. "So the deal is settled. Thank you for your services, Captain Forge."

"Pleasure's all mine. Tell me, King, what will you do with all that information?" Forge asks.

"I can think of a few things," William replies.

"And the prisoners?" Forge asks.

"Prisoners!" I muster between gnashed teeth.

"I'm sure you need new players in the Gauntlet, don't you?" William suggests.

"I certainly do," Forge says as a chorus of cheers erupts from his men.

"The Gauntlet! The Gauntlet! The Gauntlet! The Gauntlet!" they shout.

"Before I go, let me address Reign one last time," William requests.

Fire burns underneath my skin, but it has nothing to do with the lights any longer as I struggle to lift my head and stare at William's face. "Steel Reign," he starts as the screen flickers in and out. "You are at this moment sentenced to the crime of treason by allowing the murder of King Gregorio Derry at the hands of madman Dominic, formerly of The Dagmas Clan."

The screen flickers once more, and Klepjustee leans in to inspect the casing for a cause. "Must be the Dark Matter engines creating interference."

"Well, fix it!" Forge demands. He points to the floating monitor from before, which now has a noticeable red light flashing along the top of it. "We're recording for the show tonight. It makes for damn good entertainment."

"I…tried to…save him," I mutter.

"Silence!" William shouts as the screen flickers 3 more times and then returns to normal. "Your failure made you complicit with the rebellion against the Torrian Alliance. And, now, it is both inexcusable and unforgivable. Gifford made good on his promise to bring you to Forge, and *he* will be rewarded handsomely. I hope you find solace in your death." William closes his eyes. "Beyond the stars."

The entire group—minus Stink and me—reply in unison, "Beyond the stars!" as the monitor goes black.

My heart sinks, and my desire to fight back against the multitude of resisting hands wanes. In a flash, everything slowly begins to make sense.

The unlimited resources.

The timely meeting.

The Intel.

Gifford was in on it too.

As for the narrow escape aboard the *Opus*. Serias? Was she in on it as well?

I hear footsteps slowly creep forward, and I find the strength to lift my gaze once more to see who they are attached to. Forge squats over me and leans in close. "Kinda sucks, doesn't it? Finally being the ass-end of a good, cruel plan. But all is not lost, Reign. As you already know, I have your sister, Olia. And she is a damn good fighter. Almost lost her over a year ago to that smug sheat-head *Prince* of yours. She's good, but the viewers are growing tired of her constantly winning, and we require a new victor to lead the Champions."

"Fook you!" I belt, cutting him off. "I ain't running sheat."

"Ahh, no, no, no, Reign," Forge says softly. "I don't mean for you to compete in the Gauntlet, nor do I desire for an old man like you to join the ranks. I have more than enough competitors, and you just brought me a fresh recruit," he says as he looks over to Stink, who struggles to wrench free from Sawjustee's iron grip. "No, what I want from you is an execution. Olia's time is truly up and what better way for her to end her run than by being executed by her older brother in cold blood. I'll let both you and your pilot here go. That way, you'll get exactly what you came for. Your sister's freedom from my menacing hands while saving your own ass. I'll even throw in the *Concord* for free. Consider it my appreciation for a job well done. It's as poetic as it is merciful. What do you say?"

I drop my head, and the floor swims in my vision as tears fill my eye. The mix of anger, frustration, hurt, and sorrow do a good enough job to numb the burning sensation in my body, allowing me just enough strength to jump to my feet and recklessly charge at Forge. "Rah!" I scream in a fit of rage as I attempt to plant a solid kick to his face, but Forge sidesteps me with relative ease and slams a kick of his own between my lower ribs. An audible crack alerts me to the presence of two fresh fractures, and I crumble to the floor in agony.

The group laughs as Forge claps his hands and chuckles. "You old Spy...Bounty Hunter, or whatever you call yourself these days. Never losing your fight, huh?" He pounces on me, rolls me to my back, and leans in close. His voice is now directly beside my ear. "Keep fighting. I like that. Oh, and that pain you're feeling? Well, that's the DX running through your veins. You see, these lights are radiation enhanced. While they're not potent enough to harm us healthy folks, they certainly do the diligence of accelerating the disease process." Forge waves a hand at Nedojustee. "Kill the lights." The bright lights fade and the soft yellow ones return. The searing pain—although not fully removed—begins to lighten, like I had taken some sort of Kinurian sedative. "I'm not going to let you go out that easily. You see, as I mentioned before, I am merciful. You will be my guest at The Gauntlet. And when Olia runs it again, it will be her last time. And you will have the honor of witnessing her demise first-hand. Then, when it's all over, I will end the night with an execution of my own." Forge grips the sides of my face with one hand, squeezing as he speaks. "You!"

TWENTY-FIVE

I'm half-dragged, half-walked down a few spiraling turns of a pale white corridor until coming to a halt just outside a large, gray, metal door complete with a pair of soldiers parked outside armed with lightning staffs. "Open the doors," I hear Klepjustee announce as my body hangs from my arms, which are secured by a pair of grunts on either side. I pass a glance over the impressively sized bolts running along the length of the trim of the door before it slides left, revealing the dark room inside.

It won't budge, I convince myself before my mind initiates any futile action resembling shoulder charges or kicks that would only steal what little strength resides within my aching muscles. Before I was promptly escorted from Forge's quarters, his minions took the opportunity to serve up a barrage of punches and kicks to my body that stole the wind from my lungs, along with any ideas of fighting back.

Sometimes as a captive, it's best to just allow your body to absorb the blows of your abusers rather than tense up and fight back. All in all, my past experience proves that you have about a good 50-50 percent chance that either choice proves to a more palatable option. But with DX barreling through my veins and exhaustion riding shotgun, choosing the latter just doesn't seem like a more viable one at the time. Besides, I'd rather allocate any sliver of energy toward vital body organs such as the heart, brain, and lungs in hopes of facilitating healing.

But I can't lie. At the moment, I owe every member of Forge's personal guard 3 to 5 very painful counters for their excruciating acts of cowardice. As they drag me to my final resting place and toss me against a wall opposite of the entrance, I turn and meet eyes with Nedojustee as he stands in the doorway. Klepjustee hangs off his shoulder regarding me in my pain. "I hope you find your new accommodations satisfactory?" he muses.

"Oh, Nedo, give the fool a break. It's not his fault he's too basic to understand the ignorance of his mistake," she says to him until turning her sights on me. "In the future, you need to choose better friends."

"Lady, I don't usually hit women, but since you just barely miss the mark of resembling one, I'll make an exception the next time we meet," I reply, slightly coughing up a bolus of blood.

"All that fight," Klepjustee says. "Too bad you won't be able to put it to the test in The Gauntlet."

Sawjuste enters and rushes over to me. He lifts his boot to my face, and as I brace for impact, I don't blink, gazing into his eyes just before he surprisingly pulls back and laughs. "You better be lucky that the Captain wants you all to himself or I'd spread your hapless blood all over this cell."

"As a matter of fact," I say before coughing, "I'll start with you first and save the bitch for last," I mutter.

Sawjustee's eyes widen in response, and for a quick moment, I discern a glint of fear hiding behind them. Maybe he's used to people cowering at his threats. Still, I'm not like everyone else. I've traveled enough in my solar days to fight the biggest to the smallest. And the 1 thing I've come to understand most is that the bigger they are, the slower they are and I'd relish the opportunity to parry each of his attacks and return counters that would make his mother cry.

"Leave him," Nedojustee says finally, bringing an end to our school-boy game of stared and be scared.

The door slides right, and a faint flickering light overhead is my only company. I roll back over, prone, cold and alone. I successfully fight off what level of uncertainty attempts to crowd my mind. Still, after an hour or so, the voice of doubt in my head eventually wins and pummels me with innumerable scenarios in which I'll face my demise.

As trying as my alone-time is, it does afford me a moment to deal with my physical pain. Slowly but surely, my strength returns, and I'm able to stand. Propping myself along the wall with one hand, I slowly limp over to the door and place an ear against it, listening for any wayward conversation from the guards. I even throw in a few verbal jabs of my own, hoping they'd respond to me, but for what it's worth, these guards are good and highly trained, avoiding the mistakes of villainous monologuing that would normally allow me a chance to get their attention and plot an escape.

After failing to get them to break, I walk back over to the opposite side of the cell and take a seat. Knees to my chest, back against the wall and hands to my face, I find myself slipping into a state of depression I've not felt since leaving Serias behind. "Serias, damn how I wish you were here," I whisper. Not to hold or make love to, but to apologize once more in hopes that you'd give me a final, satisfying look of forgiveness. Just the thing I'd need to pass from this life in peace.

I did it.

I made a mistake.

I allowed them in.

Too many, too close.

Let my guard down, breaking all the rules of a good spy.

Against my own instincts, I trusted them. Now, I'll lose everything.

My sister Olia.

My lover Serias.

And anything I *thought* was family.

Don't worry, Mother…and Father. I won't go out with a whimper. I'll do as you taught me and give 'em hells with every ounce of my last breath.

They'll feel me. I'll make them pay.

But beyond the pain of Gifford's betrayal looms the greatest of them all. William's. Why? The question filled my brain ever since his face plastered the monitor in Forge's quarters and ceased to escape up until now, along with the image of his father King Gregorio's death looping on replay. The entire scene is remarkably life-like, and I swear I can even hear both the King and William's voices hiding in the darkness of my prison.

I sit wordlessly in my cell for about one more solar hour until the sound of commotion just outside my doors floods my senses. I sit up and eye the door as it slides left, and the bright light of the hallways pours in, beating my good eye. The silhouette of a strong slender frame enters the room and kneels in front of me.

"Brother, are you okay?" Olia asks.

"Olia!" I reply, my voice is coarse and loud.

Her hand touches my face. "You look like—"

"Sheat, yeah, I know," I say, unable to offer a smile.

It's then that my body betrays me too, overwhelmed by the surge of emotion overtaking me. I lurch to the side as my muscles fail to hold me up, and my shoulder slams the ground of the cold, metal cell. My eyes wither and close.

Darkness fills my head.

***

I awake, not knowing exactly how long I was out nor how I mysteriously returned from certain death. But Olia is with me. She sits to my left, tending to a red line leading into the vein of my right forearm. A small metal box lies along the floor connecting both the red line in my arm and another red line hanging from hers.

280

"Back from the dead?" she mocks as I stir to a sitting position.

"I guess," I grunt. "But...how?"

"Don't worry, the transfusion's almost complete, and, soon, you'll be back on your feet, ready to fight," Olia says.

"Ready to fight?" I repeat softly, doing my best to make sense of the situation. Last I recalled I was standing in front of Forge watching William weigh in on my treason. Anything after that was a blur, all except, "A message!" I stammer.

"Right, boss," Stink says from behind Olia.

"Stink?" I ask.

He moves in closer, standing behind Olia and holding a lightning staff with both hands as his head whips back and forth between me and the door while he speaks. "The message. The one from William. What did it say?"

I shake my head and close my eyes. "What the hells?"

"The coded message in the broadcast," Olia says matter-of-factly as she begins to disconnect the red line running from her arm.

"I...I do remember a message, faintly," I reply.

Olia stands and takes the weapon from Stink. "A little help here, please, baby. Brother needs some assistance," she says.

"Baby?" I grunt between clenched teeth.

Stink squats down and begins to speak with animated hands. "Remember your Optic Aug?

"Wait," I say, holding up an open hand. "What about *baby*?"

"Oh, that?" Stink says with a bright smile. "Well, when Forge sent you here, he released me to the Champions to prepare to run The Gauntlet. That's when I had a chance to officially meet Olia. She's...in a word...amazing. Just like you said, boss."

"And *baby*!" I growl louder, losing my patience.

Stink tries to explain further, but as my strength is returning, I struggle to drown out the impulse to crush his skull. "Well, our teleonotioning bond is...stronger than anything I've ever felt before. It's like we both know—"

Olia cuts in again. "What the other one is thinking and can even finish—"

"Each other's sentences!" Stink says emphatically with brows raised to his hairline as if I'd share his excitement. "We're in love, boss. Crazy, right?"

Speechless, "You called my sister baby?" is all I can muster.

"We don't have time for this," Olia chimes. "Tell him about the codex."

"Oh, yeah, right," Stink says with a snap. "During King Derry's message, remember that flickering in the signal?"

"Yeah," I reply.

"The flickering had a hidden decoded message, straight from the King himself, only visible by an Optic Aug," Stink says. "You should've been able to access it whenever you went into sleep mode."

"When the signal was finished, the message concluded, and now it's locked inside that stubborn brain of yours. Think you can retrieve it, brother?" Olia asks.

"Possibly," I say. "Don't know how well my mind is operating right about now."

"You've got Sintock blood running through those veins now, brother, and with a bevy of teleonotioning power to boot. Extracting the coded message should be a breeze," Olia says confidently.

"What's so special about it?" I ask.

"It's got a security sequence embedded in it that will drop the Dark Matter engines and disable the *Eclipse*," Olia says. "I'm sure you realize we don't have a lot of time."

I'm usually not a slow learner, but it isn't until that exact moment that the truth finally burst forth in my mind. William sent Giff to find and lead me along a path of breadcrumbs so that I can successfully get to my final destination and free Olia. Snatching up the *Concord* along the way was a mere bonus and the perfect Trojan Horse to his real plans—getting the schematics for the Dark Matter engines. Keeping me in the dark was a key component to getting all the beautiful pieces to fall into place because even though I'm a whole piece of eye-candy, I've never been one for the camera or bright lights. So my acting skills would completely suck and give away the plan, presuming I was right in my assumption.

It all made plenty of sense, but one question remained. "So Giff's in on it, as well as William, but when did you come aboard?" I ask Stink.

"Not until they kicked you to sleep," Stink says. "I was totally in the dark, but after Olia had a moment to implant the microchip and communicate with Gifford—"

"Everything fell into place," I say. I peer over at Olia and sigh heavily as a wave of pride washes over me. "And you?"

"It didn't take long to run the plan through all the rigors of probabilities of success, and with a couple of tweaks here and there, it all made good sense. Besides, I'm tired of running this place anyway," Olia says.

"Tweaks?" I ask.

Olia squats down again and disconnects the red line to my arm as the small metal box begins to chirp. "Yeah, with William's codex, we'll be able to buy about 15 more solar seconds than what Gifford projected, making the odds of our escape a little more palpable. Oh, and there's these."

Olia stands and quickly saunters over to the door. She reaches down into a pile of two bodies and pulls out three pairs of boots. I hadn't noticed Stink drag in the now-deceased guards during my most recent awakening, but the boots caught my eye for sure. "What's those?"

"Air skates and Grav boots. Once the *Eclipse* powers down, me and baby here are going to make our escape to the *Concord* using the skates while you use the boots to trail behind," Olia says.

"Baby again, huh? You guys don't mind trying to shove this down my throat, do you?" I ask, mightily uncomfortable and annoyed with Olia's gushing over her newest beau.

"It'll take some getting used to boss, but relax. We'll be brothers soon. Our teleonotioning predicts it," Stink says as if that makes the news all the easier to digest.

With the red line no longer restraining me, I stand to my feet and clench my fists, tensing the muscles in my arms as my strength returns and the pain from the DX completely absent. "Until we get free from here, let's kill the family talk for later. Agreed?"

"Absolutely," Stink agrees.

"Olia, why am I lagging?" I ask, making air quotes on the word lagging.

"Because you'll be wanting to swing by the armory to grab Martha, I'm sure," she says, flashing me a row of pearly whites.

"You know me too well, sister," I say.

"Besides, Stink's had an hour at best to master the flight of the air skates, and, well, even with a solar day of training, I'm confident you'd still end up on your ass." She and Stink share a smile as if they'd been swapping coordinated insults about me during the entire time of my absence.

"Time's a wasting, boss. Those codes, please?" Olia says as she points to her mouth. "Gifford's words, not mine."

"Giff, he's alive?" I ask.

"Yep, but he won't be if we don't hurry," Olia says.

"Wait, how come I'm not privy to this conversation? My microchip was implanted before we came aboard," I say.

"That pummeling you took back in Forge's office probably knocked it loose. It's not made to tolerate a lot of tussling," Stink says.

"The codes!" Olia barks as she tosses me a Holo-band to synchronize the 45-second countdown.

"What if I can't?" I ask.

"All you have to do is focus, boss. Like Olia said before, the teleonotioning perk running in your blood right now should make this pretty easy. Just lock in on numbers and words. But only the most recent ones," Stink says as if coaching a small child.

I take a deep breath and close my eyes, praying that I'm able to rummage through the most recent painful memories of my past and retrieve the codes. Numbers fade into view as I plunge deeper into my most recent dreams while my Optic Aug clicked into sleep mode. The words slip from my mouth slowly.

"35…92…2…Delta…64…51…Tango…8…Alpha," I say, straining to mutter.

Olia turns away momentarily, lightly touching her temple. "You get all that, Gifford?" With a nod, she turns back and spins the lightning staff once before impaling it into the concrete. "Strap up, gentlemen. It's time!"

TWENTY-SIX

The door of my cell slides open with a hiss, and as I step out, the strength in my legs returns as I steady myself for what was next to come.

"Brace yourself!" I hear Olia scream behind me as the bright, pale hallways of the *Eclipse* turn completely black.

I take a defensive position and kneel, one foot slightly behind me to prepare myself for the sudden loss of gravity. My finger tickles the button along the side of my Holo-band as I await Giff's power shut down. On cue, the overhead lights blast on, bathing me, Olia, and Stink in a sea of red flashing lights. An annoying chorus of horns wail in my ears, and I reflexively press the button on my Holo-band as I take off full speed down the corridor toward the armory.

43 seconds and counting.

Olia screams out something from behind me—cautionary, I'm sure, judging by her tone—but the wind breezing over my ears makes it totally indiscernible. Objects float by in my periphery as I speed along, and I'm easily able to weave through others that occlude my path; the Grav boots performing more perfectly than I'd hoped.

"Highly esteemed guests of the *Eclipse*," I hear Nedojustee's voice croon over the overhead intercom. "We are currently suffering a power outage. Please stay in your current quarters and remain calm. Our technicians are feverishly working to restore power. Sorry for the inconvenience."

Frantic screams fill my ears as the red lights continue to flicker, and I imagine the bewildered looks across the faces of the many passengers as they uncontrollably float skyward. The vision creates a faint smile across the corners of my mouth. This part of the vessel is off-limits to visitors, as Nedojustee explained before. Still, sooner or later, I know I'd be running into a few of Forge's goons as normal containment protocols dictate that you secure prisoners on vessels first in the case of a total power failure.

40 seconds remain.

A couple of twists down the corridor later, and I spill into a wide opening vestibule that houses my prized destination: the armory. But I'm not alone. Standing in front of the entrance is a shirtless Sawjustee, holding a lightning staff and donning a pair of Grav boots of his own. He keys in on me the moment I come to a stop and slowly begins to spin the staff between his fingers in his off-hand. A single gold light bathes his body from above creating dark recesses underneath his eyes and forming shadows that accentuate his muscular frame as if he needed it.

He points at me with his free hand. "So predictable."

"No time for this chump. I've got a plane to catch," I say.

"You want her, don't you?" Sawjustee says, gesturing toward the glass of the armory where Martha was holstered on the wall in plane view.

35 seconds left.

I've never been one for words, so in badass fashion, I bite my lip and begin to charge. Sawjustee drops one foot back and braces for my assault, keeping his staff just behind his shoulder. With any luck, he'll swing haphazardly, and if my body doesn't fail me, I'll dive underneath and drop behind him for a quick counter to snap his neck like a twig.

As I close within a foot of Sawjustee, he does the impossible and executes a forward flip in my direction that takes me by surprise. He's a lot more agile than I assumed, but I'm no slouch either and swiftly slide on one knee and duck, just as he swings his staff backward with one hand as he lands on both feet.

I roll to a standing position and eye Martha from outside the armory as Sawjustee laughs. "You're quick."

"You're stupid," I say, trying to buy myself some seconds while I contemplate making a run for Martha instead of confronting him again.

But Sawjustee doesn't afford me the time to think and descends upon me like a wild beast. This time, his wild swing connects, knocking me back as I do my best to absorb the blow with a double forearm block across my chest. Sawjustee is back upon me as I roll sideways and catch my breath, bracing myself against the wall behind me.

Brilliant blue flashing lights dance across the red floor as Sawjustee takes a few more swipes at me, but somehow misses as I struggle to dodge him while not losing too much ground from the armory. Sawjustee wedges himself back to where he first started, forming a barrier between me and the armory. My teleonotioning perks send a spike of adrenaline through my veins, and I can feel my heart rivet in my chest at a paralyzing pace, but I don't deny it as my fear and desperation makes for a perfect cocktail to execute my next move.

With perfect timing, Sawjustee changes pace and takes a full two-handed thrust in my direction, exposing his full torso. I cock back and swing with all the strength I can muster. My hand sinks into his side, just beneath his ribs, folding into the meaty part of his trunk. The staff slips from Sawjustee's hands as he huffs, and a bolus of blood splatters the ground at my feet.

Enraged and extremely pissed, Sawjustee takes a swipe at me, and as I block his attack, he grapples my arm and snatches me close to his body. He locks his arms around me and begins to squeeze. In what seems like an eternity, my body slowly loses its ability to fight back and Sawjustee's muscular frame tightens around me like an overgrown slithery animal. From here, I can appreciate the lack of proper hygiene that most people joke about concerning pirates, but instead of laughing, I wail in pain as my heart thumps against my chest so hard I swear that my sternum was going to pop.

"Don't worry, I'm not going to kill you. Just make you suffer," Sawjustee taunts as I begin to slip out of consciousness.

My eyes reflexively lock on Martha. Oh, how I wish I had one shot at this fooking imbecile.

Sawjustee tightens his grip, and just as I'm about to give up, a glint of green light reflects at me from the window of the armory. The sound of a hot hydrogen round explodes over my shoulder as heat passes just outside my left ear.

Sawjustee releases his grip and flops backward as I fall to my feet, bent over and coughing as my lungs welcome the return of fresh oxygen. I turn slightly to find the source of the blast. Standing in a black, form-fitted dress was Serias, still extending the hand cannon out in my direction as smoke billows up from the barrel.

"Serias," I muster to say between coughs.

She doesn't answer, but holsters the weapon and takes off in a full sprint in the opposite direction, her Grav boots clattering along the tile floor.

25 seconds is all I have.

I jump to my feet and race inside the armory to secure Martha. When I do, I kiss the barrel and turn the dial along the side to two. Rapid-fire, double kill.

"No one better fook with me now," I declare as I run through the hallways, making haste to find the cargo hold where the *Concord* was docked.

It takes me a few seconds more to find my bearings, but when I do, everything becomes more familiar. I know for certain, I'm only seconds away from finding the others.

Maybe by chance or possibly after Sawjustee's life signal went silent, a horde of soldiers fills the hallway before me, forming a wall between both me and the hangar bay, armed to the teeth with rifles and guns of their own. I pray like hells that the Dark Matter engines are disabled enough to allow Martha to show her ass.

I pull up short, raise my gun, and let off a few rounds of hot hydrogen. 4 men instantly fall like snowflakes and excitement washes over me. Time to provide a live demonstration on why they call me the Gunman. I squeeze the trigger, again and again, watching in glee as the wall of soldiers topple before me in a beautiful synchronized exhibition of blood and destruction. Shots whiz by as I slowly close the distance between the remaining soldiers and me. A few shots graze my legs and arms, but not enough to get in the way of my pursuit of freedom. As warm blood flows down my legs, I focus on the last two remaining soldiers and rip off two more shots, perfectly piercing the left eye of each one.

They crumble to the floor, and I pick up the pace, hopping over the downed bodies in my path. Instantly, I feel young again. It'd be pretty impossible to ask for a more inspiring adventure of gunplay such as this, and admittedly I'd secretly wished for such a mission ever since losing my sheat on Fabricius. Call it redemption or just plain ignorance, my body longed to pop heads and steal souls again, possibly redeeming my failure of protecting the King back when.

As I exit the winding hallways, I come front and center with the elevator that Nedojustee used to ascend the tall shaft leading down to the hangar bay. Darkness surrounds me, and that's when I realize that the crippled power grid paralyzed everything, elevators included. I shoot out the glass window in the back of the elevator and peer down into the dark chasm below.

15 seconds to escape.

The roar of whirring engine noise slowly fills the abyss beneath me as a pair of spotlights passes over me a few times until locking onto my position. I use my free hand to block out the lights while trying my best to aim Martha at whatever was coming. It's then that my Optic Aug kicks in, and I realize that the approaching vessel is no other than the *Concord*.

The ship cruises in and meets me with its backside as the aft door opens. Olia stands along the catwalk and offers me a stretched out hand. "Come on, brother. It's time!"

I take two steps back to give myself some room and rip off into a gallop toward the end of the stalled elevator before sticking my right foot along the edge and leap for the *Concord*. Olia catches my extending arm and swings me inside with one hand. I slide along the floor safety inside, and the aft door slams shut. Olia greets me with a smile.

"You're stronger than I remember," I say.

Olia shakes her head at me. "You barely remember sheat."

"True," I say.

"And by the way, you're heavier than I recall," Olia replies. "But, yes, training has done me well," she says and offers me a hand. "You're hit," she says, regarding the fresh wounds along my arms and legs.

"Just flesh wounds," I say.

She helps me to my feet as N.I.N.A.'s voice booms overhead. "Brace yourselves!"

Olia and I find refuge along an empty bench welded to the floor inside the cargo bay and fasten ourselves to it, wrapping our arms around it and locking our fingers in tight. I glance at my Holo-band one last time.

7 seconds until...

The *Concord* banks sharply and dives downward. My stomach swims inside my gut, and I close my eyes to fight back the urge to vomit. After surviving a few more twists and turns, the *Concord* performs a full burn for what lasts about 3 seconds and since we don't explode into pieces, I figure we successfully navigated to free space outside the *Eclipse*.

"Gifford!" I yell, reminding Stink of our stranded genius.

"I'm on it," Stink replies as the *Concord* banks again and slows to a crawl.

Just as I'm about to stand, Olia beats me to it and places a gentle hand on my shoulder. "I've got this, brother," she says softly.

I'm old and exhausted, but the adrenaline flowing through me easily allows for one last heroic gesture, but I relent to my sister's request and let her secure our friend. As the aft door opens again, the air pressure inside the cargo hold escapes, pulling with it small objects and debris. But Olia is unfazed, standing strong against the resistance, Grav boots locked along the metal grating. I tighten my hold on the bench and use my legs to press against the flooring to stabilize myself so I don't join the hapless junk floating away.

Gifford's Galley Suit slowly creeps into view from the dark sheet of nothingness just outside our ship. He quickly enters as his small propulsion jets along his backpack carry him safely inside. The aft door closes behind him and normal pressure returns.

"Hold your nuts, gang, we're outta here!" Stink screams over the comms as the *Concord* burns again and blasts clear from the *Eclipse*.

"Boss," Giff says as he runs in my direction. He kneels beside me and removes his helmet. "I'm so sorry for tricking you. But King Derry...he gave me strict orders."

I hold up an open hand and cut him off. "Chill, Giff. I'm thanking you now...not later."

"No time for kissing and hugging folks, we got company," Stink screams over the comms.

"Great, I was so lonely outside the Eclipse. So glad that Forge and his cronies decided to make up for lost time," Gifford jokes as I fail to share his humor.

"Did your balls freeze off?" Stink asks with a chuckle.

"Don't know, haven't had time to check. You got a free hand?" Gifford says.

"Good one," I chime.

Gifford stops laughing and looks over at me. His face is solemn. "I'm glad you made it, boss."

"I am too, Giff," I say with a sigh. My heart grows heavy as I ask my next question. "Was she in on it too, Giff? Serias?" He hesitates for a moment as if trying to find a delicate way to answer. But when he takes too long, I jump in. "She was there...tonight. Saved my ass right in the nick of time."

"She was boss, but only at the last minute. Right before she debarked at Terrius 7, I spilled the beans on the plan. Funny thing is, she didn't seem too surprised or shocked."

'What do you mean?" I ask.

"Let's face it. The chances of survival were about 3 million to one. And she didn't bat an eye when I told her about it," Gifford says with a shrug.

"Then, she did know. Damn good spy she is," I say.

"Did you get a chance to talk to her?" Gifford asks.

I nod silently as the *Concord* begins to pick up speed. Olia storms off toward the cockpit before I can stop her. "Hey, what are you doing?" I yell out after her.

"Saving our asses again," she yells.

"Again?" Gifford questions. "I think I have something to say about that."

I glare at him. "Stow your pride, Giff, let's move."

We give chase to Olia and come to a stop at the cockpit of the *Concord*. "Sitrep!" I bark, bracing myself on the consoles along the right side as Gifford secures himself on the left. Stink rides pole position in the command chair while Olia is strapped behind him in the back seat.

"Multiple bogies emptying from the *Eclipse*, making a B-line for us," Stink says.

"How many?" Giff asks.

"Does it really matter?" Stink asks.

"12 fighter craft of varying designs," N.I.N.A. answers. "Most of which I'm unable to classify."

"Courtesy of pirate technician's piecemealing together stolen ships," Olia says. "The customization makes it difficult to isolate weaknesses."

"Peachy," I murmur, just as my eyes spot a field of asteroids nearby. "Look, over there," I say, pointing. "Let's use the asteroids as cover."

"Um, those aren't asteroids, boss," Giff says, quick to correct me.

"Then, what are they?" I ask.

"Debris from destroyed Capital ships. Shortly after you guys boarded, the *Eclipse* opened fire and destroyed them with some large hydrogen-based energy blast from its core," Gifford says.

"Why would he do such a thing?" I ask. "What's his play?"

"Olia?" Gifford asks.

"Hells if I know. It's not like we shared commentary over lunch in between Gauntlet runs," she says.

My eyes land on the overhead console, which displays the radar systems. 6 red triangles close in from behind with more blinking in from the periphery, heading straight for the green circle in the center. Us. "Can we get there before we're blasted to pieces, Stink?" I ask, ignoring the conversation between Olia and Giff.

"It's going to be close, boss, they're gaining, and I can't pull any more juice from the *Concord*," Stink replies.

"You might not be able to on your own, but *we* can," Olia says. In a flash, Olia and Stink's chair slide forward and backward, but instead of swapping positions as Stink and Gifford did previously, they park side by side. "N.I.N.A., give us the juice!"

"You got it, baby," N.I.N.A. replies.

"Baby!" Gifford and I reply in kind.

The nose of the *Concord* lifts, and the sea of starship remnants disappear from view. I'm not completely sure of what's about to happen, but my Hunter's instinct tells me that Giff and I would be best served to find the floor right about now, so I reach over and grab him by the waist before we both crash to the ground.

298

The world around us begins to waver and fade, becoming semi-transparent as the stars become visible and burn brightly, threatening to blind us. I shut my eyes and tense my body as the *Concord* rattles and shakes.

"Boss!" I hear Giff yell, a prelude to a sonic boom.

And just like that, the *Concord* performs the impossible. A singular, non-solar space fold.

EPILOGUE

When the haze settles, and the *Concord* slows to a halt, everything returns to normal as the metal underneath me presses hard against my body. N.I.N.A. blares an update over the comms. "Greetings, passengers. You are safely in Torrian Alliance space. Should I set the autopilot for Fabricius, Stink?"

"Absol-fooking-lutely," Stink replies, sounding somewhat drained as if the life had just been sucked right out of him.

Both Olia and Stink's chairs return to their previous position as Giff, and I sit up. Olia cranes her head in my direction. "You okay, big bro?" she asks with equal desperation in her voice.

"Yeah. How are you feeling?" I ask.

Olia rubs the back of her neck. "I'm not completely sure."

Stink's chair spins around. "Baby, are you hurt?"

"No, my love," Olia replies.

"Um, what the hells?" Gifford asks.

"Don't ask," I tell him.

"I didn't think it was possible," Gifford says faintly.

"Well," I start, "they've been entertaining this teleo-what's-it crap—"

"Not that, boss," Gifford says, cutting me off. "I mean the Gallop fold. It was rumored to be in Beta testing for some time now."

"Consider us the Beat testers then," Stink says.

"So this thing has a name? I heard whispers about it for a while now as well, but they quickly faded as the physics behind such a feat discouraged further talks," I say. "How did you know about it, Olia?"

"I don't know. It's like some little voice in my head took over, and before I knew anything, N.I.N.A. had prompted me to initiate it," Olia says.

"I felt it too," Stink says. "Weird."

"You're just full of surprises, aren't you, sis? And can you explain to me how you busted me outta jail?" I ask.

Olia shrugs. "Forge may control the *Eclipse*, but I hold center court over the jailers. Males are so easy to manipulate. Even though he kept us confined to the Champion quarters, I used my assets to occasionally slip out and roam the ship."

"Whoring is never the right option," I say.

"Says the man who made a name for himself as the Stellar Pimp," Olia replies.

"Okay, straight pimping. I see you," Stink jokes, pointing in my direction, suddenly more alert.

Olia reclines a bit and closes her eyes. "But ease your mind, brother. Unlike you, I never gave up the goods. Only made promises to. Kept those boys salivating like starving babies for their mother's milk."

"Incoming hail from Ontarius," N.I.N.A. announces. "Should I patch it through?"

"Go ahead," I say.

A haggard-looking face of an older man appears on the screen. "Starship *Concord*, you are cleared for landing," he says through a full, gray beard that covers his lips so much that if not for his words, I'd find it difficult to believe he was even speaking. "King Derry would like to see you. Job well done."

NOT, THE END...

ABOUT THE AUTHOR

Braxton A. Cosby is the award-winning author of YA, superhero, and Sci-Fi fiction. He is a devourer of speculative fiction and a wordsmith, desiring to deliver vivid worlds and stories that readers can both see and feel. Braxton lives in Atlanta, GA with his amazing wife, four children, twenty fish, a dreamy cat, and a rambunctious dog.

FOLLOW Braxton @:

Instagram:

braxtonacosby

Twitter:

@BraxtonACosby

Facebook:

https://www.facebook.com/BraxtonACosby

Websites:

www.braxtoncosby.com

www.theredgeminichronicles.com

www.cosbymediaproductions.com

BOOK 2

STEEL REIGN: PREFLIGHT (THE COMIC)

OTHER BOOKS FROM THE RED GEMINI-CHRONICLES SERIES

PROTOSTAR

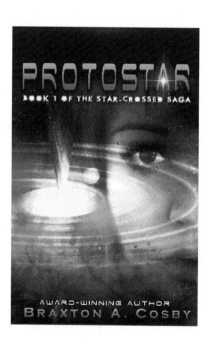

SUPERNOVA

SOLSTICE

BROKEN PRINCE: A RED GEMINI CHRONICLES NOVELLA

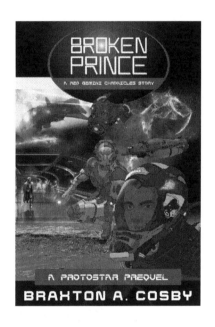

FOR MORE WONDERFUL SCIENCE FICTION
STORIES, GO TO:

www.cosbymediaproductions.com

Made in the USA
Columbia, SC
25 May 2023